Feet on the Ground

E.M. Phillips

I0550376

Cover photograph by Marcus Parry

TO CARO AND ROBIN

FOR THE GIFT OF THEIR FRIENDSHIP

My thanks to: Dick Purdue for editing,
Sandra Jacques for proof reading,
and special thanks to Diego (aka Heathcliffe)

Other titles by E.M. Phillips

A Year Out of Time

And All Shall Be Well

Matthew's Daughter

The Changing Day

A Very Private Arrangement

Return to Falcon Field

A Very Artistic Affair

The Turning Point

Feet on the Grouind

———

E.M. Phillips

Feet on the Ground

Published 2012 by Sagittarius Publications
62 Jacklyns Lane, Alresford, Hampshire SO24 9LH
Tel: 01962 734322

Typeset by John Owen Smith

ISBN 978-0-9555778-8-8

Printed by CreateSpace

PROLOGUE

Kate Shaw examined her eyes in the bathroom mirror, patted concealing cream over the dark smudges beneath them, then sat back to view the effect. Not bad, she thought, for a woman who was at the back end of forty-three and still suffering the emotional equivalent of being hit over the head with a blunt instrument.

She finished dressing then went downstairs to wander around aimlessly; tidying papers, stacking magazines, wiping a cloth over the black lacquer coffee table that attracted dust like a magnet. As she hadn't bothered to make like a housewife for a week or more the dust had now reached an impressive depth on all surfaces.

It was when she straightened the French carriage clock on the mantelpiece that she discovered the small porcelain shepherdess, still whole and hidden behind a gold-lettered invitation to view paintings by a particularly aggressively *avant-garde* Croatian artist.

With great care she took down the figurine, weighed it for a moment in her palm then let it crash onto the tiled hearth. Dusting her hands briskly she said 'The hell with you, Paul,' then burst into tears.

1

October

Trawling through the less-than-enticing positions available for an experienced, proficient in two languages, obviously over-qualified PA, Kate decided that job-hunting on the internet was akin to her frustrating search through www.homesteads.co.uk for what might be the home of her dreams, providing it was a) cheap, and b) not actually falling down, only to discover the Bijou period cottage in Islington that she fancied: Sit.Rm., Gal.Kitch., Bth., 2bds., courtyard gdn – a snip at £300,000, was actually a nineteen-twenties jerry-built two-up, two-down, with a leaking roof, suspect plumbing, the garden a few feet of soured earth used by generations of the neighbourhood cats as a powder room.

*   *   *

The phone rang as she was about to bite into an avocado and brie sandwich from the *prêt a manger* on the corner. She ignored the first half dozen rings then sighed, put down the sandwich and picked up the handset.

'Kate, dear, *must* you leave your phone off the hook for hours on end? I've been calling you since early morning.'

Her mother's plaintive voice with the painfully ironed Essex vowels and familiar undertone of I'm-not-complaining-*but...* had Kate immediately on the defensive. She struggled to keep the impatience she felt out of her voice.

'I've been working hard,' she said. She hadn't, it was an auto-matic response. 'What do you want, mother? I'm terribly busy right now.'

'It's Megan; she's not been well – her asthma, you know.' Ellen's tone made a slight shift from hard-done-by to earnestly concerned, 'She's taking her doctor's advice for once and spending the winter in Italy.'

Kate said, 'Glad to hear it,' and took another bite of her sandwich.

'We-el, there is a problem; the kennels at Poltreven the dog usually goes to have closed. We agreed that as you were mooning around in London doing nothing much, you could house sit and look after Heathcliffe while she's away.'

'Hang on…' Tilting back on her chair Kate stretched out an arm for the bottle of Merlot on the kitchen side and refilled her glass. 'I'll do a lot for Megan, but I can't just drop everything at a minute's notice.'

Her mother's voice strengthened into stubborn. 'Don't pretend you have anything to do but feel sorry for yourself. It will do you good to get away from London and that awful man and you can do with some peace and quiet to think about your future.'

Kate shut her eyes, did a rapid count to ten and put on her best professional voice: businesslike but soothing, 'Paul and I have just called it a day in a civilized and sensible manner, that's all, and to put your mind at rest, in a fortnight he leaves to tour Canada and the US.'

'And thank God for that…I said to your father: all that hair – '

'I'm very sorry about Megan's problems,' Kate interrupted, 'but I prefer to stay in London, particularly during the winter. Paul and I may have split but I still do have friends, you know.'

'How many of *those* will want a jilted, middle-aged woman spoiling their seating plans?'

'I was not jilted, neither do I consider myself middle-aged – and all the friends that matter most wouldn't know a seating plan if it got up and bit their arses. I'm sorry, Mother, but spending all winter in the House of Usher on a storm-blasted Cornish headland is not my idea of fun. '

As though reasoning with a recalcitrant child, Ellen gave a little sigh, 'I should think you'd be glad to get away from London; people may be kind but it won't be very nice having to show you are alone after all this time.'

Kate winced. Trust her mother to put her finger on the most painful spot. '*You* could go to Cornwall,' she countered, 'or you could fetch Heathcliffe back to Colchester.'

'Oh darling, *please*; you know how I hate Pendragon at any time of the year, and last time Megan brought Heathcliffe here he dug up the roses, smashed two vases and ate the remote control – and he is so HUGE.'

Kate poured another glass of wine and stared moodily at the wall calendar, knowing she was hamstrung. Her parents couldn't manage Heathcliffe for three days, let alone weeks – or indeed months if Megan decided to sit out the whole of the winter in Italy. She heaved a sigh. 'Exactly how long will Megan be away – and should she be travelling alone if her health is so poor?'

8

'She didn't give any firm dates and she isn't alone; that nice Frank Barclay is with her.'

Kate repressed a snort of laughter. If dear old Frank was going along he'd be too busy chasing every pair of tight trousers in Tuscany to be the slightest use if Megan was taken ill. She capitulated somewhat gracelessly. 'All right, I suppose I shall have to say yes. When does she leave?'

'Well actually, she left yesterday. Some old chap called Sam Trevene is looking after Heathcliffe and holding the house keys until you can get down. He has promised to chop wood for you and leave the shed filled with logs. I *think* Megan said he was something to do with farming. I know I put his address somewhere....' There was a sound of scrabbling through papers. 'Oh dear, where *is* it? – I'll call again when I find it. Oh, I *do* wish your father would stop tidying up...'

Kate mentally closed down and let her mother's recital merge with Radio 2 and a reporter's honeyed tones sucking up to the latest bimbo to be turfed off the Big Brother chicken ranch. Oh, great, she thought, all I need is some hoary old man reeking of manure to chop my wood and bang on about a life tilling the soil. Fixing her eyes on the view of the garden through the kitchen window she waited for her mother to run out of steam before asking reasonably, 'Can't this old Sam go on looking after that bloody maniac of a dog until Megan comes back?'

'No; unlike *some*, he has a job to go to. Besides, Pendragon is too isolated to be left empty for any length of time.'

You're telling me, Kate thought. Isolated didn't even begin to describe the location. 'Let me talk to dad, will you?'

'Wait a minute – I'll call him.'

'Stop hiding behind mother,' she snarled at Douglas Shaw's cautious "Hello," 'Megan is your cousin and I hold you responsible for this cock-up on the house-sitting front.'

'I'm sorry, lass, I did point out it was bit much but you know your mother...'

Kate heard her mother's indignant squawk in the background and sighed again. 'I know, I know.'

'Be honest, Katie: it will do you good to get away, now won't it?'

'Will it? I've never spent a winter in Cornwall and I'm not crazy about making it the first...and it isn't just for a few weeks is it? More like a bloody life sentence.'

'Take plenty of thermal underwear and a raincoat,' he advised, 'the last time we stayed with Megan it was either blowing a gale, freezing cold, or raining buckets; sometimes all three at once. And that was in August.'

Kate groaned, 'You can't think how much I hate you right now, daddy darling,' she said. 'I shall buy you a really crap tie for Christmas,' and cut the line before he could reply.

*   *   *

She spent what remained of the day packing her warmest clothes; stuffing them along with her essential Reeboks into a large hold-all, then squeezed an Orvis duffle, a crushed velvet hat and a large woolly scarf into a nylon flight bag. Packing never had been one of her strong points, she acknowledged ruefully. Zipping her laptop into its carrying cover she tucked a couple of new drawing blocks and pencils into her briefcase then, remembering that Barbara Pym and Ivy Compton Burnet were about as contemporary as Megan's reading got, added a few paperbacks to tide her over until she was able to raid the Penzance library.

Despondent, she surveyed the two lumpy bags of clothing. For the past eight years Paul had always seen to their packing, dovetailing shoes, smoothing and folding clothes, making it all look so *simple*. For a moment she wavered as a sob rose in her throat. While she spent the coming months shacked up with a great smelly hound for company, Paul would be screwing the brains out of his drippy harpist in hotel bedrooms from Montreal to Acapulco.

Hefting bag, laptop and both pieces of luggage she struggled down the stairs and out of the handsome front door. Slamming this with unnecessary vigour, she stepped out on the first stage of her journey to the as yet untested delights of Cornwall in winter.

2

Andrew Parradine closed the zip on his canvas hold-all, cast a final glance around the hotel room to check he was leaving no oddments of his life in that anonymous place, hefted the grip in his good hand and made his way down to the lobby. Five minutes later he had paid his bill, left a cryptic message at the desk to be passed on to any caller, particularly any female caller, assured the very pretty receptionist that he had indeed enjoyed his stay and would do his best to Have a Good Day, and stepped out into the mid-morning bustle of Charing Cross.

Momentarily closing his ears to the ceaseless rumble of traffic, he let his mind take a sudden leap to Cornwall and the clear air and tang of windblown spray over the cliffs at Porthcledra. He quickened his pace: if he could catch a cab within the next five minutes he might make the earlier train and be at Rosscannan by late afternoon.

He reached Paddington with just a few minutes to spare. The train was crowded and he hurried along the platform searching in vain for an unoccupied seat until he reached the first carriage. Flinging himself through the doors on their final hiss before closure he wrenched his so-recently healed shoulder. Swearing aloud he leaned against the back of the nearest seat, waiting for the pain to subside before making his way through the compartment in search of that elusive seat, finally running one to earth at the far end. Taking care to avoid the elegantly booted feet belonging to the woman by the window, he heaved his grip up onto the parcel ledge then sank down into his own seat and closed his eyes

*   *   *

Kate watched the man stumble through the closing carriage doors with a loud and explosive 'Bugger!' then, wincing visibly, lean against the nearest seat for a half minute before heading down the length of the compartment towards the single unoccupied seat beside her own.

Determined not to get trapped into conversation, she hastily opened her shoulder bag and taking out her book gave a good impersonation of a woman deeply engrossed in the unravelling of the Da Vinci Code, a book she had been meaning to read for at least five years, and had already decided by chapter two that it was a huge hunk of enjoyable hokum.

But with only a grunted, 'Excuse me,' as he lowered himself into his seat and without a second glace in her direction, the late arrival leaned back, closed his eyes and within seconds appeared to fall into a deep and untroubled sleep.

At the first faint snore Kate cautiously put down her book. Angling her head to read the dangling label on his one piece of luggage she gave an exasperated sigh at the neatly printed: A. PARRADINE, PORTHCLEDRA, PENZANCE. So, she thought, his highly polished size ten Pavers were going to be crowding her size five and a half Russell & Bromley's all the way to the end of the line. Closing her own eyes against the watery sun struggling through the clouds, she willed herself to loosen up.

But it was no use. In reality the break-up with Paul had been far from the civilized affair she had made out to family and friends. Her fury on returning early from a weekend of lectures on Italian Renaissance Art to find her lover snuggled under the duvet in their king-size bed with Alberta Opie had been immediate and violent; his reaction equally and predictably so. Insults had been hurled from both sides; anything remotely fling-able had been flung and the neighbours had a field day.

Screaming like a banshee, wrapped in Kate's best Janet Reger negligee, Alberta had bolted to her Honda through the hail of invective and crashing glass and leaving behind a tar-melting trail through Ealing to her own apartment in Kingston, whilst Kate went ten rounds with the man who was now quite definitely her ex-lover.

Eventually, running out of missiles, she had prudently locked the bedroom door against Paul's mounting homicidal fury. At mid-day, nursing a bruise the size of a billiard ball on his noble forehead, he had packed his entire wardrobe into the best luggage and followed Alberta. Flinging the cases into the Mercedes he roared away, yelling out of the window in his excruciatingly bad Polish/American, 'Focking beetch... for you did I gif my HALL, Katarina, and thees you do to me for such a leetle mistake!' After which un-lover like farewell Kate had resumed her rampage through the house, smashing what was left of his extensive collection of porcelain.

She was, she told herself repeatedly, better off without the double-dealing swine, but after eight turbulent, exhausting, but in the main ragingly sexy years, his departure had left an enormous gap in her life and she still felt a vital part of her was missing. It had been hell to wake each morning alone, to eat a solitary evening meal in the wine bar on the corner, to have a silent house without the sporadic strumming of the piano and the "Tum, tee-tum-tum-TUM" of Paul's sonorous baritone going through a score.

But it was at the day's end she missed him most: the drive home after an evening concert. The slow winding down as they ate and drank and talked over the evening: how it had gone, the good parts: the so-so moments, which soloist had come in too soon; which one fluffed a note. And she missed his unpredictability: how sometimes he would rage, at others laugh uproariously. How all the tensions of the day would melt away when he at last swept her off to bed to make love to her for half the night.

In the days following the break-up, tears would course down her face at the most inconvenient times and in some of the most embarrassing places, and there was nothing and no-one to help her through the long lonely nights. She even found herself missing the vitriolic verbal battles that had punctuated their years together.

At such moments of howling despair, she had to remind herself hard of what an utterly self-absorbed lunatic bastard he was. That he had until recent weeks been fantastically good between the sheets, she did her best to forget. The trouble right now was that her best just wasn't equal to the task.

Now, thanks to her mother and Megan, it looked as though she was in for an unspecified number of even lonelier weeks than those she had just passed, with only a large and extremely hairy dog for company. She supposed it had been fortunate that the break-up had come so close to Paul's long North American tour and that he had so far left her in peace. However, she knew her man; when he did return he would almost certainly cancel the lease of their house and she would be left homeless; but even that would be better than having him share their former love nest with Alberta bloody Opie and her sodding harp.

She wouldn't have minded quite so much if the woman had been something out of this world; so stunning that no man could resist her charms. Losing one's long-term lover to a lusty teenage bimbo would have been painful but understandable. Losing him to a thirty year old over-ripe blonde slapper with big knockers, a Barbie Doll simper, callused fingertips and, in Kate's opinion, all the charisma of a dyspeptic traffic warden, was just plain, fucking insulting. Alberta Opie, she brooded, must screw like a Black and Decker if she could give the bastard more than *she'd* been giving him for the past eight years.

Well, to hell with them both, Kate indulged in a silent snarl. She'd get organised in Cornwall, then make a trip back to Ealing well before Paul was due home She would clear all that was hers out of the house, find a place of her own, and when Megan returned, would be ready to get on with her life without the great Verdassey.

The one bright spot in the whole lousy mess was that while Alberta Opie was a passable harpist and may be hiding a sexual appetite to rival Annabel Chong, she was no Kate Shaw where a first class organizational and business brain was concerned. Without his efficient partner and PA to host his dinner parties, dovetail all the multifarious strands of professional and social mores into a smooth and seamless whole, soothe his hypochondria and massage his ego, Kate thought with a great deal of satisfaction that by the time the US tour ended, Paul Verdassey would have torn out a fair amount of hair from his arrogant head and quite possibly broken his baton over Ms Opie's ample and pneumatic arse.

*   *   *

At midday she stepped over the apparently still comatose A. Parradine and went to the dining car for lunch. Continuing to use her book as a shield against a tendency to conversation by the elderly couple who shared her table, she drank the glass of slightly sour Sauvignon Blanc, ate the overdone roast chicken served by a young man in a white jacket and a bad case of acne, and tried not to think about all the other journeys and meals she had shared with Paul.

For a girl from the suburbs, his lifestyle had at first been daunting but she had swiftly become used to the pleasures of living the high life. Quick-witted, an eager pupil, she soon lost her lingering Essex vowels and learned to fit in with all types of people, in all kinds of places. With a wry inward smile she recalled how on tours they always travelled first class, stayed in the top hotels, drank the best wine and dined off *haute cuisine*... Oh well, she brushed a few stray crumbs of her British Rail roll from her lap and recognized that in future it would be second class all the way. For a while longer she continued to sit, staring out of the window at the passing countryside: the barely-glimpsed local stations flashing by, the occasional herd of cows, a lone horse in a paddock, grazing sheep – all seemingly oblivious of the silver monster racing across their territory. Eventually she rose, and slinging the strap of her bag over her shoulder, headed for the toilet. Time to freshen up and get back to the zonked out A. Parradine, though how any man could sleep *that* soundly out of his bed was beyond belief.

*   *   *

14

She would have been surprised to know that, apart from an initial brief cat nap, Andrew Parradine had been awake and very much aware of the woman seated beside him, who for the first hour at least had radiated equal and uncomfortable amounts of tension and repressed fury. As she walked along the car toward him now, from beneath almost closed eyelids he took inventory.

She was tall he saw, had had a lithe, slender body and knew how to dress. The high-heeled leather boots, long caramel cord skirt and cream high-neck cashmere sweater were worn with careless throwaway elegance beneath a black, full-length military-style wool coat with big brass buttons. Although certainly past the first flush of youth and by no means a beauty, she had a good face, with sculptured cheek bones, a small straight nose and smoky blue eyes, her dark brown hair cut in the fashionable shaggy gamine style. As a lifetime observer of his fellows, Andrew found her intriguing. Just what might have happened, he wondered, to have such an all-of-a-piece-looking woman strung so tight?

As she stepped over his feet he caught a fresh whiff of newly applied perfume: *Oscar*, he hazarded: mature, subtle, not too heavy… he let his lids droop closed again. He could live with that for the next couple of hours; it would take his mind off the house and what the hell he was going to do with Toby, that bloody-minded streak of hostile adolescence Vanessa had saddled him with. If the little sod got caught smoking pot again, he thought grimly, he'd break the habit of a lifetime, risk the Charter of Human Rights, and belt him right where it hurt. He moved slightly, easing his arm on the padded rest. Stupid to have risked a fall just to catch a train; now his shoulder, and George, would give him hell for at least a week.

*   *   *

Kate came to consciousness with a start. She couldn't believe that she had been asleep: had actually slept, probably with her mouth wide open and showing her fillings. Worse, A. Parradine was tapping her arm gently, saying, 'As you and I appear to have reached our destination, I think you would be wise to get off.'

'Sorry!' she shot to her feet, grabbing at her shoulder bag. He clicked his tongue reprovingly.

'You shouldn't do that; it deprives the brain of oxygen.' He stood and with one hand hauled her brief case, laptop and bags from the overhead shelf and onto the seat. His glance flickered over the untidy bulges of her baggage. 'Going on safari, are you – you'll need a camel to transport this lot!'

'Thank you. A porter and a taxi will do.'

'A porter?' he raised his eyebrows. 'Where have you been for the past few years? The only place you'll find one of those now is in the British Museum.'

Biting back the retort that porters were still in plentiful supply if one travelled first class on Eurostar, she shouldered the straps of her brief case and laptop and bent to lift the two bags. He clicked his teeth again.

'First oxygen deprivation, now a slipped disc; you do like to live dangerously, don't you?' He brushed her aside and, picking up her heavy holdall with his own bag, suggested, 'You take the smaller one – and better hurry. The queue for taxies will be a mile long by now.'

She said 'Shit' under her breath and he grinned. 'Quite,' he said, 'so isn't it a good job I've transport in the car park and can give you a lift?'

Back into her stride she answered sarcastically, 'Bit rash aren't you? You don't know how far I'm going.'

He flipped the label on the holdall. 'PENDRAGON, PENMARIC, PENZANCE,' he read aloud and grinned again. 'Now that trips lightly off the tongue. Come on.' Without waiting for her reply he started down the carriage.

Kate seethed, of all the bloody nerve…if she hadn't been so flat out and pissed-off she would have told him what he could do with his lift, but the pull of Megan's centrally heated old house and any half-decent meal she could rustle from the store cupboards was strong; set against the long queue already forming for the few available taxies, it was overwhelming. Swallowing her pride she followed him towards the car park. Of course, she mused, eyeing the tall, broad shouldered figure striding ahead, he could be a rapist or mass murderer who cruised B.R. looking for victims, but somehow the darkly pleasant looks and easy authoritative air didn't quite match up to either image.

She uttered aloud a sound between a groan and a sigh. It was too late to pull back now, because the blasted man now legging it towards the car park had the larger part of her luggage held very firmly in one of his capable hands.

*   *   *

His "car" was one of the old heavy Mark Two Land Rovers, battered and with a liberal splattering of mud up the sides. Paul, she thought with sudden childish glee as she climbed onto the step-up, wouldn't be seen dead in it. As A. Parradine slung her bags into the back then climbed behind the wheel, she said rather stiffly. 'This is very kind of you. I have first to find Hawthorn Cottage in Maury's Lane, and pick up a dog and the keys to Pendragon, but I don't have a clue where the cottage is, except that it's somewhere near Godolphin Point so it can't be all that far from the house.'

'Hmm,' he took a map from the dash and began tracing a finger along a thin green line of road, 'well here's Godolphin Point and this track *here* must be Maury's Lane; no problem, it's only a couple of miles or so short of Penmaric and a couple more by the main road from my place.' He held out his hand. 'Andrew Parradine...and you are?'

She took the proffered hand. His grip was warm and firm. 'Kate,' she said, 'Kate Shaw.'

He started the motor and the engine roared into life. 'Glad to know that,' he raised his voice over the din. 'With the vibes you've been giving off I thought the K might stand for K.G.B.'

'And I,' she answered tartly, 'thought Parradine might be Ugandan for sleeping-sickness.' She gave him a sideways glare, saw he was grinning again and added meanly, 'and you *snore.*'

The grin didn't waver as he answered her with a laconic, 'So my wife tells me.'

'She has all my sympathy,' she said sweetly, then, apart from brief snatches of general conversation, they both relapsed into silence for the remainder of the journey to Hawthorn Cottage and old Sam Trevene.

*　　　　*　　　　*

Twenty minutes later he stopped the Land Rover before a squat cottage that crouched menacingly behind a rickety fence. Lacking a gate, the fence appeared to be held upright only by a solid hawthorn hedge.

With her hand on the door of the Land Rover, Kate hesitated, seized by a disquieting sense of *déjà vu.* As she stepped from the safety of the vehicle little ripples of apprehension ran through her and her hands turned cold and clammy inside her lined leather gloves. She had been here before, she realized, on one of the holidays spent with Megan when she was a child.

She couldn't have been more than ten when she'd ridden her bicycle well beyond the allowed limits set by Megan and stopped by this hedge to break off a sprig of hawthorn to take home. A terrifying old man had leaped swearing from behind the fence, catching her a whack across her back with his stick and yelling: "Get yur thieving 'ands off, yu little bastard." She'd wet her knickers with terror, leaped on her cycle and fled sobbing hysterically all the way back to the safe haven of Pendragon. She hadn't told anyone, even Megan, about the old man but, as children do, had tucked the incident away in some dark recess of memory…until today.

She became aware that Andrew Parradine was staring at her, his bright eyes suddenly sharp and alert. 'Are you all right?' he asked, 'you've gone hellish pale.'

With an effort Kate brought her thoughts back to the present. That had been thirty-five years ago and no one was likely to send her bolting for safety now. 'Yes, I'm all right. It's nothing.' God, but this was a gruesome-looking place; she wished she had the gall to ask him to come with her…recovering herself she made to reach into the back for her bags, but he put a restraining hand on her arm.

'Hey, not so fast – you don't want to be stranded here, do you? You won't want to haul your luggage *and* a dog all the way to Penmaric in the dark.'

The relief that she wouldn't be left alone for long in this ghastly hovel was enormous, and despite the fact that her heart was still leaping around her chest like a ferret on crack, she almost smiled. 'If you're sure you don't mind…I have to warn you, it's a damned big dog and hairy with it.'

'I'm in no hurry, and a full-sized pony straight from a bog could hardly make a difference to the interior of this heap.'

She opened the door and swung down into the lane. 'I'll be quick as I can once I've collected Heathcliffe from old Sam Trevene. Do you know him?'

'Sorry, no, I'm more or less a stranger around here myself these days, but as I said, take your time. Right now that's something of which I have plenty.' He settled his head deeper into the collar of his overcoat to watch her progress up the moss covered brick path, then leaned out of his window and called, 'Give my regards to old Sam, whoever he is!'

'Oh, sure, I bet he'll be thrilled to hear that,' she muttered. Banging on the rusty knocker she stood shivering in the damp night air, entreating silently, Come *on* old Sam and get it over with before I pee my pants again.

The door opened suddenly on a figure that at first glance appeared to be on nodding terms with a scarecrow, but on closer inspection the gaunt figure outlined against the light became a tall gangling young man, his long tow-coloured hair tied back in a ponytail. Slanted doe-like brown eyes inspected her with distant enquiry through John Lennon spectacles. Drawing herself to her full height Kate forced a smile. 'I'm Kate Shaw. I'm looking for Old Sam – '

The scarecrow regarded her gravely. 'He's over in the churchyard.'

'At *this* time of night?' She was incredulous.

'At any time of night: he's dead.'

'Oh, shit…I mean, I'm sorry to hear that.'

'No need; he's been that way for years.'

His face remained deadpan but his eyes were laughing at her. She gave him the kind of steely look she had given Andrew Parradine, a look that in the past had, on occasions, made even Paul proceed with caution.

'Let's start again, shall we…' She articulated carefully as though speaking to a backward child. 'I was told that old Sam Trevene lived here and – '

He interrupted. 'I'm Sam Trevene. *Old* Sam was my grandfather.' He opened the door wider. 'Come in, Kate, I've been expecting you.'

'If Heathcliffe's ready I'll take him straightaway – I have someone waiting for me,' Relieved, but furious with her mother, who had as usual got it wrong and made her look a fool, Kate stepped from the porch straight into the small living room.

He closed the door behind her. 'Megan said you didn't have a car and would come by train and taxi; 'fraid I couldn't help; I only have a motorbike. Heathcliffe's things are ready in the kitchen. I've just given him his dinner so if you sit down here for a minute, I'll let him loose when he's finished…I always find it safer to sit when Heathcliffe tells you hello.'

She said feelingly, 'Don't I know it.'

He disappeared through the door which apparently led to the kitchen and she took one of the two easy chairs by the log fire, bracing herself for the expected onslaught when the door would re-open.

A swift glance around the room, at the scattered papers, books and CDs on the table; the piles of clothes stacked on the couple of upright chairs, confirmed this was quite definitely a bachelor pad. For such a male domain she thought it odd that the windows were fitted with shelves and crowded with seed-trays and earthenware flower pots, giving the chilly air inside the house an earthy tang.

Her musings were interrupted by a joyous '*Woof,*' as with a scattering of rugs, thirty kilos of hair and muscle was upon her and

Heathcliffe's hot ecstatic tongue slavering over her face.

'Down, you great ox, *down*!' Kate fought him off and reluctantly, with a couple of valedictory wipes of the tongue, the shaggy grey Briard subsided to loll against her legs. She rubbed his rough head. 'You and I,' she said severely, 'have got to come to an understanding about all this, or one or other of us will have to go!'

Panting, he gazed adoringly up at her and Sam grinned. 'I wish I could keep him and save you the trouble, but I have to work.'

Kate looked up and smiled. 'Farming?' she queried.

He shook his head. 'Nothing so grand; at present I'm filling in time at a garden centre in Penzance until I can get on a college course in garden design.'

A sudden smile sent a network of lines around his eyes and mouth and she realised he wasn't quite as young as he'd at first appeared. She returned the smile and stood up. 'I wish you luck, but I should go now – I caught a lift off a total stranger and I've left him out there in the cold. Thanks a lot for looking after Heathcliffe. Perhaps I could pay you back with a meal sometime.'

'I'd like that.' He handed her a large plastic carrier. 'His bowls and the remains of his feed are in this, and you'll find a new sack of his kibble in Megan's cellar; but I daresay you know where everything is. She told me you visited a lot.'

'I used to, but I haven't actually taken a holiday here for almost five years, although we always meet when she comes to London.' Kate took the bag and studied him for a moment. 'As you and Megan seem to know each other well I wonder why I haven't met you before.'

He shrugged. 'I've known her, on and off, since I was a kid, but I come from Maundsley and I've only lived here for a couple of years. Sam died in the early 'nineties and left this place to me, but it had to be rented out until I was free to move here permanently.'

Kate took a firm hold on Heathcliffe's collar. 'Well, thanks again, but I mustn't keep the chauffeur waiting. I'll call round some time if that's all right, and fix a date for that dinner.'

He gave his slow grin, 'Sounds good to me.'

Sam waited at the cottage door until woman and dog were safely aboard the Land Rover parked by his non-existent gate, then gave a brief wave and stepped back inside, shutting the door firmly.

'Very nice,' he said aloud, 'Megan was right; she's quite something…' He sat down and stretched his toes to the fire and thought what a clever old bird Megan was to have found a way to give Kate

Shaw the space and time to sort her troubles. Megan hadn't seemed to know in any great detail what had caused the bust up between the apparently self-assured Kate and the mad musician, and just who had walked out on whom. Maybe Kate herself would unbutton and tell him over that dinner she'd promised.

He yawned and reached for his book from off the floor. Better to keep off the confidences; she probably wouldn't want to talk about that any more than he would want to talk about the circumstances that had kept him so long from claiming his inheritance.

Secrets, he thought, we all have them.

*   *   *

When the cottage door opened and Kate re-appeared, Andrew jumped down from the Land Rover and, expertly fending off Heathcliffe's lunge for his shoulders and canine attempt at French kissing, dropped the tailgate and unceremoniously bundled the dog inside. 'Sit!' he commanded in a tone that had Heathcliffe sat back on his haunches and quivering.

'Bloody *hell*,' Kate exclaimed admiringly, 'how did you do that?'

'Practice…' he secured the tailgate then helped her into her seat. 'I've been dealing with something like his human counterparts for most of my life. Actually, I'm not really a dog person…now cats; they are something else again. Cats and I are like *that*.' He crossed two fingers and grinned.

While he was fitting back into his seat and re-starting the engine, Kate took the opportunity to take a really good long look at Andrew Parradine. Hazarding a guess she put his age somewhere around fifty. Beneath the expensive overcoat he looked to have a surprisingly lean muscular frame for his years. He wasn't handsome, despite those extraordinarily clear grey eyes and lean dark face. The nose was a little too large, and although the long upper lip had a humorous slant, it was immediately contradicted by a hard stubborn jaw; a face of strength rather than masculine beauty; one of contrasts that, once seen, would not easily be forgotten.

Frowning slightly she looked a little harder at his profile and the thick, greying dark hair that looked as though it was used to being cut short and close, but was now beginning to creep into the nape of his neck in bristly curls. Odd, but somehow he was vaguely familiar. She asked curiously, 'I think I might know you from somewhere. Are you anything to do with show business – in the widest sense, that is?'

He said with dry dismissal, 'Not in any sense; nor am I at present

21

in any kind of business…by the way, how was Old Sam?'

Kate wasn't put off by this neat spot of evasion. 'Old Sam's in the graveyard, thank God; that was young Sam,' then, still with her mind on show business, asked, 'did you ever wear a wig?'

'No, and I didn't wear false teeth or a wooden leg either. May I ask what *you* do for a living, and if you propose doing it in Cornwall? Or is this just a flying visit?'

Smart, she thought, but if he could keep wraps on the way he earned his daily bread so could she. To say she had been lover, PA and right hand woman to a famous musician, had just been massively jilted and was at present swelling the ranks of the unemployed, might trigger all kinds of unwelcome questions. She shrugged and said vaguely, 'Oh, this, that and an occasional spot of the other…but I'll not be doing any of it in Cornwall – just house-sitting for my aunt.' She saw in his eyes a faintly sardonic answering smile. Not an easy man to fool, she thought, and wondered again what he did for a living.

Not that it mattered. Marooned as she would be in Megan's storm-blasted eyrie, with only a thick-as-two-short-planks hound for company, it was highly unlikely that their paths would ever cross again.

*   *   *

Andrew stopped before the closed gates of Pendragon and cast a doubtful eye over the rusting ironwork. 'I hope you have a key for those things because I'm not about to scale even that modest height of wrought iron with you, your baggage *and* that hairy mutt on my shoulders.'

She confessed, 'There was a key once, but Megan lost it long ago. All they need is a shove in the right place. Hang on and I'll do the honours.'

She opened her door and jumping down swung the gates open with one quick heave. 'Real state of the art security,' he said as she clambered back into her seat, 'I don't suppose there is such a thing as an alarm system for the house either.'

'How did you guess?'

'Let's just say I have a nose for such things.' He shifted gears and drove up the short curving drive, slowing to a crawl as the house came into sight. *'My God!'* he peered through the dusk at the looming pile that was Pendragon. 'You're surely not intending to stay alone in this place; it's straight out of *Psycho!'*

'I think I'm old enough to manage – and I shan't be alone; I have

Heathcliffe on my side!'

'And what do you imagine *he'd* do to any intruders – apart from try to shove his tongue down their throats?'

She retorted tartly, 'He has his moments; he *can* be quite fierce.'

He grunted. 'In a pig's eye, he can.'

'Look,' Kate felt her temper begin to simmer. 'I appreciate you going out of your way to help, but you don't need to take it further. So I'll just thank you very much for the lift and let you get to your own home, which I am sure is fitted with flashing lights, security cameras and probably a brace of Dobermans patrolling the grounds.'

He didn't answer, although she was aware his shoulders were shaking a little as he pulled up before the front door. Kate jumped down and, not waiting for, or wanting him to follow, hauled her luggage efficiently from the back seat and dumped it all on the drive before releasing Heathcliffe, who leapt from the tailgate with a joyous howl and flung himself up the steps.

As he again slipped his disreputable vehicle into gear, Andrew Parradine leaned an arm on the open window to grin down at her. 'Goodnight, Kate Shaw, sleep well.' He cast a last look up at the over-the-top Victorian Gothic of Pendragon. 'If I were you,' he called encouragingly as the Land Rover began to move, 'I'd keep an eye out for Norman Bates – and for God's sake don't take a shower or go up into the attic!'

Kate watched his taillights disappear around the bend in the drive, her pique fading, dispersed by the laughter in his voice. She chuckled. 'Bastard,' she said equably. Shoving Heathcliffe aside she opened the heavily panelled door and dragged her luggage into the tiled hallway.

Enveloped by the warmth of Megan's super-efficient central heating she straightened, stretched luxuriously and gave a contented sigh. Winter or no winter, it was good to be back in the old house again.

Forbidding Gothic horror it may seem from its external appearance, but inside was an oasis of comfort and charm. Curtains were heavy and well lined, the couches and easy chairs plump and soft, the mixture of late Georgian and Victorian furniture polished to an impressive shine – the handiwork of Ena Trevone, who came twice weekly to 'do' for Megan. Which was just as well, Kate thought as she made her way to the kitchen, for *she* was certainly no hand with a tin of hard polish and a lot of elbow grease: a blast with someone's All Purpose Cleaner followed by a quick wipe with a duster was more in her line; a failing in her housewifely skills that had more than once driven Paul to the verge of apoplexy, particularly when applied to his

23

Bechstein grand.

In the big square kitchen an oil-fired Aga pulsed heat, and Heathcliffe made straight for his personal rug spread before the range. Flopping down he lay his head on his paws and gave the canine equivalent of a human sigh of content. Home, his expression said, home at last.

Kate gave him a sardonic look. 'It's all right for you to take it easy pal, but I've some unpacking to do, and a meal to get before *I* can flop and let it all hang out!'

She humped her luggage up the long staircase to the blue-painted bedroom that had been hers for many past summer vacations. Drawing the curtains she unzipped the bags and tumbled her belongings onto the wide four-poster. Thanks to her inexpert packing, almost everything but the sweaters would have to be re-ironed. Well, she'd bother with that some other time, until then they could stay out of sight in the chest of drawers. Taking up a bundle of creased shirts, she stood for a long minute holding them to her breast, letting the solitude and silence of the old house settle around her.

No one to bother her here; no demands for attention, for food, for love; no need to argue, to fight, to wound...She buried her face in the clothes that smelled of London and Paul and home.

It had been good while it lasted, and it had lasted a long time, the hurled insults and fights all part of the passionate, all-consuming loving, although to be honest, love had died some time before the advent of the lady harpist; died, she remembered with a sudden piercing pain, two years ago almost to the day...

A squall of wind from the sea buffeted the house, sending a scattering of rain against the windows. Dropping the shirts into a drawer she closed it gently and returned to the kitchen, where the old schoolhouse clock on the wall ticked away the minutes and Heathcliffe twitched and yipped and chased rabbits through his dreams.

3

By the time Andrew reached Rosscannan it was already dark and rain was gusting in from the sea, but apart from rattling the casement glass, even a sizeable gale made little impression on the solid Regency house.

Zacharius Parradine, Andrew's great-grandfather and owner of the most prosperous tin mine in South West Cornwall, had built Rosscannan in the mid-eighteenth century. Since then it had provided a home for successive generations of Parradines; or had done so until the nineteen-seventies, when Andrew's father, James, with a great disregard for his family's wishes and increasingly pressing demands from the Inland Revenue, had moved to Italy.

Since then, the house and extensive grounds had been let to a succession of tenants aspiring to acquire the status of local squire, but for the past year it had stood empty. Now, at the beginning of the twenty-first Century and with the UK country house market booming, James Parradine had decided Rosscannan should be put to rights with a view to an eventual and hopefully lucrative sale.

A few weeks before his meeting with Kate Shaw, and nearing the end of a protracted convalescent visit to Italy, Andrew had sat on the terrace of his father's colonnaded villa while James gazed contently at the Tuscan landscape and mapped out his plans for Rosscannan's future.

'Overseeing the work will give you something useful to do. After all, the place is part of your inheritance and when you've got it up to scratch I'll give half of the sale price – more than enough for you to retire here, buy yourself a decent place and relax in the sun.'

Andrew demurred mildly, 'I'm not cut out for sitting around letting the grass grow under my feet. I'll need to find something else to keep me busy.'

James poured himself another glass of wine. 'You've taken a bad knock. Later on you may feel differently. After all, you can live anywhere you choose and do anything you like when you no longer have the demands of Army life and Vanessa's wishes to consider.'

Andrew settled back in his chair and let it ride. He knew, and James knew, that with or without his soon-to-be-divorced wife he wouldn't settle to a life of lotus eating.

A week after that conversation he was on his way back to

England; to a house he'd left as a teenager and hadn't seen for more than thirty years, an almost ex-wife about to take off for California with a new husband, and to top it all, the unwelcome burden of having sole care of a teenage son already sliding rapidly into delinquency; the very last scenario needed to help a convalescent invalid back onto his feet.

*   *   *

Approaching Rosscannan, he reflected morosely that although he and George had been in residence for more than a month, they had done little more than list the somewhat daunting amount of decorating, both inside and out, to be done if the house and neglected grounds were to be restored to their former glory. Tenants, even the more considerate amongst them, had shown a tendency to let the place go, and twelve months without an occupant had accelerated the general air of decay.

He realised that George must have been watching out for him, as the gates swung wide before he had time to leave the car to key in the code or use the entry phone. He couldn't help a wry chuckle as he drove through and they closed silently behind him. The acerbic Kate Shaw hadn't been all that far off the mark about the security of this place, although the CCTV cameras, light-sensors and entry phone were the brainchild of the last tenant, a somewhat paranoid ex-chief constable. However, she'd been wrong about the Dobermans, although George could be a pretty good substitute for any guard dog.

He drove quickly down the gravel driveway. Drawing up before the house he turned off the engine and gave an audible sigh of relief. He was bone-tired after his long day, the nagging pain in his shoulder insistent as a bad tooth.

Beneath the portico, the front door was open; George already waiting, his skinny form outlined in the light streaming from the hall-way behind.

'About time,' he complained, beginning to hobble down the steps, 'I was near to gettin' the fuzz out looking for yer!' This sally was followed by a strangled laugh and a bout of wheezy coughing.

Andrew climbed out, slamming the car door behind him. 'Get inside, you bloody old fool; I've no time for nursing one of your famous bouts of bronchitis. Remember, I'm the invalid around here.'

George fussed around him officiously, taking the holdall from his hand and dropping it on the hall floor before easing the coat from his shoulders. 'You go on in to the fire an' get a drink, while I fetch your supper.'

A few minutes later Andrew stood before the drawing room fire, a glass of single malt in hand, while George drew up a small table and set a steaming dish of *bœuf stroganoff* before him. Andrew savoured the first mouthful, musing that, as well as taking on the self-appointed position as major domo for Rosscannan, for a deplorably subversive batman, ex-corporal George Riley made a very satisfactory cook.

'Shoulder giving you trouble, sir?' The beady, darting eyes noticed him wince as he sat. 'I'll give it a good goin' over later.'

'It's okay. My own fault – I slipped getting on the train and gave it a bit of a wrench.'

George stood with folded arms, watching him eat. 'Saw you on telly at the palace,' he said, 'thought you looked a right ponce; all bleedin' tarted up again in uniform.'

'Your sentiments warm the cockles of my heart. But it was for the last time and marginally better than clarting around in a frock coat and top hat like some of the other poor sods.'

George sniffed. 'What else you find to do in London then, 'cept 'ob-nob with 'er Majesty?'

Andrew shrugged. 'Nothing much; I had a meeting with pa's solicitor and a final hospital check-up. Had a hard time dodging the counselling sessions that any poor sod who gets shot or generally duffed up is automatically supposed to need or want.'

'So that's it – you've finally re-joined the 'uman race!' George cackled. 'So what you goin' ter do next?'

'Make a proper start on this place. I've got a local chap coming up soon to give an estimate on putting in the new boiler and replacing the old radiators. Meantime I'll continue cleaning up generally: repair that spot of dodgy panelling in the dining hall, fill the odd hole in the walls, stuff like that. Pa's dealing with the financial side of things, thank God. I don't think we'll have to scrimp on costs…we are just here to make a plan of what needs doing, then hand the place over to the experts.'

George sniffed. 'Nice to know *he's* doing something apart from sittin' on his arse in the sunshine while we sweats it out 'ere, sir.'

'You're a miserable old sod, aren't you, George!' Andrew moved his empty plate to one side. 'I thought you'd be only too pleased to start lording it over this place...and for God's sake drop the sir.'

'It's n'abit.'

'Maybe, but you and I are in civvy street now. These days nobody but waiters at the Savoy and butlers to the gentry calls anyone sir.'

'What am I supposed to call you then?' George pondered a moment then slapped his thigh. 'I know, 'ow about guv'nor?'

Andrew said irritably, 'Call me what you like. I'm bushed. Think I'll have a bath and turn in.'

'Right, guv'nor.'

Andrew got to his feet. George, he thought, was about the only sane thing left in his life. They had been in hard and dangerous places together for many years, now he had assumed a many-sided persona including part nanny, part bully, part servant – and a good and much-needed friend.

He smiled suddenly and laid a hand on the older man's shoulder. 'That was a great homecoming meal. Thank you George, when a man can cook as well as that, he's entitled to call me anything he wants.'

George sniffed again. 'I'll be up with the embrocation and a brandy in 'alf-'n-hour.'

*   *   *

Andrew lay in the deep bath, lazily content to be back again in his boyhood home, remembering the first fifteen years of his life spent in this house before his father had dragged him, his sister and their mother to Italy. Not that he had anything against that beautiful country; he loved it. He just hadn't wanted to live there permanently. He had been heartbroken at leaving Rosscannan, a sentiment shared by his mother and sister, but while he and Fliss had eventually made their escape back to England, their mother had stayed and died under that Tuscan sun. The diagnosis had been cancer, but a younger, angrier, and less tolerant Andrew had blamed his father for tearing her from her roots and leaving her Cornish home to the care of strangers.

Now he was back, and finding the old house balm to his soul; he slept better here than he had in months, even if he couldn't completely beat the dreams that still haunted him from time to time. Perhaps, he mused, he should have taken that counselling when it was offered, but he'd never been good at baring his soul to anyone…except perhaps to confide in the odd barracks moggie from time to time. He liked cats; they were sensible, independent creatures who took life as it came; soon as he was settled somewhere for good, he'd find himself and George a feline companion.

Idly he filled the sponge with water and squeezed it over his head, wondering where he could live and what he could do with his life once the house was sold. The army, the centre of his universe for all of his adult life, was in the past; there would be no more postings to different parts of the world. His roots now were back where they had always been in spirit, if not in fact: here in Cornwall. Specifically they were here in this house.

Since his return he had begun to toy with the idea of staying once the house had been put to rights. No doubt his father would kick up and there would be one hell of a row, but he'd have to cross that bridge if, or when, it came. Totting up his financial assets in his head he reckoned if he used his share from the sale of the Hampstead house, which had been bought for a ridiculously low sum during the nineties slump, the proceeds, plus his pension, should allow him to live comfortably: how to pay what might be his father's share from any prospective sale would be the problem.

It wasn't one of the larger country houses in this part of Cornwall; just a pleasant, beautifully-proportioned Regency House, standing in some five acres of park and woodland and built for the fair-sized families of the times. The five main rooms and six bedrooms with the servants' quarters above would make a comfortable, if over-large, home for the three of them now, with ample space for guests; but what possible use could he make of the stables and hay lofts, the barn and the old wooden grain store raised on granite staddle stones? He couldn't just leave them to decay any further than they already had. It would be sheer vandalism to have them pulled down, but perhaps they too could be put to some financial use…

He had just stepped from the bath and was knotting a towel about his waist when the telephone rang. Frowning he stepped from his bathroom into the bedroom and, hitching onto the side of the bed, picked up the handset. Now who the hell was calling at this hour? If it were Vanessa he'd drop the bloody thing from a great height… 'Parradine here,' he announced grumpily.

'What a sweet old darling you are!'

Andrew's frown vanished. 'Fliss! How did you know I was back from town?'

'I called your hotel and got the rude message you left at reception to say you'd died and not to send flowers, just a cheque, so I knew where you must be; I suppose you left that little gem for Vanessa.'

'You suppose right; just a gentle reminder that her loaded boy-friend is paying for the divorce and she can forget any idea of alimony. Anyway, how are you?'

'So, so,' she hesitated, sounding off-hand and Andrew's senses immediately sharpened. He asked quickly, 'Everything OK up in the Highlands?'

'Sure,' again that slight hesitation. 'How is dear Vanessa?'

Andrew stopped pushing…he knew his sister; if something was troubling her he'd hear, but all in her own good time. 'I've no idea,' he answered, 'it's too much to hope she's been abducted by Aliens.'

'And darling papa?' she pursued.

'Fair to middling as usual, bursting with rude health and full of ideas as to what I should do and how I should live my life.'

She giggled. 'I must be permanently *persona non grata* to the old bugger because he never bothers me from one year to the next.'

Andrew said equably. 'He thinks only idiots and Royalty choose to live in Scotland, darling. He's all right in his way; it doesn't happen to be either yours or mine, that's all.'

Felicity's voice softened. 'Are *you* all right now?'

'Uh, huh: almost.'

'There was a lovely picture of you outside Buck House in last week's Sunday Times…all done up like a dog's dinner and clutching your medal.'

'George said I looked like a ponce.'

She giggled. 'Sounds like George. Really I called to make sure you've actually got rid of Lucrezia Borgia at last.'

'More or less, the decree will be absolute in a week or two. I gather the nuptials will take place in the New Year down on the family estate in Old Virginny – an out-of-doors affair with arches of roses and Van dressed head-to-toe in Lady Di off-white crushed meringue. It would *have* to be off-white, wouldn't it, although grey bordered with black might be rather more the ticket.'

'Honestly, Andy, you can be such a bitch.'

Privately he thought he was being pretty restrained, considering Van had been screwing every bloke she fancied behind his back for years – and now had the nerve to leave him Toby as a farewell gift. He said, 'Did you know Toby got himself nicked last term for smoking pot in the bogs?'

'He told me. Give him a chance, big brother. You weren't exactly a paragon of virtue at his age, were you?'

'Perhaps not, but I at least had the sense not to get caught out in any of my extra-curricular activities.' Using his free hand Andrew began drying his hair with the end of the bath towel. 'Damn it, Fliss, you know we're practically strangers. Apart from the odd weekend I've hardly seen the boy in the years since Vanessa and I parted company, now he'll be here for every damned holiday. Still, looking on the bright side, I can at least pack the stroppy little bastard back off to school afterwards.'

'Poor Toby: a cow for a mother and you for a father! That surly adolescent act is mostly show you know; he isn't really like that. Duncan and I had him here all last summer. He was sweet with the boys and they adored him.'

'Yeah, Okay, I'll cope.' He turned as the door opened to reveal George, a bottle of his secret and noxious concoction for pain relief held aloft in one hand, a large glass of brandy in the other. 'I'd better go now. George is hovering. Give my regards to Duncan and a hug for the brats. I'll call you some time over the next few days.'

'Yeah. Sure. Give George a big kiss from me!'

Andrew put down the handset. He leered. 'That was my sister. She says to give you a big kiss from her.'

'You try it,' said George darkly, 'and I'll bung the brandy on your back and you can drink the horse liniment – guv'nor.' He stared at the fresh bruise across a shoulder already sporting two deep, livid scars. 'Now how did you manage to do *that*, you stupid old bugger?' he demanded fiercely.

Andrew groaned and rolled onto his front. 'Just shut up and get on with it, Florence...and don't forget to blow out your lamp when you go!'

*   *   *

He dreamed that night that Kate Shaw's long smooth hands were massaging his back with Oscar de la Renta perfume, only to wake at dawn with a shoulder like a well-roasted leg of mutton, the only perfume on his sheets a mixture of menthol, eucalyptus and various other odours he'd rather not think about.

He swore and turned over, pulling up the duvet against the cold, perversely wishing for Tuscan sunshine, a cool marble terrace and a leggy, slender woman lying beside him in a miniscule bikini, minus the top half...

No chance, he mused: that sort of woman always had a man around somewhere and these days he steered clear of competition. Twenty years back, Vanessa, blond and bosomy, her bikini line waxed to her ears, had lain topless beside him on a Malayan beach – and look where that had got him.

George may have his drawbacks, but at least he wasn't about to take off with a millionaire Yank, leaving him to cope alone with a dope-smoking teenage zombie...

After a while he went back to sleep and dreamed of Kate Shaw again.

4

Kate slept deeply and awoke to a misty Cornish morning; the kind of morning that experience told her would turn into a bright clear day before noon. From the kitchen directly beneath her bedroom she could hear Heathcliffe making the peculiar keening yowl that meant he needed out.

Groaning a little she pushed up from the pillows and sat for a moment cross-legged, yawning and combing her fingers through her hair before swinging her legs from the bed and feeling for her fleece-lined moccasins. Wriggling her feet into their warming depths, she snagged Megan's thick wool dressing gown from the door and belting its ample folds around her, padded downstairs.

Heathcliffe was lying in wait. Rearing up and thumping his front paws on her shoulders as she entered the kitchen, he managed a couple of quick wet laps before she could beat him down and battle across the room to the garden door. Shooting the bolts she flung it wide. 'Out!' she yelled and he charged through, his tail landing a brisk slap across the back of her left knee in passing.

She shrieked, 'You bloody thing!' Limping to the table she collapsed into a chair, rubbing her knee and complaining aloud, 'God Almighty, Megan, if you must have an animal that size around the place, why not get a nice quiet donkey?'

'Anything wrong Miss?'

Without turning her head Kate recognised the sepulchral voice of Ena-the-cleaner and groaned inwardly. She'd forgotten all about the ghastly early morning arrival of the lugubrious Mrs Trevone, by whose standards an eight a.m. start was passable, eight-thirty verging on the slothful, and nine … positively degenerate. She squinted blearily at the clock. It was seven forty-five and she hadn't even heard the old hag's key in the lock. Summoning a weak smile she prised herself from her chair. 'Hello, Ena, I guess I overslept.'

'Aye, it's a fair old journey Down Here from Up There – but don't you mind I, you just go on up an' dress and I'll have a nice cup of tea and breakfast ready for when you be down again.'

Christ, seven forty-five… Kate moaned softly as she climbed back up the stairs, *and I've got to put up with this every Tuesday and Saturday morning, come rain or shine…*

After a very hot bath, she felt almost human again and once dressed in warm cords, a wool shirt and the beautiful new blue cashmere sweater of Paul's he'd overlooked in his hasty packing, she felt brave enough to return to the kitchen and face the mug of strong stewed tea, pale toast and leathery bacon and eggs, which by Ena's reckoning was what constituted a proper breakfast.

Heathcliffe, once returned from his *toilette à nécessaire,* was a great help. In the intervals when Ena's back was turned, at least three-quarters of the egg and bacon disappeared down his obliging gullet, while the dried flowers in a vase on the dresser received a mug of pure tannin by way of nourishment.

Breakfast satisfactorily disposed of, Kate took laptop and briefcase into Megan's study and shut the door firmly, leaving Ena free to thrash the carpets and furniture into submission to the accompaniment of "Jerusalem," sung a full octave too high and belted out in rousing Women's Institute style.

*   *   *

By the time Ena left at noon, Kate had accomplished nothing more inspiring than finding two possible, but not probable, and definitely not well-paid enough PA jobs on-line, and a great deal of doodling with an HB pencil on a sheet of Megan's best notepaper.

The fact had to be faced that now she and Paul were no longer an item, she would have to start looking seriously for other employment. As Paul's partner she had enjoyed a luxurious and mortgage-free life-style, and as his official and efficient PA, earned the kind of salary that would be hard, if not impossible, to match elsewhere. Moreover, while most of her life before Paul had called for economy and a plain and at times positively frugal lifestyle, enchanted with her status as partner of the rich and carefree spender Paul Verdassey, she had spent as she earned, with little need to save for what had seemed a safe and financially secure future.

She sighed, closed the laptop and brushed a hand through her hair, and picking up the sheet of doodles she studied them more closely.

Amid whorls and spirals and horizontal figures of eight cascading down the paper, her caricature of Andrew Parradine stared up at her, exaggeratedly large nose, deep-set eyes creased at the corners, long, mobile mouth half-curved into a smile, just as he'd looked when he'd left her last evening. Further down the page and nestling amid a riot of

Hawthorn blossom appeared young Sam: narrow-faced, with tilted faun's eyes, sardonic grin and long, straw-coloured hair.

Pensively she added a few more lines to the first face, and longer eye lashes and a small pair of goat's horns to the second, then looked from one to the other. She felt a twinge of guilt over her abrupt dismissal of A. Parradine. He had after all gone to considerable trouble on her behalf, and she needn't have been quite such a cow. It wasn't his fault that she'd been in a foul mood. Bad timing, she thought and sighed. Even if she had been interested in forging a beautiful friendship she couldn't have made a better balls-up. What twat, she wondered, had first coined the phrase "Life Begins at Forty"? – her forties had begun an insidious slide into chaos a couple of years ago, with little prospect of getting back on track in the immediate future.

After Ena the cleaner's departure she abandoned her PC and returned to the kitchen to rummage around the meagre stocks of food in store cupboards and fridge, following this with a visit to the freezer, a monstrous affair kept out of sight in the cellar. This, when she had prised the ice-sealed lid open with a screwdriver, revealed reposing in its depths what had to be the oldest pizza in Cornwall, six monster packets of frozen peas and a leg of lamb in the last stages of frostbite.

Kate was unsurprised by her findings; even when younger Megan had been a notoriously lazy cook. The Market Inn Pub or the chippy in nearby Maunsley village, or at a pinch, and if the car started, any one of the myriad eating places further afield in Penzance generally provided her lunches and evening meals. All very well if one had limitless amounts of cash to eat out and the price of petrol no object, thought Kate, but if she was going to have anything like a reasonable but economic diet over an unspecific number of weeks, she would have to go supermarket shopping in a big way.

She dumped the lamb, pizza and peas into a handy plastic bag for removal to the dustbin, switched the freezer to defrost then climbed back into the kitchen, where a cup of instant coffee and a sandwich made from some rather elderly cheese, together with the scrapings from a jar of piccalilli, made a passable lunch.

The village shop she knew of old was hardly a cornucopia of exciting delicacies and while she ate she made a list of all those Things Most Needed for Survival that might be found in one or other of the Penzance supermarkets. It was a long list. Even after the deletion of several expensive and not strictly necessary items, she realised with sinking heart that there was no way she could struggle on and off buses then walk almost a mile from the nearest stop carrying half the contents of the Co-op in plastic bags. She would have to take Megan's car.

The clapped-out nineteen seventy-something Triumph Herald Convertible, perpetually smelling of dog and mildew, was only just bearable in high summer with the hood down. In mid-winter, when wind and weather made their remorseless way through the gaps where the hood met, or rather failed to meet, the main body of the car, it would doubtless resemble nothing so much as an odorous travelling icebox. Just the thought of the journey ahead made Kate shudder. Although Paul's luxurious sweater, her woollen tights, duffle coat, scarf and thermal gloves might just keep her on the right side of hypothermia, she realised too late that her elegant town boots could only invite instant frostbite. Her present get-up was a long way from being sophisticated, she thought morosely, but she'd be damned if she would descend even further into sluttish mediocrity by wearing her Reebok trainers to slog around Penzance. Why the hell, she demanded of an unheeding Heathcliffe, hadn't she thought to buy a pair of fleece-lined waterproof boots before leaving civilization?

She remembered that Megan had always kept a collection of boots, waxed jackets, hairy tweed coats, various dog blankets and bits of old harness from an extant pony and trap, in the old scullery off the kitchen. In desperation and holding her breath she opened the doors of the musty cupboard in the corner of the scullery and plunged into the depths, emerging after a minute of frantic burrowing clutching a stout pair of sheepskin-lined boots to her bosom as though they were the Holy Grail.

They were a size too large, but after cleaning out the dead spiders, flies and other creeping wildlife long expired in their depths, with the addition of a second pair of socks they became wearable. Feeling like Michelin Man in all her layers of clothing, she shut a loudly complaining Heathcliffe in the kitchen and trudged large-footed to the garage, ready to do battle with Megan's answer to Paul Verdassey's Mercedes.

*   *   *

Andrew Parradine was also compiling a list of essential DIY items; he enjoyed working with his hands and looked forward to doing some of the lighter tasks around the house himself, although there had been an acerbic exchange that morning between himself and George, whose dire warnings that Andrew would cock up his shoulder even further and put himself on a fast track back into hospital had tipped his employer over into temper. George, he said waspishly, was talking out of his arse. While he, Andrew, still had one good arm with which to work, that was what he intended to do; with or without George's flaming approval.

George had stomped off muttering "awkward old bugger" and taken his revenge at breakfast by serving, alongside the grilled bacon and scrambled egg, several rounds of black pudding, Andrew's least favourite breakfast food, then watching hawk-eyed to make sure he ate it.

Now he eyed his employer as he climbed into the Land Rover, and sucking his teeth audibly, another thing Andrew detested, observed, 'What you needs now guv'nor, is an automatic. Bunging that bloody gear lever in and out that ol' gearbox won't do you no good, you'll see.'

'Yeah, yeah, I'll find myself a nice little old Austin – one of those blue jobs driven exclusively by senior citizens wearing flat caps or knit hats!' Andrew shoved the lever into first and tried not to wince. Goaded by pain he added, 'and while I'm about it, I'll go to the job centre and find a nice, sympathetic, clean-living lady housekeeper to do for me and you can shove off into the Chelsea bloody Pensioners; that's if they'd have you, which I doubt.'

George muttered, 'I ain't old enough fer them yet, and any landlady would probably do for you all right – and she wouldn't be clean-living for long with you around!' Andrew affected not to hear him, nor to notice the two-fingered salute he got as he drove off. There were times, he thought sourly, the black pudding lying heavy on his stomach, when he could cheerfully throttle George, but then what would he do without him? And the old devil was right; this was one cow of a heavy vehicle and he definitely shouldn't be driving it at this stage in his convalescence. Tough, he thought, he'd be damned if he'd give up his recently clawed-back independence. Now he was finished with hospitals and being bossed around by well meaning doctors, nurses and every kind of therapist known to man, the time was well overdue for his return to being the one doing the bossing and having the last word. Not that that would cut any ice with George but Toby might be a case for reverting to his normal persona of top dog.

During the drive into Penzance, Andrew thought about his son. It was true that he'd seen little of him over the years since he and Vanessa had agreed to part, although he could never lay claim to their ever having had what one might call a close father/son relationship. Army life hadn't exactly been conducive to that kind of parenting.

Perhaps they might have been closer had Vanessa not insisted the boy should be sent away to school as a boarder at eight. With bleak unhappy memories of his own schooldays spent in what amounted to a penal colony for small boys in the depths of Hampshire, Andrew had fought her over that, but had been forced eventually to give way, first to a preparatory school in Hampstead, then a later move to a minor public school near Shaftsbury. As Vanessa had coolly and logically pointed out, her social life did not include a growing boy forever hanging about the place, and with Andrew seldom around when needed, a day school was out of the question. The poor little sod, no wonder he's a mess, Andrew thought with rare compassion. I should have fought his corner for him a long time ago; too damned late now…

Still pre-occupied with the looming problem of what to do with the ill-named Tobias for all those future vacations, Andrew negotiated his way through the Penzance traffic in search of a parking space.

5

The supermarket car park was full, but Kate eventually found a parking bay on the far side, where she discovered that, apart from the boot, none of the locks on the Triumph doors responded to her attempts to lock them. She knocked superstitiously on the walnut dash and hoped the car would still be there on her return. A fairly safe assumption, she mused as she collected her trolley; any would-be thief or joy-rider would need to be either severely visually-impaired or intellectually challenged, possibly both, to even chance opening a door, let alone actually sit in the thing. Sure enough, when she emerged half an hour later to push her laden trolley across the car park, there stood Megan's car, unmolested and clearly undesired. Encouraged, she locked her six plastic bags into the boot, returned her trolley to the rack and went in search of coffee.

By the time she left the little café in Market Street, the sun was out and for an hour or more she walked around the busy town, renewing her acquaintance with some of the older and more familiar shops still open for business. She was standing before the window of the art shop she had first visited as a young girl, when she heard her name spoken and turning around was caught in the gaze of Andrew Parradine's penetrating grey eyes.

'Hi,' he smiled at her startled expression. 'I wasn't sure if it was you...all that gear...' he gestured, smiled again. 'I like it; it suits you.'

'Thanks,' she gave a return grin. 'I thought I'd try merging into the local scenery.'

'The woman about country looks as good as the woman about town,' he commented, then passed a slow, narrow-eyed, lingering look over her from neck to toe and back again before flicking his eyes back to her face. 'It's almost lunch time,' he said.

You cheeky, eye-stripping bastard, thought Kate. Controlling an immediate desire to kick his shin with one of her enormous boots, she studied her watch for a moment. 'So it is,' she said briskly. 'Time I finished my shopping then. Goodbye, Mr Parradine.'

'Annoying you seems to be a habit with me,' he said cheerfully. 'I'm sorry. If you're not in a hurry perhaps you'd let me stand you a lunch?' George, he thought, would play hell for the rest of the day if he were not back at Rosscannan by noon, but so what...

Kate cast a speculative eye over his now amiable and guileless expression. 'All right,' she said eventually, 'you're on.'

Now why on earth, she wondered, had she said *that*? If she stayed away too long Heathcliffe would probably pee all over Ena's nice clean kitchen floor, just to show who was boss.

She watched her companion as he studied the bar menu in the Queens. He *did* have a familiar face and it irritated her that she couldn't place him. She had a good memory and an almost instant recall of faces, at least in the music and theatre world. But he couldn't belong with the luvvies, musical or theatrical, she reasoned, otherwise she would have tagged him the first time they met. Perhaps with that seemingly well-muscled body he was someone's bodyguard, or something equally hush-hush and brutal, although if that were the case, surely his face wouldn't be familiar to anyone outside his own field?

His clothes gave no clues. Yesterday he had worn a dark suit and overcoat, with a sober tie and starched shirt collar; all of it expensive. Today, with old cords tucked into his Hunters, a check shirt under a Guernsey and a worn Barbour jacket, he looked the perfect country-man; all that was needed to complete the picture was a Labrador. She knit her brows at his bent head.

Without looking up from the menu he said conversationally, 'To answer at least one of your questions, I am a deranged serial killer on the run from a maximum security prison hospital. This morning I murdered a harmless old man, breakfasted off his blood and stole his clothes.'

Caught out, Kate blushed which was something she very rarely did. 'I didn't mean to gawp; it's just that I'm sure I've seen you before…I have a very good memory for faces, and it's been bugging me that I can't place yours.'

'There you are then,' he gave a close-mouthed smile. 'I expect you saw my pictures when I went to trial – there was one in the Sun that I was quite pleased with; it showed my best side.'

'Don't be ridiculous. I was only curious about where I'd seen you before, that's all.'

'Well, we all have a *doppelganger* somewhere.' He put down the menu, adding 'You should do that more often.'

'Do what more often?'

'Smile.'

Despite herself she laughed. 'For a married man you have a nerve, asking a strange woman to lunch then trotting out a horny old cliché like that!'

'Nothing wrong with a horny old cliché if it gets results,' he murmured, aware that he was actually flirting with Kate Shaw. A nice old-fashioned word, flirting, he thought and wondered if anyone under the age of fifty used it anymore. Toby would probably say he was on the pull. He could almost hear him, drawling in that horrible, bastardised English and fractured grammar which now seemed *de rigueur* with his generation, *Flirting? Man that is so-o-o not cool; know what I mean?* He dragged his attention back to the menu. 'Shepherd's pie,' he said firmly. 'You can't beat that on a cold day.'

'Beef Curry,' she countered, 'for my money you can't beat that on any kind of day.'

'One Shepherd's Pie, one Beef Curry it is then.' He signalled to the waitress. 'I like a girl who knows her own mind.'

'Just as well,' she said dryly, 'seeing you are stuck with me for as long as it takes me to eat.'

Was he making a pass she wondered; he hadn't risen to the bait when she'd knocked his status as a married man, she noticed, yet somehow he didn't appear the philandering type, anymore than a serial killer...

At that moment he looked up, a lazy smile lurking behind his eyes, and a warning bell began to ring. She was not about to go down *that* path again, she reminded herself severely. Self-preservation, was the name of the game, and the sooner she got rid of the blinkers she'd worn for the past eight years and remembered how to play it, the safer and less stressful life would be.

*　　*　　*

That evening Kate settled into a voluptuously comfortable armchair before the fire, wondering how many evenings she was destined to spend alone in Megan's house, her only companion the creature now stretched full length on the couch, his head hanging sideways over the edge, his enormous tongue hanging from drooping lips.

'On occasions you really are a remarkably unattractive creature, you know,' she told him. She gazed broodingly at his inert form. God, now she was talking to a *dog;* but perhaps people who talked to their animals weren't crazy, after all. As they didn't talk back there was less likelihood of misunderstanding than when talking to humans. She sighed and sank further into her chair. Heathcliffe woke at the sound, heaved an answering sigh and rolling off the couch with all the lumbering grace of a bear fresh from hibernation came to lean his head on her knee. Absently she rubbed his ears. 'What do you recommend I do to earn an honest penny, Heathcliffe?' she asked him, 'go back and sweat it out in London, or move right out, perhaps even out of England; try something totally different.'

It was odd to realise that she had only left Ealing such a short time ago but was already dreading a return to the old faces and places. Despite Paul's myriad failings, in the past eight years, where work and life in general were concerned, she had always known exactly where she was at. Now she was adrift and rudderless, without any clear sense of direction and trailing a sophisticated lifestyle behind her like so much useless flotsam. She had to face it; she was forty-three, an unemployed P.A – and God knew, *they* were two a penny – a musical genius's ex-lover; childless, loveless and unloved, with no idea of where to go next…and despite all that had happened, she still missed Paul; missed him terribly.

For a few minutes she allowed herself a good wallow, then sat up and gave Heathcliffe's head a brisk pat. 'Tomorrow you and I are going to take a walk over to Sam Trevene and leave a note inviting him for that dinner I promised. I could do with a friend and he's young enough to be just that and no more.'

Shrugging off her attack of the blues, she jumped to her feet urging, 'Come on Heathcliffe; we'll see what we can rustle up for a not-too-intimate little dinner on Saturday. I may be crap with a tin of furniture polish and I don't have tits like Nigella, but I'm a demon in the kitchen and can give any TV cook a run for his or her money any day of the week.'

6

Toby climbed down from the bus without any clear idea of what to do next or even where he was going. It had said Maunsley on the front, and as it was the last one leaving Penzance that afternoon and going vaguely in the right direction, he'd boarded it. Now he hadn't a clue as to how he was to get to a place he'd never heard of until a few weeks ago, let alone find a house he'd never seen. If only he'd had enough dosh to get up to Aunt Fliss in Scotland…

The bloody bus driver hadn't been much help. "Rosscannan – never hea'd of it, m'dear; I'm from Mous'le meself." Scuzzy old git. Toby slouched along what seemed to be the only street in this divvy town. No bloody shops open, except the chippy. He felt the few remaining coins in his pocket; he was hungry, but there wasn't much left after the train and bus fares and he couldn't risk leaving himself totally skint. If the old man cut up really rough he might have to do another bunk.

The bus had turned and was grinding down the street; as it passed Toby gave the driver two fingers. He wished he still had the bottle of voddy, the discovery and confiscation of which had been the cause of his present lousy predicament. He thought with moody dislike that the head had probably guzzled the lot by now, the boozy old bugger.

The smell from the chippy made his stomach contract with hunger. He scuffed at an empty lager can and sent it rattling into the gutter. Trust that old twat of a matron to go turning all the mattresses in search of porno mags, now he'd been sent down and there'd be all hell to pay with the old man. It was pure luck there'd been no answer when the head telephoned the house, but if they'd thought he was going to hang around until the next day and wait for daddy to collect him like some bloody parcel, they'd another think coming. He'd go home, if that was what you could call it, under his own steam. That's if he ever found the place.

It began to rain. He shivered, pulling up his blazer collar against the cold. If only he'd been able to get down to the locker room to fetch his coat and perhaps nick that pair of fur-lined leather gloves old lard-arse Collins had got for his birthday…but there had been no chance of that when the only way of escape had been through the sickbay window.

He peered through the half-open door of the chippy. The guy

behind the counter was enormous and looked like he could double for the Incredible Hulk. There was only one customer, a girl, and he waited until she came out and watched her stroll off, her bum in the tight micro skirt rolling from side to side and up and down at every step. Immediately his mind turned to sex, which it did anyway about every other minute. What he'd really like, he mused, was to have so much of it that it almost got boring. Not very likely for a bloke who hadn't managed anything more than a quick grope around the navy blue knickers of Vicky Spencer, his housemaster's daughter. She was reputed to be the college bicycle but she'd never offered to give him a ride.

Sighing, he levered himself off the doorframe and ventured into the chippy. ''Scuze me,' Better do the polite bit, he thought. 'Do you know if there's a house called Rosscannan near here?'

The Incredible Hulk looked him over without interest. 'I know it. But it ain't nowhere near here, sonny.'

It was true, Toby thought, hearts really did sink: right now his was sloshing somewhere around his knees. He asked gloomily, 'It's quite a way then?'

'Too right; ye'll not get there tonight – not before dark, ye won't.'

'I have to,' he tried not to sound as desperate as he felt. 'If you just tell me which direction…'

The Hulk took a chip, tested it with his fingers then transferred it to his mouth. He shrugged. 'Rather you than me, me 'andsome!' Wiping his hands on his apron he came to the door and pointed back down the street toward the sea. 'Go to the end and turn left, then keep goin' along that old cliff road for a couple o' miles until it narrows into the track signposted Penmaric: ye don't go along there but take another left turn onto the A-road towards Porthcledra. That takes ye inland for a mile or so before it turns back towards the sea. The 'ouse is about another mile on and ye can't miss it 'cause there's a ruddy great pair of iron gates wi' ROSSCANNAN on 'em.'

'Thanks…' Toby swallowed hard. 'I'd better get going then.' He nodded at the Hulk then turned, and leaving the light and warmth of the chippy, began to trudge miserably towards the cliffs.

*   *   *

Kate woke early on Saturday morning to a slate-grey sky and a stiff wind coming in from the sea. Determined to beat the lugubrious Ena, she raced through a shallow bath, dressed at breakneck speed and by the time Ena arrived, was at the kitchen table finishing a normal breakfast of toast and coffee.

'I'm walking Heathcliffe now,' she said quickly before Ena could reach for her favourite culinary weapon, the frying pan, 'so I'll be out of your way for a bit.'

'Where you going then, m'dear?'

Kate would like to have told the nosey cow that was none of her business, but if she must suffer her visits, it would be as well to keep her sweet. Shrugging into her duffle she said, 'Hawthorn Cottage at Godolphin Point, do you know it?'

'Old Sam Trevene's place? Course I knows it; half o' Cornwall knows that mucky old ruin.' Ena began wrapping her voluminous apron around her considerable avoirdupois 'You want to keep away from there…time after time I've told Missus Baxter, bad blood will out and that young Sam's no better than 'is dirty old grandfather before him, but do she listen to me – no she dos'en't, she 'as him up here doin' her garden an' choppin' her wood…asking for trouble, she is.'

'He seemed all right to me.' Kate was instantly intrigued, her interest now thoroughly aroused by Ena's tightened lips and obvious desire to spill the beans. She egged her on. 'What's he done?'

'What 'asn't he more like!' Ena crossed her arms over her mighty bosom. 'Spent all his time with that poaching, swearing, woman-grabbing Old Sam – and 'is own folk good God-fearing Chapel people with his dad a lay-preacher. Broke his heart, that boy did.'

Kate perched on the kitchen table, 'Go on,' she urged, hoping to cut to the chase without being forced to wade through the entire Trevene family history. 'What did he *do* exactly?'

'Got hisself in with a wild crowd over in Penzance, drinking an' suchlike, then the old man died sudden and left him the house. He moved in an' took up with Aiden Pascoe's young Rosie: both of them bare seventeen they was when he got her pregnant, then they neither of them would do the right thing and get married. Sam forged his dad's signature on a cheque for her to have an abortion at some posh place in London; a wicked thing in the eyes of the Lord.'

Kate said quietly, 'She obviously thought that better than having an unwanted baby. You can't blame Sam – or Rosie for not wanting to be tied down at that age.'

Ena sniffed. 'Look before you leap's my motto. But she was well rid of that tearaway, because within the year he was up to the magistrates for smoking that mary what's-it stuff.'

'Marijuana,' supplied Kate helpfully. Big deal, she thought, who hasn't.

'Very serious that was. He was going to get sent to one of them delinquent places but Tom Trevene went bail for him, took him home an' took off 'is belt to him...' Ena paused for full dramatic effect. '...so you know what that boy done then?'

'Tell me.'

'Near broke Tom's jaw, he did, then set fire to the 'ouse and run off to London! Police found him tho' and he done five years for assault and arse-what'sit. The cottage was let and we didn't hear nothing more of him 'til he turned up again a couple of years ago now. Gawd alone knows what he'd been up to between prison and coming back here.'

Kate was impressed. Whoever would have thought young Sam had such a colourful history. Not that she necessarily believed all Ena's gossip, which had doubtless gained colour over years of repetition. She would like to have asked how Megan came to have befriended such a desperate character, but thought she'd have to pass on that one for now if her morning was to go to plan. Given the chance Ena would talk for hours.

Twenty minutes later she had finally managed to ease herself and Heathcliffe out of the house and was striding along the headland path towards Godolphin point, the dog only leaving her side occasionally to forage down a rabbit hole or dive into the tall coarse grass and put some resting bird to flight. Apart from an excursion or two down onto the beach to examine some particularly interesting looking flotsam washed up by the tide, Kate walked at a brisk pace, the cold wind buffeting her body with an icy blast that took away her breath and made her eyes water. Above her head gulls swooped and cried while the wind drove the incoming tide foaming and tumbling over the rocks. An hour or so and the waves would be pounding half way up the towering cliffs, to hang for a breathless moment in a blinding flurry of spray before plunging back onto the rocks below.

She thought how Paul had loved just such mornings as this; how on one visit in their early days he had stood on a great flat rock jutting out over the sea and conducted the crashing waves, shouting and laughing uproariously until she thought his enthusiasm would take him over the edge and into oblivion.

There was nothing, she mused, as sad as a love affair ended in anger, with no chance to repair or to heal the hurt. She wondered, given the chance, if she would go back and for a moment thought she might, until she remembered all those porcelain figurines she had slaughtered: Paul's pride and joy, hunted for and found in antique shops and market stalls all over Europe.

He was impossible and exhausting and had a temper a Rottweiler with toothache would be ashamed of, but she still longed to feel again the sheer energy and exuberance of him and that warm vibrant body in her bed.

'It's only the sex you miss,' she scolded herself aloud, safe in the knowledge she would not be overheard; that no other idiot would be walking the cliff path on a morning like this. 'Well, you're a big girl now, so you must either learn to live without a man, or stop whingeing and find yourself an occasional spot of nooky.'

But she knew she needed more than that, much more, but it would be a long time, if ever, before she would commit again to just one man. Few seemed to have the staying power and it hurt too darned much when it ended.

*   *   *

Between her own and Heathcliffe's several diversions, it took her well over an hour to cover the distance between Pendragon and Hawthorn Cottage. While she was still some yards off the dog raced ahead and she let him go, figuring that if Sam was at home and didn't yet know how to defend himself, he'd have to take the consequences. She was startled when the dog shot back through the non-existent gate and hurtled to her side whining and shaking. Kate didn't need a degree in dog psychology to see he was badly spooked and the hair on the nape of her neck began to prickle…what could have scared him like that… some kind of wild animal; an escaped lunatic; a dead body?

Taking a firm grip on her nerves and Heathcliffe's collar she started down the path.

Nearing the cottage she could see what appeared to be a heap of clothes piled in the shadowy gloom of the deep porch. Relieved, she shook the dog's collar. 'Heathcliffe, you big wuss,' she scolded, 'don't you know a bundle of old clothes when you see one?' and taking her invitation to dinner from her pocket she stepped up to the door, then screamed and leapt backward as the heap moved, grew arms and legs and was revealed as a youth wearing a saturated school uniform and a glazed expression.

He peered up at her with uncomprehending blue eyes.

'What the hell…,' his speech was slurred and slow. He made to struggle to his feet. 'D'you reckon you could…that's if you would….' his voice tailed off and before Kate's fascinated and horrified gaze, his eyes closed and he slid back down onto the damp flagstones.

She thought it unlikely that Sam was in, but pounded the door with her fist, then looked again at the boy, who had collapsed at an awkward angle, knees and head slumped sideways. Kneeling, she pushed the damp hair from his forehead, feeling his skin cold and clammy to the touch.

'Damn…' she squatted back on her heels. It was obvious he was in desperate need of warmth, and possibly medical attention, but the last house she had passed was a good half mile back along the cliffs, the next at least another 500 yards or more on down the lane...and her mobile was at Pendragon in the bag she hadn't bothered to bring with her.

She looked at her watch. Almost nine-thirty and Sam had obviously left for work. Who the hell was his mysterious visitor and how long had he been on this freezing doorstep? More to the point, how was she going to get him off it and into the house?

She thought hard. Would Sam keep a spare key, and if he did, would he hide it somewhere complicated and difficult to discover, or somewhere obvious where any would-be intruder could find it? 'He's a man, isn't he?' she muttered aloud and getting to her feet reached up to run a hand experimentally along the beam over the door. 'Hah, now that *is* original!' Triumphant, she retrieved a large iron key and waved it under Heathcliffe's nose.

Despite her lean build she was a strong woman. Unlocking the door and pushing it wide she hauled the youth's slack body more or less upright and staggering a little under his dead weight, managed to get him over the threshold and into an armchair without too much difficulty. For a few moments she stood looking down on him, wondering how old he was, hazarding a guess at fourteen, perhaps a little older; his features hadn't yet fully metamorphosed from puberty to adult and he still had the over-large nose, pimples and prominent ears common to early adolescence.

She shivered, suddenly aware that the room was bleak and cold, the only source of warmth a wood fire smouldering sullenly beneath a dampened covering of coal slack; but there were dry logs stacked beside the hearth and next to them a businesslike pair of bellows. A minute's work with the latter and the careful placing of several of the smaller logs soon brought the fire to life.

The boy in the chair stirred slightly; Kate dusted off her hands then leaned forward and shook his shoulder gently until his eyes flickered and opened.

She smiled. 'Hey, stay with me this time, will you.'

He looked around and, giving a faint moan, made a half-hearted effort to rise. Kate pressed him back onto the chair. 'I said stay with me, not run a marathon!'

He look confused and definitely not with it. 'You're new here; where's matron?'

'I'm slightly less new than you, buster – and I'll pass on the matron tag.' She regarded him thoughtfully. 'Are you a friend of Sam's?'

'Who's Sam?' His eyelids drooped again. 'Shit, but I'm tired.'

This was one of those situations for some straight talking. Using the Royal We she said briskly, 'I think we should get you out of those wet clothes. Come along; sit up and I'll help you.'

It was fortunate she thought, as she helped him struggle first out of his blazer then his shirt, trousers, shoes and socks, that he was sufficiently far gone not to be either coy or alarmed at being stripped to his boxers by a strange woman, then wrapped in the hairy rug she'd found thrown over the back of a chair.

So far so good, she congratulated herself as she stood back to view the boy, who again appeared to have lapsed into unconsciousness; now to find a doctor who actually made house calls. In London those were rare as hen's teeth; she could only hope the country version might be more co-operative. She looked around for a phone, wondering under which particular pile of clothing or paper it might lurk.

She hunted carefully and thoroughly around the small sitting room. No phone. Cursing aloud and followed by Heathcliffe, who, making it quite clear he wasn't going to be left alone with the corpse-like figure by the fire, stuck to her like glue, she went into the kitchen, which was reasonably tidy and almost clean, despite a proliferation of plants crowding the window sill and wooden draining board, but similarly devoid of a phone. Reluctantly and with an uncomfortable sense of prying, she climbed the steep and narrow stairs, peered briefly into the bathroom, where even she didn't expect a result, then opened the last door onto what was Sam's sparsely furnished, and in contrast to the rest of the house, almost clinically clean bedroom.

No phone.

'Oh, *bugger*,' she said aloud. 'Wouldn't you just *know* it – useless or what?'

'Who is?' Sam's voice enquired from the foot of the stairs and she whirled around, glaring down at him with accusing eyes.

She said bitingly. 'Only *you* would invite someone to stay then forget to be home when they arrived – and you must be the last man on earth who doesn't have a telephone.'

Before he had time to reply Heathcliffe left his exploration of the bedroom. Launching himself down the stairs he pinned the newcomer against the wall and began moaning and slavering into his left ear.

'Okay, okay, take it easy,' Sam detached himself from the hound's enthusiastic embrace and grinned up at Kate. 'Can anybody join your party…I assume that *is* your Toy Boy zonked out by my fire and minus most of his clobber?'

'It is not.' Kate joined him in the sitting room and together they stared at the boy, who was either asleep or in a coma. 'I found him on your doorstep, soaking wet and looking as though he'd been there all night.' She added stringently, 'He's very confused, and so am I.'

'Me too, I've never seen him before in my life.'

'I thought you said you worked every day.'

'I do, but I only work the afternoons on Fridays – I've been down in the back garden and greenhouse since breakfast, so the guy could easily have been out front all night.' He took a packet of papers and a tin from the pocket of his oiled jacket and began to roll a cigarette. 'The question now is: what are we going to do about him?'

Equally baffled they looked at each other in silence. Eventually Sam suggested. 'His school gear…it probably has a name in it.'

Kate shook her head. 'I looked; just a number – like a convict,' she said, then realised she might have been more diplomatic.

Her companion's mouth curled slightly. 'Sounds like one of our minor Public Schools; the kind devoted to the regimentation of the young – all doomed to failure, of course. The young are now well past being regimented.'

Kate thought briefly about her own non-regimented and somewhat chaotic schooldays in a large mixed comprehensive ruled over by a benign but bemused headmistress, and silently agreed. Regimented wasn't a word that sprung to mind in describing the *ambience* of the Alderman Roberts Comprehensive. Perhaps Sam's unexpected guest had decided he wanted out and done a bunk, but from where? And how on earth had he managed to end up on this particular rugged and sparsely populated headland? She said, 'I think one of us should try to get a doctor.'

Sam took a closer look at the comatose one and gave Kate a quick wink. 'He may have been out of it when you first found him,' he murmured, 'but right now I think he's playing possum.' Squatting down he put a hand on each of the boy's knees, squeezing hard. 'Okay,' he said loudly, 'game's over chum, you can wake up now.'

The boy's eyes shot open and he glared at Sam. 'Hey, you don't have to break my frigging kneecaps!'

'Where were you heading when you decided to kip on my

49

doorstep, mate?' Sam's asked, his voice easy and unthreatening

'Some dump called Rosscannan,' the boy answered sulkily,

Sam raised his eyebrows. 'That place – it's been standing empty for over a year.'

'Well, it isn't empty now. My father lives there.'

Kate asked, 'Won't he be worried that you haven't turned up?'

The boy gave an indifferent shrug, 'Shouldn't think so; be well pissed-off though.'

Judging that Sam might get further with this cagey brat if she made herself scarce she offered. 'I'm going to make us all some tea,' she was carefully casual, 'are you hungry?'

'Yeah: a bit.'

'I'll see what I can do – all right with you, Sam, if I root in your kitchen?'

'Fine, help yourself. If you need anything, just yell.'

Sam waited until the kitchen door closed behind Kate then seating himself on the other side of the hearth fixed his guest with a gimlet eye, 'Okay, I can guess you're on the run from school, so let's start with your name.'

'Toby.'

Sam took a deep breath; he said bluntly, 'I don't do patient mate, so...which school and where?'

'Brandon House...it's near Sherborne.'

'That's a bloody long way to run – what happened; drugs? wakky baccy? porno mags?'

'Nah,' Toby almost smiled, 'a bottle of Voddy, under the mattress!'

Sam grinned. 'Careless, and bloody uncomfortable I should think...come on now, how did you get from Sherborne to my doorstep.'

'Walked across country to the next station, then rail with a couple of changes to Penzance; took a bus to Maunsley from there but it turned around in the village and I didn't have any dosh left, so I had to walk –'

Sam interrupted, 'Christ, that's miles from here, you idiot – and a damn sight further to Rosscannan.'

'I didn't know that, did I?' He was sullen, then his mouth began to tremble and suddenly all the smart talk was gone. 'I just kept walking in the dark then it started to piss with rain and I sort of lost the track...think I must have turned off before I should. I saw this place but it was all dark and I thought it was empty so I kipped in the porch until that woman came along...' he looked wildly at Sam, 'Shit,

50

man, she took my kit off!'

'Don't worry,' Sam was soothing, 'I'm sure nothing you might have came as a surprise to her. By the way, her name is Kate Shaw and mine is Sam Trevene; it might be a good idea if you told me yours – all of it.'

He hesitated, shooting a glance at the closed kitchen door. 'Toby Parradine,' he said at last, 'but don't tell anyone…my dad 'ud kill me if I got even one line in the local rag!'

'Parradine?' Sam repeated; 'Big bloke – Army – been in all the papers?' Toby nodded and Sam's mouth twitched. 'Okay, but if you've been missing since yesterday he must be a pretty worried man, so we need to get you home PDQ.' He stood up. 'I'm going up to find you some dry clothes now, then, when Kate's fed and watered you, we'll deliver you to your dad.'

While the visitor ate a couple of boiled eggs washed down with tea, they decided Sam would take Kate to Pendragon to collect Megan's car, hoping that by their return Toby would be recovered enough to face the journey home and whatever fate awaited him there.

Poor little sod, mused Sam as he watched him eat, no wonder he's shit scared of returning home. So would I be if I had that bloke for a father.

Sam knew all about Andrew Parradine; practically everyone in this country and beyond did; but hero or no hero, Sam didn't approve of any man who had any connection with war in any shape or form. All in all, he thought he would leave Toby's delivery to Andrew Parradine in Kate's capable hands.

*   *   *

Thankful that she was wearing trousers and not a skirt, Kate braved the icy journey to Pendragon on the back of Sam's ancient motorbike. Only stopping to drop her at the steps he rode off noisily, trailing a cloud of sludge coloured exhaust fumes and leaving Kate to follow in the Triumph. With feet and hands numb with cold, she drove slowly back to the cottage along the rutted track, swearing monotonously and consigning Sam and his unspeakable motorbike to the furthest and hottest corner of hell. Reaching the cottage at last, she climbed shivering from the car and staggered through the front door.

The boy was asleep on the rug before the fire with Heathcliffe lying along his back, while from the kitchen could be heard the sounds of a man at work. Skirting the somnolent pair on the hearthrug, Kate dropped her duffle on the littered table and crossed to peer around the kitchen door. 'Any chance of a cup of something hot?' she asked plaintively.

Sam jumped, almost dropping the plate he was drying. 'Don't *do* that, I've already had enough shocks for one day!'

'Sorry,' she came in, shutting the door behind her. 'I was trying not to disturb the love birds in there,' she jerked her head back towards the living room. 'There should be a law against motorbikes; I'm bloody freezing.'

'Sit down and I'll make some fresh tea.' Sam began to set mugs and milk jug on the table; clearing his throat he said much too casually, 'I hate to ask, but would you mind taking the kid home by yourself, I've got quite a lot to do before I go in at lunch time...' his voice tailed away at the look on her face. 'Sorry,' he repeated lamely, 'but it isn't far; only a few miles and I can write the directions down for you.'

'It isn't the journey I mind, more the reception I might get when I arrive,' she snapped. 'I imagine his parents won't be exactly overjoyed to find that while they've been tearing their hair out their darling boy has been a half dozen miles away, kipping on your doorstep.'

'I can't help it if I only have a mobile and that you left yours *and* your bloody car, at home,' he retorted sharply – then added: 'I'll probably be finishing up in the greenhouse when you get back.'

'Then I'll do my best not to disturb you. All right if I leave Heathcliffe here for now and pick him up on my way back?'

He flushed. 'Sure. Take no notice of me; you've been brilliant.'

'Hey, don't you worry about a thing...all I need to round off my healthy morning stroll is an outraged parent spitting nails.' With a dramatic gesture Kate flung her scarf around her neck. 'Now if you can just lend the bolter a warm coat, or failing that a half-way clean rug to keep him from freezing to death in Megan's morgue wagon, I'll deliver him, pick up Heathcliffe then get back to Pendragon and have a nice quiet attack of hysterics, all by myself.'

Wordlessly, Sam rose, took a rescued-from-Oxfam type overcoat from a hook by the back door and handed it to her. 'Thanks.' She took it, looked down for a moment, then raised her eyes to his. 'Sorry, you've been brilliant too. Actually,' her mouth quirked into a smile, 'I only came over to invite you to dinner,' and she handed him her invitation, now rather creased and grubby.

He laughed. 'I did rather wonder at the early morning call.'

'Will next Saturday do – or will you be working?'

'I am working but it would be fine if you could make it lunch. I work eight to seven Saturdays; it's a long day so I'm pretty knackered at the end of it, but I get a two hour break around midday.'

'Okay,' she said breezily, 'lunch it is – time it right and you'll be sure to miss our Ena!'

*   *   *

Kate drove away from Hawthorne Cottage with Toby slumped beside her, his head drawn down into the upturned collar of Sam's overcoat, giving him, she thought with an inward smile, the air of a beleaguered tortoise.

Her thoughts turned to Sam and his Spartan existence. On Saturday she would make him a good substantial lunch, something to take him through the long day. Whatever he had been in the past, she mused, he certainly seemed to have turned his life around now. She would like to have given him a good dinner, with wine and an evening before the fire, instead of lunch around the kitchen table. Although to be honest, she thought with a tinge of guilt, she'd just as soon spend Saturday evening slobbed out before the fire with a good book, a bag of sherbet lemons and Heathcliffe for company.

7

Toby sat silent beside Kate as she drove him home, huddled down into the overcoat which smelled vaguely like the pong that hung around school cloakrooms. He wished he could figure out everything that had happened yesterday; he remembered changing trains, then a bus and a big bloke in a chippy, but after that it was all muddled and a bit weird. He still felt shivery and light-headed, but was reasonably warm, both inside and out, apart from a nasty cold spot around the pit of his stomach every time he thought about the inevitable meeting with his father. All hell would have let loose when the school discovered he'd pissed off, and he bet the Head had managed to find and call dad the minute they'd missed him.

He shuddered, clutching the plastic bag containing his wet clothes and shoes to his chest. Trust the old man to bury himself in the country just as ma was clearing off to the States. With him about all the time, Toby thought, it would be fucking awful; he'd be on my neck day and night, although having old George around would help.

Gradually he became aware of the Kate woman's perfume and took a surreptitious sniff, surprised and pleased at the comfortably erotic glow it produced, then blushed darkly at his hazy remembrance of the expert way she had whipped off his clothes. Stealing a sideways glance at her face he wondered if was true that older women fancied younger blokes – and if it was, how did you let them know you were up for it? Were you supposed to make a pass or leave it to them – but how *did* you make a pass and how would you know for sure if *they* were up for it?

His mother would know the answer to that one, he thought, she'd always liked the young hunks of stud muffin. He wondered if the man at that cottage – Sam something – was the woman's bloke...

'How are you feeling now?' Kate interrupted his erratic, not to say erotic, train of thought. 'I guess you could do with a good long sleep once you get home.'

'Not much chance of that if dad's ready and waiting,' he muttered. She gave him a sympathetic smile and for a moment the pleasing fantasy of being seduced by an older woman got another nudge in the right direction, until he realised this one looked, and sounded, just a bit too businesslike to be interested in toy-boy rumpy. Anyway, he thought disparagingly, she was too skinny and probably too old for it as well.

Dispirited he picked morosely at an emerging spot on his chin; thinking about his mother and the so not-brilliant muscle man she'd buggered off with…like something out of a Rambo movie he was, thick as shit but *loaded*. He picked his spot again, drawing blood. The daft cow must be ten years older than Hugo bloody Kremmer the Third. He wouldn't, he told himself, have gone with them if they'd begged him. Even dad had to be better than that…

With a horrible sick-making start he realised the car had stopped before a pair of high wrought iron gates with ROSSCANNAN worked in a fancy scroll at the top. Set into the wall beside them was one of those entry-phone things. Christ he thought, naff or what?

Beside him his companion gave a gurgle of laughter.

'Your father wouldn't by any chance be a Pop Idol determined to keep out hordes of screaming fans would he?'

He answered sourly, 'Anyone bonkers enough to mob *him* would need to get a life!'

'Like that, is it? Well. No good putting off the evil moment,' she grinned. 'Out you get and announce yourself.'

He crawled reluctantly from the car, relieved to hear his halting greeting answered by that funny old guy George, who swore loudly and told him to get his arse into the house PDQ before the boss returned.

'Dad's out,' Toby slumped back into the car. 'George is here: he's okay.'

'Glad to hear it.' Kate was equally relieved. She could do without any more hassle, particularly from someone who was beginning to sound like a cross between Vlad the Impaler and Attila the Hun.

The gates opened smoothly and silently and she covered the long drive at a fast lick. Anxious to off-load her companion and make a swift getaway she swore aloud when a half-dozen pheasants appeared from the bushes and began to zigzag in front of the car as though playing dare across the M25. 'Will you just look at those idiots?' she demanded, 'why in hell d'you suppose God gave them wings when they spend ninety percent of their lives on their bloody feet?'

Toby didn't think an answer was required. He was beginning to feel sick and his headache was back; he didn't care if the place was stiff with pheasants; all he wanted was to curl up somewhere and sleep and sleep…

Kate slowed the car to take in the building that rose out of the encircling trees. Even at this time of year it was beautiful, a perfectly proportioned Regency country house set in terraced lawns fringed with flower beds and mature trees. The window frames needed a coat of paint and it did have a rather neglected air, but lucky Toby, she thought, to have all this to come home to.

Stopping the car before the steps she slid from behind the wheel as a man who had obviously been waiting for them, hurried down to open the passenger door. 'You little bastard,' he snarled. 'Where the blue blazin' 'ell 'ave you bin since yesterday morning?'

Kate protested. 'Hey, take it easy buster. What this boy needs now is a hot bath, some TLC and a good long sleep. He's had a rough time you know.'

The man bared his teeth in a ferocious smile. 'He'll 'ave an even rougher one when the guv'nor gets back. He's bin searching the countryside for the bugger from 'ere to Dorset an' back since noon yesterday.'

'Shit!' Toby staggered and lurched toward the door. 'Get me in George – quick, before he gets here.'

Giving the boy's shoulder a parting squeeze Kate reluctantly surrendered him to the fierce little whippet of a man. 'I'm sure he won't be mad for long – just glad to find you are home safe and in one piece.'

'Derr,' Toby squirmed again, 'as if!'

'Very nice of you to bring him back, miss,' the man George appeared suddenly to remember his manners. His small sharp eyes darted from her face to her feet and back again. He leered. 'I reckon the guv'nor 'ull want to thank *you* personally when he gets the chance.'

'That's all right.' Kate's reply was crisp, with the unmistakable underlying message of *don't you try it on with me, my man.* 'We were only too glad to be of help. But Toby has been quite ill and he really should be seen by a doctor.' She turned back to the car then stood for a moment with her hand on the door. Suddenly she pivoted on one foot and gave George a dazzling smile that punched right in under his ribcage. 'But I'm sure *you'll* take good care of him now and save him from the guv'nor, won't you?' she purred.

'I will that, miss,' he winked at her and giving Toby an affectionate shove commanded, 'Get inside then, you daft sod, and I'll run you a bath.'

Kate restarted the car. 'I'll be off, then. Goodbye, Toby.'

'Goodbye – and thanks for everything.'

Still hugging the carrier bag full of his wet clothes he watched the Triumph out of sight and wondered wistfully if he'd ever see her again.

There was no sign of Sam when Kate retrieved Heathcliffe and she drove back to Pendragon, relieved that the absence of the owner of Rosscannan had spared her a meeting with a man who sounded as though he could give Idi Amin a run for his money. Really, she thought with exasperation, what was it with some men that they could chuck their weight about and expect to rule wives and children like some power-mad dictator. Although no woman had been in evidence at that beautiful house she supposed the unfortunate Toby must have a mother around somewhere: most probably she'd been slaving away in the kitchen, wishing she'd never said those two little words: "I do…"

She pondered on the disturbing fact that she, Kate Shaw, couldn't have chosen the men in her life all that well either, because so far there seemed to have been quite a few of them with one or more of those unlovely male attributes, Paul Verdassey being a prime example. Could it be she wondered, that in some strange way she attracted, and was attracted to, the masterful type? She shuddered. If so, then she really should take time out to re-evaluate her life and loves.

*   *   *

Andrew Parradine was not a happy man; was in fact a very worried and angry one. As he drove the Land Rover back towards Rosscannan he vacillated between an awful gripping fear that his son had met with some terrible accident, and a periodic overwhelming desire to remove the little bastard's head from his shoulders when he did catch up with him.

He had passed a very stressful twenty-four hours since his return from that luncheon with Kate in Penzance, when his arrival at Rosscannan in a convivial frame of mind had been shattered by George cautiously relaying the phone call from his son's headmaster alerting them to Toby's disappearance.

He had driven straight to the school, listened in stony silence to the litany of his son's sins that term, culminating in the discovery of the vodka and his subsequent flight. Considering the headmaster's limp-wristed way of dealing with the delinquent little sod hadn't helped and Andrew had left the school in the worst of tempers to begin his own search for his runaway son.

Armed with a recent school photograph he'd spent the remainder of that day painstakingly tracing Toby's progress from school to trains, from trains to bus and from bus to Maunsley village. Arriving there in the in the pitch dark and pouring rain, he found the only lighted windows were those belonging to the pub, a fish and chip shop, and the short row of council houses opposite. Figuring the chippy was the most likely haven to be visited by a hungry runaway, Andrew had entered and placed Toby's picture on the counter.

In reply to his by now rather weary, 'Have you see this boy– he may have been here sometime this evening,' the Cornish equivalent of a Sumo wrestler presiding over the fryer grunted, wiped his ham-sized hands on his apron and picked up the photograph. Wrinkling his brow he admitted grudgingly, 'Might have. Who wants him – the police?'

'No,' said Andrew coldly. 'I do, I'm his father.'

'He was here couple of hours or more ago. I gave him directions to the old Parradine place. Last thing I see of him he was walking down towards the sea.'

'Thanks.' Andrew took a card from his pocket. 'If he turns up again will you hang onto him and call this number?'

'Yeah, okay.' The Sumo wrestler shook his head. 'Little bleeders, ain't they?' he asked, and silently Andrew agreed with him.

Reasoning that if Toby already had a head start of at least two hours, any attempt to track him down in the dark would be a waste of time, Andrew gritted his teeth and stilling his fears with the thought that the boy wasn't a complete fool and would undoubtedly have made for cover of some kind he returned home to unfairly vent his frustration on George, meeting his enquiringly raised brows with a snarl. 'Before you ask, I haven't any idea where the little fuck-wit has taken himself to, but when I do catch up with him I'll break his bloody neck!'

George had sucked his teeth with disapproval and picked Andrew's drenched trench coat from where he had flung it on the floor. 'It's no use you sounding off an' cussing at me; that don't do nobody no good.' He cast a shrewd and expert eye over Andrew's face, which was grey and drawn with exhaustion and pain. 'You've got a n'eadache, haven't you? Have a bath then get some sleep. He'll have found shelter somewhere and you can't do nothing more now until the morning.'

Next morning, cursing George for letting him sleep late and brushing aside all protests, he had swallowed a cup of black coffee and a couple of codeine, then climbed into the Land Rover to resume his search. By the time he reached Maunsley again his headache was still with him, and after enduring the jolting of the Land Rover over the pot-holed coastal road for a few minutes he decided to leave it on the headland and continue his search on foot. Wrapping his scarf more tightly around his neck he put his head down against a buffeting wind and continued along the track he had driven with Kate Shaw only a few days back. If Toby had been looking for shelter it would be at one of the scattered cottages along the way, he reasoned, or if he had kept going to where the coast road ended and risked the narrow cliff path he could even have fetched up at Pendragon. There was a slim possibility his son might have found shelter for the night in one of the sheds or outhouses.

He covered the ground swiftly at first, but by the time he had called without success at the few cottages in sight of the track his pace was slowing and he trudged on with weary feet, while the pain in his shoulder began to spread across his back, increasing with every step.

When there was no answer to his ring on Kate Shaw's doorbell he waited for a few moments before walking around the house to check the various sheds and outhouses, but both house and outbuildings were clearly deserted.

Frustrated, his thoughts swinging erratically between fear that something terrible had happened to his son and anger at Toby's stupidity in leaving the safety of the village to make this ridiculous journey in darkness over unknown territory, he retraced his steps. Stopping every few yards he squatted down to peer over the edge of the cliff, scanning the ledges and rocks below for any sign of an inert body.

It was well past noon when muddy, cold, dog-tired and empty handed he returned to Rosscannan and climbed wearily from his vehicle, cursing when he realized he had forgotten the remote to open the gates; in his dazed and fraught state he couldn't remember the code. He jabbed a frozen finger at the entry-phone. 'Parradine,' he said tersely when George answered. 'It's a no go. I've drawn a blank.'

There was a pregnant pause, then the gates began to move and George said flatly, 'He's here and sleeping like a baby...'

A stream of oaths seared through the speaker. George raised his eyes to heaven. ''Ere we go again,' he said resignedly and opening the front door, prepared for big time fall-out.

Andrew's entrance into the house was on a par with that of Raging Bull leaving his corner of the ring for the first round: every muscle tight and tensed, murder lurking beneath a thin veneer of control. He took off his mud-caked coat and gloves and laying them carefully over a chair demanded, 'Where is he?'

George stood firmly between him and the staircase.

'I told you, 'e's asleep,' he repeated, 'so leave 'im be for a while yet.'

Andrew moved forward and made to go around George, who side-stepped in front of him and stood his ground saying doggedly, 'Sir, 'e's 'ad about as much as he can take for one day.'

Andrew took another step forward. 'That makes two of us. Move,' he said softly, 'or I'll break your frigging neck.'

George's patience snapped. 'Aw, shut-up, you unreasonable bastard, and use your bloody head before you go sounding off will you!'

Andrew stopped inches away from him and spoke through teeth gritted so hard they hurt. 'Take my advice, George; *when* I sack you, which I am very close to doing right now, don't apply for a job in the Diplomatic Service, because take it from me, cocky, you haven't the qualifications.'

'An' right now *you* haven't the qualifications even to be a halfway decent human being. Fine bleedin' apology for a father you are!'

George was almost dancing with fury and as Andrew's tired gaze took in the enraged, determined figure still barring his way, the light of battle slowly faded from his own eyes. Wearily he brushed past him and sinking down onto the bottom stair, rested his head in his hands. 'George,' he sighed, 'just get some bleedin' coffee brewing will you, before I throw you out on your bleedin' ear!'

Half an hour later he walked quietly into his son's room. Toby lay on his back, duvet pulled up to his chin, eyes staring vacantly at the ceiling. As Andrew sat down on the side of the bed he had the distinct impression that if it hadn't been for his own weight pinning the boy down beneath the covers, the son and heir might have levitated half-way to the ceiling.

'Duh – like, shit – what is it man?'' Toby was disorientated, his eyes glazed with fright as he took in this new menace. Andrew sighed.

'I don't have time to get an interpreter, so just forget The Simpsons and try speaking the Queen's English, will you.' He looked intently at Toby's flushed face and feverish eyes, then laid the back of his hand against his forehead. 'You've got one hell of a temperature there.'

Toby clutched the duvet even closer to his chest. 'I feel c-c-cold inside.'

Andrew's smile was grim. 'Well now, that's probably just funk, but you're warm enough outside – too warm. You'll have to sweat it out until I can get a doctor.'

The boy made a feeble attempt at defiance. 'I don't need a doctor.'

'You don't need a temperature, but you've got one – and don't argue with *me.*' Andrew glanced around. 'Know what this room is, do you?'

'No.'

'It's the old nursery. Kind of appropriate that George put you in here, don't you think?'

'I'm not a kid,' Toby muttered.

'Yes you are, and a bloody stupid one – you left a trail a mile wide, from the school to the chippy in Maunsley. I suppose you got yourself lost after that.'

'Worked it all out, did you?' Toby stuck out his lower lip. 'All right, get it over with. I might as well have the grilling now.'

Andrew stood up and walked towards the door. 'Stay where you are,' he said over his shoulder, 'move and I'll have your hide.'

He called two of the G.P. surgeries in Penzance and got lucky with the third. After a courteous but determined tussle with the receptionist, he obtained the information that Doctor Chundura was already in the area and would arrive within an hour. Putting down the phone, he turned to the hovering George. 'I'd better pay the son and heir another visit,' he said, 'and clue up on how he got in that state and where he's been all this time.'

'No need to bother him; I already know as much as he does, and that ain't much when all's said and done.'

Andrew jerked his head toward the kitchen. 'Come on then, make some fresh coffee and give with what you've got.'

'*Kate*?' He stared in disbelief at George, who was thoroughly enjoying himself. It wasn't often he was one step ahead of his boss and he was making the most of it. 'Are you *sure* that's what he called her?'

''Course I'm sure – not senile, am I? Don't ask me where she come from though, 'cause she didn't say. She were off like a rat up a drainpipe soon as he was in the house. Bossy sort she was; knows how to use the charm when it suits her, but she got a tongue on her could cut steel.'

Tell me about it, thought Andrew. 'Anything else?' he asked.

'Nah, not from her; the boy said 'e'd walked 'till 'e couldn't walk no more – thinks he must have wandered off the path somehow and ended sleeping on someone's doorstep. All he remembers is that this

Kate who looked after him had a bloody great dog with her. He says she took his wet kit off and some bloke called Sam gave him some dry clothes.' He looked suspiciously at Andrew. 'You know the bloke or something?'

'Not exactly, but the lady and I have met.' He frowned. 'Why didn't you get a bit more information from her?'

'Didn't get the chance; like I said, she just took off.'

Andrew rubbed a tired hand over his face. 'Actually George, I couldn't care less if he was kidnapped by Martians and given a brain transplant, which in any case could only be an improvement. I'm too knackered to try and work it all out now.'

He was suddenly aware that he was ragingly hungry, and that his own immediate need before Dr Chundura arrived was for a large whisky and anything hot that would fill the aching void in his belly. Discovering what had actually happened and why Toby's rescuer had been in such a hurry to leave would have to wait.

Privately, he thought that nothing Kate Shaw might be involved in was ever likely to be straightforward and uncomplicated, and that when he ran her to earth, which he fully intended doing the next day, he would probably end up with an even bigger headache than the one she was giving him right now.

*   *   *

Kate drew the heavy curtains in the sitting room, moved one of the roomy armchairs closer to the fire and set her glass of wine on the low table beside it. Tucking her legs beneath her she sat down and, opening Dan Brown, began to read from where she had left off the night before.

The house was silent; even the wind had dropped, the only other sound in the room, apart from Heathcliffe's rumbling snores, was the occasional shifting of logs in the grate. She read a few pages, then sat back and closed her eyes, listening to the silence, remembering summers long ago, when Megan and this house had been her escape from the stultifying world of suburbia; a haven where she could read, and daydream and walk the long sandy beaches by day, then in the evenings sit out on the grass under the cedar tree to listen to and laugh at Megan's anarchic stories of when she was young; for years Kate would spin her own fantasies about the child Megan growing up in that crazy old house and playing in the peaceful garden above the wild Cornish cliffs.

Kate smiled in recollection: delightful, scatty Megan, with her dogs, cats and chickens, her seemingly inexhaustible energy…and all those lovelorn admirers, who after the death of Johnny, her charming, feckless, gambling husband, would turn up at all hours, with chocolates or whisky and their arms full of flowers …Oh, to be somewhere between eight and sixteen again thought Kate; lying out on the grass, listening to that lively voice and in total ignorance of what the future held.

'I'm beginning to *feel* middle-aged, even if I'm not,' she said aloud. 'I am homeless and in the very near future will not only be broke but probably menopausal as well. I am alone and loveless and I haven't a clue where I go from here.'

How did a forty-three year old woman start again from scratch, she wondered, and what could she do to change her life around when all she had done in the past eight years was excel at organizing people and events, charming the pants off the press and TV, and overcoming all those other little tasks scattered about the path of a talented musician?

Now the musician had gone, leaving her marking time with a wardrobe full of beautiful clothes she would seldom wear again, unless she found another artist, director, actor or businessman, either too lazy, too busy or too incompetent to organise his own life.

Of course, her mother would recommend she should stop wasting herself on what she dismissed as arty-farty jobs and unsuitable men and get married; as if marriage ever solved anyone's problems. The very last thing she needed now was for some Sir Galahad to appear and make an honest woman of her. If any such man did appear, she thought sourly, he would most likely, once his armour was off, turn out to be just as mean, moody and considerably less magnificent than Paul and the rest of her late-unlamented lovers.

It didn't help to know that she had no one but herself to blame: she had never wanted marriage, not after a childhood and adolescence passed observing the lifestyle of her own parents: her father a quiet, unassuming assistant bank manager, who played bowls every weekend; her mother an ex- nursery teacher who had given up work on marriage and apparently found all the fulfilment she needed thereafter by having a finger in all the charitable pies Colchester had to offer. In her own way, Kate cared for and loved them both, but didn't understand either, any more than they understood the clever, artistic cuckoo that had arrived so unexpectedly into their settled middle-aged lives.

Moreover she had felt stunned and betrayed, when her two closest women friends had taken the matrimonial path; watching in horrified fascination their metamorphosis from bright liberty-loving women to split personality wives and mothers, desperately trying to balance marriage, motherhood and career, but beaten in the end by the sheer impossibility of managing any one of them either efficiently or well.

And what have *I* done that is so different? Kate queried with silent sarcasm. Apart from the kids and the wedding rings she'd eventually done the same thing as both her friends. After a succession of male companions, both straight and gay, friends and lovers, Paul Verdassey's eyes had met hers across a crowded theatre foyer, and for her at least, that had been that.

Thoughtfully she picked up her wine and took a long drink. 'I,' she announced to the sleeping Heathcliffe, 'have been a prize twat, and now I think it's time, as the Yanks put it, to get up off my butt and do something about it.'

She would use the time she had before Megan's return to do all the things she had enjoyed doing before the break-up; only now she would be doing them in her own time and for herself. There would be no return to the old life, no more living through and for someone else. Why, she might even return to her first love, the theatre. At least there she could do the job and stand on her own two feet.

Tomorrow she would begin; in the morning she would run again, get back on form and forget time wasted in mooning and bitching at fate; tomorrow would see the re-birth of the old Kate Shaw, the one she had been before Paul Verdassey erupted into her life and turned it upside down.

She stood to face herself in the mirror above the fireplace and raised her glass. 'Bottoms up then; let's drink to the all-dancing, all-singing and about to be *totally* re-invented Katherine Francesca Shaw.'

8

The next morning, Andrew left the house armed with little more information than on the previous afternoon. The doctor, a quiet, gentle, turbanned Sikh with an impeccable Oxford accent, had insisted that his patient be kept in bed for at least another forty-eight hours. A light diet, plenty of rest and, he had added with a stern sideways look at Andrew's ominously lowered brows, absolute peace and quiet if the young man was to recover quickly from his ordeal. Grudgingly admiring the doctor's diplomatic but firm stand, Andrew took the hint and left his son alone and unquestioned – for the time being.

Weary from his own stressful day, he slept soundly again, only waking when George clumped into his bedroom to fling back the shutters and announce in ringing tones that as he was now not only head cook and bottle-washer but a bloody nurse as well, the sooner people were out of bed and downstairs the better. Seeing George was spoiling for a fight, Andrew gave him one, and after a satisfying exchange of snarled insults, peppered by heavily sarcastic 'sirs' from George, took a long shower, shaved and dressed, then made his own toast and coffee before heading straight for the maddeningly elusive Kate Shaw.

He left the main road and took the minor road down to the headland where, about to turn in at the open gates of Pendragon, he glanced towards the vast stretch of sand left by the outgoing tide and gave a low appreciative whistle. Jumping from the Land Rover he moved closer to the edge of the cliff to get a better view of the distant figure running along the water's edge, a large dog bounding alongside. 'Well, Well!' he murmured, 'now isn't *that* a sight for sore eyes!'

She was running as though not quite warmed up, he thought, or was perhaps out of practice, then smiled when he saw the almost imperceptible shift as she crossed the barrier from warm-up into the smooth graceful stride of a practised runner. Watching until she was out of sight, he looked for and found the steps cut into the cliffs below the house. Once on the beach he selected a handful of flat, polished stones and began walking along the strand in the direction the runner had taken, skipping the stones out over the calm water.

By the time she reappeared he calculated she must have run the two miles, the length of the beach at low tide, and run it pretty steady, there and back. As she came within speaking distance, he slid down from the outcrop of rock where he had been sitting and looked at his watch.

'You must have kept the pace if you made it right to Nanquidno and back,' he said as she came to a halt a few paces away from him, Heathcliffe skittering to a stop beside her.

'Only just!' she bent, putting her hands on her knees, breathing deeply. 'But don't imagine Heathcliffe did the lot – he stopped after a few hundred yards, had a nice snooze and waited for me to come back!'

She was wearing grey tracksuit pants and a loose blue sweatshirt, her damp hair sticking up in all directions where the salt wind had blown it. As she looked up at him, face flushed beneath the creamy skin, her eyes lively and bright, Andrew Parradine thought he had never seen anything so gloriously sexy in his whole life. Forget about topless bimbos in lycra thongs, he thought. This was some woman...

Exhausted by her run and happily unaware of his thoughts, Kate collapsed onto the rock. 'Out of training,' she said breathlessly. 'I used to do a turn around the common most mornings, but I haven't run for anything more than a bus in over a month.'

He sat beside her and Heathcliffe gave a warning growl. Andrew scratched the dog's ears and felt him relax. 'It's more than three months since I took any serious exercise,' he said.

Kate remembered the impression she'd had of a muscular body beneath the city suit. 'Perhaps you should start again; the beach is the best place in the world for running.'

'Maybe I will.' He smiled. 'I came looking for you,' he said, 'but we mustn't sit here talking; you need a warm shower or you'll seize up.'

'Why should you come looking for me?'

He hesitated, 'It's...complicated.' An hour ago, he told himself, you were ready to give this woman the third degree; now look at you; as Toby might put it: 'get real, mate' or he'd lose the advantage.

Kate stood, dusting sand from her jog pants. 'Well,' she said with a trace of irony, 'if it's complicated you'd better come up to the house, although what you can possibly have to say beats me; I've only been here five minutes and so far as I know, have done nothing *worth* talking about.'

Oh haven't you, he thought with an inward cynical smile, *then let me tell you, Miss Kate Shaw, that you don't know the half of it yet!'*

*   *   *

66

While she showered and changed Andrew wandered around the kitchen, filled and put on the kettle, found the bread and breadboard, hung his Barbour over a chair and sat down to wait. Kate returned in less than ten minutes wearing a plaid shirt and old, but beautifully cut, tan slacks. *Fifth Avenue,* thought Andrew. Married to Vanessa for the best part of twenty years, he knew a thing or two about style and where it came from – and how much it cost.

He continued to watch and admire while she made coffee, cut and toasted bread then set the kitchen table with plates, mugs and cutlery; all done with an offhand efficiency accompanied by a run of innocuous small talk that marked her out as a practised hostess, one used to producing food at the proverbial drop of a hat. She didn't ask if he wanted breakfast, just put the toast, a jar of dark Oxford marmalade and butter dish centre table and left it at that. Andrew found he was hungry and appreciated the butter, as George had a distressing habit of veering toward the kind of cholesterol-reducing spread that tasted of nothing at all except cholesterol-reducing spread. He also appreciated the fact that she ate heartily and didn't feel the need to continue the small talk while she did so.

She finished her toast, poured her second cup of coffee and looked at him enquiringly. 'Well,' she said, 'what do you want to know that I may be able to tell you?'

'I want to know,' he said carefully, 'where, when and how you found my son, and I want you to tell me why you couldn't wait to drop him into George's tender care and take off like a scalded cat.'

'Your *son* – that boy is your son?' She put down her mug with a clatter. 'Why the hell didn't he say? All I got when I asked him his name was "Toby,"' she mimicked the teenage mumble perfectly.

'Sounds familiar; chatty at that age, aren't they?' He hunched forward in his chair, 'but I'd still like to know why you were in such a hurry to leave.'

Kate took a deep breath. 'I left your house pronto because, from the impression I'd got of you, from both your son and that skint-eyed flunky you keep in place of the Dobermans, I was happy to give you a miss. I'd had a hard morning and wasn't in the mood to go a couple of rounds with Attila the Hun.'

'Jesus,' he said admiringly, 'George was right; you do have a tongue that could cut steel, but I'm sorry you got that impression of me,' he spread his hands in rueful defeat. 'Toby doesn't really have much reason to be wary of me; it's just that we don't know each other very well. You see I've spent my life in the army, he's been away at

67

school and we've not had very much contact until quite recently. I've been the bogey man called in to sort him out when he gets into trouble, which for the last couple of years or so he's being doing on a regular basis.'

'It seemed to Sam and me that he was scared stiff of you.' Kate commented

He sighed. 'I *can* have that effect on people, but beneath this terrifying exterior I'm a pussycat at heart.'

'Huh!' she returned his mild, guileless look with a disbelieving stare. 'Maybe, but I have to say that if the chips were down I'd be on Toby's side. How is he, by the way?'

'Recovering; the doctor thinks a few days of care and attention will see him good as new. But he isn't communicating with me and I need to piece together what happened.'

Kate shrugged indifferently, 'Does that matter now?'

'Yes, to me it does. It was such a hare-brained and stupid thing he did – taking off without any idea of how he was going to find me.' Suddenly the grey eyes were steely. 'It occurred to me he might have been on something.'

'Drugs?' Kate shook her head. 'No, he was feverish and disorientated but I'd have known…' she gave a thin smile, 'I wasn't born yesterday; I know a user when I see one.'

'I do have my reasons for asking, but thanks for putting my mind at rest,' he was mildly sarcastic. 'Now, if you wouldn't mind, I'd like you to take me through what happened at Mr Trevene's cottage.'

She was silent for a few moments and he watched with interest, recognising a mind as professionally ordered as his own clicking away behind those expressive dark eyes. Kate Shaw, he surmised, wasn't anyone's fool and would have her answers absolutely spot on and in order and be unlikely to tell him anything she didn't think he needed to know.

Kate was well aware of his scrutiny. She guessed that he hadn't been just any soldier, but one with considerable clout; well used to being in command and almost certainly very good at getting his own way. 'Okay,' she said at length. 'I will, as you have asked so nicely, take you through it from the time I found him.'

Andrew propped his chin on one hand, watching her as she talked, thinking that he could listen to that voice all day; wondering again how she'd managed to get so pally with Sam Trevene, and in such a very short space of time.

When she finished speaking he sat for a few moments, slotting what she had told him into what he already knew, realising that Toby had merely acted on impulse in putting as much space as possible between him and the school in order not to suffer the additional humiliation of being collected by one very angry parent.

And that parent hadn't handled it particularly well; could have done very much better in fact. He cleared his throat.

'Thank you, it does fill in a few gaps, but as Toby has only the haziest idea of how he fetched up at Hawthorne Cottage, I imagine we are never likely to know the full story. However, thanks to you and your friend Sam he arrived back not all that much the worse for wear...which reminds me...we still have some of Mr Trevene's clothes. I'll return them to him tomorrow.'

Kate said quickly, 'I shouldn't make a special journey. He's hardly ever there – but he's coming here to lunch on Saturday, so I could collect them sometime before then and save you the trouble.'

'In that case,' his answer was just a quick and very smooth, 'perhaps you will come back to the house now and pick them up. I'm sure Toby would like to see you again – and Heathcliffe too, of course.'

Kate had met an immense variety of people in her forty-three years, but army types hadn't figured largely in the circles in which she moved, and she was more than slightly miffed at this one's irritating habit of being subtly but very definitely in control of any and every situation. She said casually, 'All right. I'll drive over later.'

'Oh, I shouldn't do that if I were you,' he was straight faced. 'I noticed the other day that your tax disc is out of date. Unless in the meantime you have returned to Penzance to renew it, I don't think you should be driving that heap anywhere until it's good and legal, do you?'

'Thank you for noticing. Taxing a car is a task I've seldom had to bother with.' Fuming inwardly but determined not to show it, she answered him with cool sarcasm.

'I'd be more than happy to take you to Rosscannan and back this morning – I feel I owe you that much at least. If you like to get the papers together now I could also run you into Penzance to get the tax sorted.'

Kate thought rapidly. There only two ways out of this *impasse*: she could tell him to sod off, but that might embarrass Sam when Andrew turned up at his cottage with the borrowed clothes, which he undoubtedly would, or she could concede the bloody man a temporary victory and combine getting the car taxed with collecting Sam's gear from Rosscannan – but very much on Mr Parradine's terms. She shrugged, finished her coffee and put the mug down with a decisive click. 'Heathcliffe and I will be very pleased to see Toby again. I'll just see if I can find the necessary papers.'

You may have won that round, she communed silently as she left the room, *but don't get too cocky chum, because you won't catch me napping again in a hurry...*

She went to the study where a swift search through Megan's desk revealed the papers for the car in a neatly labelled envelope, together with a cheque for a year's tax. Kate smiled: so typical of Megan to have organised everything then forgotten the most important part of the exercise.

When she returned to the kitchen Andrew asked. 'Will you still be here at Christmas?'

'Unfortunately yes, although I may have to go back home before then to attend to some business.'

'Hmn; you'll have an odd kind of Christmas, won't you, all alone in this place?' He gave his sudden smile, 'I guess mine will be almost as odd. Rosscannan will take quite a while to get straight; not all tenants are careful as one would wish, and it has been some thirty years since my family left.'

'Sam said he thought it had been empty for some time...'

She gave him the kind of enquiring look that not only invited an answer but made it almost impossible not to give one, and on the journey back he was aware she had not only got him talking about the house, but at any sign of flagging, kept him going with just the right amount and degree of politely interested questions.

By the time they reached the drive gates he realised that although he'd managed to keep his private life fairly well intact, he had described the changing fortunes of his home over the past thirty years in considerable detail. Such expertise on her part, he decided, would make future exploration of how *she* came to be spending Christmas alone in that mausoleum a positive pleasure.

At their first meeting, then later over their lunch together in Penzance, she had been cagey about her life: what her work was, where she lived, and whether she did so alone or with someone else. Such reticence, he reasoned, was unusual in an attractive and apparently self-confident, and by the look of her wardrobe, a wealthy woman of Kate Shaw's type and age.

Shrewdly, he placed her as late thirties, early forties, and although there was no sign of a ring on her finger that meant little these days. It was simply that experience told him no woman who looked and acted as she did would arrive at this point in her life without some kind of past, either romantic or professional or both.

The one absolute certainty was that beneath the rather remote, coolly sexy exterior she presented to the world, there lurked a possibly vulnerable woman, with above average intelligence and a flash-point temper of considerable force.

*　　　*　　　*

Kate was beginning to enjoy herself. The exchanges with Andrew Parradine were rather like the kind of verbal fencing she did so well in her job – her late job, she corrected herself. It was always fun to draw people out; to find what was behind the façade – and how such revelations might be used to advantage. Quite why she was doing it with this man she wasn't sure. Certainly she was intrigued and interested in someone who owned a house like Rosscannan, who had been, perhaps still was, something pretty senior in the army, had a quite extraordinarily villainous looking manservant, a son for whose safety he had been obviously concerned although he didn't appear to be a fond parent...and had so far made no reference to the wife who told him he snored.

It might take a little longer to move from an in-depth chat about the house to an in-depth chat about his life, she thought, as the gates of Rosscannan came into sight, but without such pleasant diversions to look forward to, life in the long term at Pendragon without Megan *in situ* might be hideously dull.

'Still no Dobermans?' she murmured as he climbed back behind the wheel after punching in his code.

'No,' he replied blandly, 'they would be superfluous; as you say, I have George!'

'Ah, yes: George...' she gave him one of her sideways glances. 'He reminds me of a very evil tempered Jack Russell terrier my father once owned.'

'Ah, but his cooking is pure *cordon bleu.* '

'Well, from our one brief meeting I'd say he would need to have some kind of talent not immediately discernable to the naked eye, otherwise he'd be in a cage.'

Andrew raised an admonitory finger. 'Very unkind of you,' he said solemnly, 'George has a heart of gold. To know him is to love him.'

The weasel, as Kate had privately named him, had the door open before Andrew put the brake on the Land Rover and now stood at the top of the steps like some downmarket Jeeves welcoming Bertie back to Blandings Castle.

'Boy's gettin' restless, guv'nor,' his gimlet eyes fastened on Kate and a faint sneer hovered over his lips. 'I suppose you'll want coffee for two, then?'

'You suppose right.' Andrew held Kate's elbow with the lightest of touch and walked her into the house, 'Welcome to Rosscannan,' he said.

He guided her through the square high-ceilinged hall and into the drawing room. This had a large ornate central chandelier, but like the hall was sparsely furnished, with two small side tables and a low table set before the fireplace, a few delicate upright chairs, a silk covered high-backed couch with plump cushions and tasselled ends, while a similarly high-backed brocaded armchair stood either side of the fire. Although the whole building had the hollow, echoing air of an almost empty house, Kate felt immediately that there was a quite extraordinary warmth and tranquillity about Rosscannan. She cast a critical eye over the wallpaper, which was, or rather had been, beautiful but was now marred by smudges where furniture had stood and careless hands rubbed against it.

Andrew followed the direction of her gaze; he said apologetically. 'Bit of a mish-mash, isn't it? Most of the original furnishings were stored on the third floor and kept safe under lock and key but the decoration and paintwork had to take their chance. When we arrived we just fetched a few things down to make it habitable until all the repairs and redecorating are done. Toby is up in the old nursery on the top floor, because it has a huge airing cupboard that helps keep it warm. We'll go up and see him now while George brews our coffee.'

The staircase was covered in a floral carpet that looked totally out of place, and ascended in a long curve with a series of short runs onto odd little landings, with two or three doors off each. Kate ran a hand along the banister rails and found them grimy and sticky to the touch: set Ena loose on this lot, she thought as they reached the main first floor landing with Heathcliffe bumping suspiciously at her heels, and *she'd* soon sort it out. She cast an eye over the walls, noting that as in the drawing room the delicately-striped silk paper was scuffed and faded, but so badly here as to be irreparable. 'A wicked thing to contemplate, but you should strip that,' she murmured, 'wash the walls in pale colours instead…'

'Excuse me?'

'Sorry,' she waved a vague hand, 'just thinking aloud…that wallpaper: it's beyond repair. You'll have to lose it. Replacing that, or anything remotely like it, would cost a fortune now, and a modern

72

substitute just wouldn't do.'

Andrew was regarding her with a kind of comical disbelief. 'Are you by any chance an interior designer – a sort of female Llewellyn-Bowen who runs riot through people's houses with swatches of material and an enormous budget?'

She grinned. 'Why? Do you need one of those?'

'If you discount the enormous budget, yes,' he paused to give her a thoughtful look. 'Better come clean,' he advised, 'you *are* an interior designer, aren't you?'

'No, but I studied art a zillion years ago; I wasn't all that good as an artist, but I'm interested in architecture per se. This has been, is still, a beautiful house,' she touched the banister rail with the tip of one finger. 'I loathe housework, but this makes even me want to wash it down and attack it with a tin of polish!'

He grinned. 'All in good time; I plan to do some of the minor repairs myself, but completely redecorating the interior and repairing damaged plaster work will need scaffolding and that I shall leave to the experts; likewise replacing window frames and repainting the exterior. I have a feeling the whole thing may take longer than originally estimated to make the place as attractive as possible to any potential buyer.' He resumed his journey along the landing, and over his shoulder asked casually, 'I suppose you are not looking for a job?'

'Why? Are you offering?'

'I might be.' He opened a door at the end of the long landing onto another staircase, this one steep and uncarpeted, the treads worn into shallow hollows at the centre. 'Up here, apart from the nursery and a little room off for a nanny, are what were the servants' quarters; not that there were ever many of those, not in our time anyway; there are only four rooms and one bathroom, so God knows how they squeezed them all in. After the war no one wanted to know, and who could blame them.'

She said ambiguously, 'Slavery takes all forms; I daresay that, like most of us in one way or another, a fair number still ended up pandering to the needs of others but got paid more for their efforts, which of course made it all worth while.'

'You're a very cynical woman.'

She gave him another of her sideways glances. 'One lives and learns.'

At the head of the stairs he threw open the first door and, as he stood back to let her pass, got a drift of her perfume. He took a deep breath and made fists of his hands to keep from touching her and as she passed him. Kate felt the vibes clear and strong, as though he had actually brushed a hand over her shoulder. Unheralded, an old familiar sensation segued briefly beneath her ribs before plunging downward, so that only her habitual self-control sent her past him and into the room.

She said 'Hello, Toby. Nice to see you looking better,' congratulating herself on managing to sound just like someone's great aunt, when her insides were still churning.

Toby was up, dressed in jeans and sweater and sitting in an easy chair by the window. With a welcoming howl Heathcliffe flung himself across the room and across his lap and the boy hugged him with unrestrained pleasure. 'Hey, big boy, great to see you!' then looked up over the dog's shaggy head and blushed. He stammered 'Uh, huh, hi...it's you again!'

'It certainly is.' Kate answered amiably. She smiled, 'I thought I'd come and satisfy myself you were OK.'

He gave her a dazzling, wolfish, young man's smile before his blush deepened and he buried his burning face in Heathcliffe's fur. Andrew looked from his son's bent head to Kate, then back again and felt laughter rise in his chest. Well, well, he thought, the boy has taste after all...with sudden fellow feeling he came to his son's rescue. 'How about we leave Heathcliffe with you while I show Kate over the house?' he asked,

'Yeah, ace.' Still avoiding eye contact Toby concentrated on stroking Heathcliffe's great head. 'I'm starving; I could do with coffee too – and some of George's cake.'

'I'll pass the message on,' Andrew caught Kate's faint sympathetic grin for his son's gauche embarrassment and when they were safely on the other side of the closed door he gave her a long, quizzical look. 'Do you always have that effect on young men?'

'Not since I was an equally young woman,' she answered. 'But that was a very long time ago.'

'Not long enough!' he said. 'Now, we'll just see George about that coffee and cake; then you shall have the sixpenny tour.'

She demurred, 'Only the sixpenny one?'

He said firmly. 'Definitely only the sixpenny one; this isn't Blenheim, you know, although we do have stables and a barn and rather a lot of garden. But we can do all that another day.'

9

Megan Baxter relaxed in her chair in the comfortable lounge of her hotel in Florence, wondering idly how her niece was managing at Pendragon and how her first meeting with Sam had gone.

Usually Megan had little patience with people who messed-up on their lives then took such an unconscionable time to haul themselves back into the world, but then Sam was different, always had been; even as a little boy he had marched to a different drummer, much to the despair of his respectable, hard-working family. Even now they shrank from any closer contact with their son than an occasional visit. She hoped his girl would continue to stick by him; she'd only met Anita once…a pretty little thing: even more important than looks, she had intelligence and, if Sam was to be believed, a commendable capacity for hard work.

She took another sip at her gin and vermouth; it was delicious and she congratulated herself that although in her late seventies, she was still able to enjoy the finer things in life. Indulgently she gazed at her companion, who had succumbed to his post-luncheon nap and was sleeping peacefully with his mouth open, emitting the occasional fluttering snore. Dear old Frank; even at his advanced age he seemed to be having a wow of a time, chatting-up and buying drinks for any number of the fetching young men in tight trousers and smelling of *Rochas pour l'homme* who hung around the palazzo of San Croc in the early evenings.

Her thoughts drifted back again to her niece and the devastatingly attractive but impossibly demanding Paul; no wonder Kate had stayed with him for all those years; just the type *she* would have fallen for fifty years ago; had, in fact. Johnny Baxter had been every bit as handsome and charismatic and equally impossible and demanding, but he had been fun, and rich, and left her very well provided for. She sighed. Even while she applauded her niece's independence it had been obvious from the beginning that with a pair as explosive as Kate Shaw and Paul Verdassey, the possibility of total nuclear wipe out had always been on the cards. A wedding ring would at least have tempered the cold wind of financial hardship.

But she knew her Kate; knew her courage and determination; knew too that she would rather starve than ask her, or her parents for a handout. Kate may have taken a very hard knock, in the bank balance as well as the emotions, but Megan had not the slightest doubt that in one way or another she would survive.

She emptied her glass and was just pondering the wisdom of another before she went for her customary afternoon stroll around the city, when her attention was caught by a man who had just walked into the bar and was ordering a whisky in a rich, dark *basso profonda*. His back view offered only a long bony figure in well-cut Italian-style tweeds, one thin brown hand holding a narrow-brimmed Borsalino, the hat so beloved of Italian men.

There was something about the man's voice, the set of his head and shoulders, that stirred a memory and she was still staring in some puzzlement when he swivelled around on the bar stool, his gaze making a lazy sweep of the room. Their eyes met and for a moment a small frown etched between his brows; then he slipped from the stool and came across the room, a smile lighting a face so scored with years of good *vino* and burned from the Tuscan sun that it might have been carved from mahogany.

'Megan…' he stopped beside her chair; held out both hands, 'what a breath of old England, and here of all places.'

'James Parradine,' she looked up into faded but still arresting blue eyes. 'You *have* gone native, haven't you?'

'That's the complimentary Megan I remember so well…God, it must be over thirty years. I recall we left England just after old Johnny's funeral.' He cast a slightly disparaging glance at the sleeping Frank, 'I didn't know you'd married again.'

'I haven't. He's just a friend and gayer than springtime, which makes him the perfect travelling companion.'

He laughed. 'That's very un-p.c. of you Megan!' he looked at her empty glass. 'What are you drinking?'

'Gin and It, and if you are staying for goodness sake sit down.'

He signalled a waiter, gave the order then sat, hitching his trousers meticulously over his knees. He smiled again. 'You are still a handsome woman, Megan Baxter.'

'Huh!' she fluttered dismissive fingers. 'None of that, James; we're too old, at least you are, and both have more wrinkles than an elephant's backside for that sort of nonsense.'

'True,' he sat back, lacing his long fingers together. 'Are you still living in that mausoleum?'

'Yes, although lately I've begun to wonder why. Cornwall isn't what it was; too much traffic on the roads, too many tourists – and you would weep if you saw what one particularly soulless *entrepreneur* has done to Lands End.'

He gave a light shudder. 'I can imagine. I've just packed Andrew off to Rosscannan; given him the job of getting it ready for sale –' he broke off as the waiter brought their drinks, '*Grazia*,' and paid him, tipping generously – 'I didn't want to go back to see it looking less than perfect. Andrew thinks I don't care about the place; I do, but it was always an albatross about my neck and post-war it just bled me dry.'

'Um,' Megan was thoughtful, 'I've heard the house is looking pretty neglected, and from what can be seen from the gates the grounds are much the same.'

He said shortly, 'Andrew seems keen to work on it. Thinks he's fit enough to do some of it himself, but I doubt it. Still, it gives him something to occupy his time; he won't take kindly to being put out to grass.' He frowned. 'He should never have got into that racket. The only good thing to come out of it for him is early retirement on a decent pension.'

'The Army is hardly a racket,' she demurred, 'and you, James Parradine, should be proud to have a hero for a son.'

'I am, but that doesn't stop me thinking he was a bloody fool in his choice of career.' He snorted, 'Getting divorced as well, and not before time; did you know?'

'I heard; amicable is it?'

'Not particularly.' He knit his brows, 'Cow of a woman. Don't think she ever wanted that boy of theirs; not even sure she ever really wanted Andrew. I daresay it was all down to their hormones at the time; it usually is when two totally unsuited people can't wait to get each other into bed. Trouble was Andy cocked it up by marrying her. Anyone with half an eye could see she wasn't the type to stick to any wedding vows: been playing the field since she left the classroom.' He glanced across at the still slumbering Frank. 'How long is he likely to be out of it?'

'I should think for about an hour or so, if he runs true to form.'

'Then supposing we leave him to it, finish these drinks and take a stroll while the sun is still shining.'

Megan raised her glass and eyed him over the rim. 'That sounds like a good idea.'

'I have an even better one; suppose you and the Sleeping Beauty come to dinner with me tonight? My place is only a half hour drive away.'

She said with a smile, 'I doubt if Frank will come. He likes his evening prowl – totally harmless now in fact, but hope eternal helps keep him from falling off his branch along with the rest of his contemporaries!'

'Just you and I, then; I can give you the grand tour of my Tuscan Castillo.'

She gave a huff of laughter. 'Yes, just you and me, James, then after dinner we can chase each other around the terrace on our zimmer-frames!'

He sighed, his eyes twinkling. 'Ah, where did all the romance go?'

'Ours,' she said dryly, 'went nowhere more than forty years ago.'

'Ah, yes,' he stood and offered his arm, 'but I remember it well!'

10

'We'll do the ground floor tour now.' Andrew led Kate back into the entrance hall. Apart from the elegant drawing room, Rosscannan boasted a panelled dining hall, leading off this a relatively small room that Andrew introduced as the snug, the walls of which held a dozen or so glass cases filled with a variety of stuffed creatures, a couple of easy chairs covered in faded cretonne and a games table with chessmen arranged in place on the board, ready for someone to make the first move. In one corner was a pianola, next to it a scarred and battered wooden table supporting an old-fashioned projector, beside it a box piled high with metal spools of film.

Kate smiled back at Andrew over her shoulder. 'This looks like something of a blast from the past.'

He grinned, 'Pure nostalgia. It was the first room I got sorted when I came back. George created hell when I hauled a load of what he called rubbish down from the attics. It was mine and my sister's downstairs lair when we were kids. We would shamelessly entice any visitors in here – I ran cartoons and cowboy films on that old projector, while Fliss did her stuff with the pianola. We charged everyone sixpence and did rather well at large family gatherings.' Closing the door of the snug, he opened another directly opposite. 'This is the study, and as you see very much a male domain.'

Kate looked around, thinking that any male was welcome to it, furnished as it was with several heavy carved wooden chairs, quite the longest, deepest and most worn old leather chesterfield she had ever seen, and an enormous leather-top desk with an ornate silver inkstand. A Turkish carpet, verging on threadbare, of great age and probably worth a fortune, covered most of the floor. In contrast, a state of the art computer, laser printer, scanner and fax machine stood on a polished wooden bench by the windows. Bookshelves filled to overflowing lined one wall with works by novelists and essayists: Aldous Huxley and Howard Spring, H.V. Morton, Evelyn Waugh, James Thurber and A.L. Rouse amongst them. A nice diverse collection, Kate thought, and gave a mental nod of approval to the absent James Parradine.

'Not my favourite room,' Andrew commented. 'I had too many run-ins with my old man in here, but as it is well away from the main rooms it's a good place in which to work and keep all my files.'

The surprise was an unexpectedly long and spacious gallery which ran the whole width of the back of the house. Andrew said, 'An addition my grandfather made in the days when such things as dances and musical evenings for the young ladies of the house were on the agenda. At Christmas we always had an enormous tree in here and on Christmas Eve my mother played the piano and we all sang carols, my father exceedingly loudly, with great feeling and very few of the right words, which as he had a voice like a corncrake must have been a trial for my mother who was very musical.' He gestured towards a Bechstein Grand, older than Paul's, but equally highly polished. 'I had to hire experts to get that down and re-assembled and the piano tuner had a fine old time getting it up to scratch.'

'My voice wouldn't exactly make Kiri Te Kanawa lose any sleep,' observed Kate, 'but I can tinkle the ivories along with the best of them!'

'I might hold you to that; George likes a sing-song. It reminds him of drunken parties in the NCOs mess on Friday nights.'

Kate chuckled. 'How did he end up working for you?'

He shrugged. 'He'd been my batman, later my driver, for a total of ten years, but was invalided out a couple of years back with dodgy lungs; not surprising as he'd chain-smoked from the age of ten. When I knew I was leaving the army it seemed logical to have him keep house and cook for me, which he does brilliantly. In return I look after *him*, pay him well and let him think he rules the roost.' He took her arm, 'Before I introduce you to the little parlour, the boot-cum-gunroom, and George's kitchen, where we'll chase him up about that coffee, there's time to show you the bedrooms. I can't think,' he continued as he began to climb the main staircase again, 'why great, great grandpapa's architect was so keen on stairs.'

Kate said sagely. 'They were in those days – I couldn't believe Jane Austen's home at Chawton. It's quite a small house and it must have been hell negotiating all those twists and turns and corridors in the dresses they wore then.'

When they returned to the drawing room again Kate sank down onto the long velvet-covered couch before the log fire, while Andrew poured the coffee George had set on a side table. She held her hands out to the warmth of the fire and thought about that unexpected sexual charge she'd felt as she passed him at the door of Toby's room. The whole thing had been over in seconds, but the memory of it, and her instinctive response, lingered on.

She couldn't remember ever being taken so completely by

surprise in that way, but reasoned that in her present state of enforced celibacy it could have happened with anyone and at any time. Such an abrupt and traumatic end to her sex life had been bound to cause problems, but because Andrew Parradine happened to have pressed the right buttons at the right time, didn't mean she had to let him know he'd got lucky.

Andrew sat at the far end of the couch, avoiding the temptation to gaze at her legs. He wondered if she had picked up on his sudden surge of healthy lust back there in Toby's room. He hoped not; at this point in his life he didn't want any complications with any woman, particularly the enigmatic Kate Shaw.

Kate settled deeper into the cushions. Deliberately keeping her voice neutral, she said conversationally, 'I didn't expect to find Toby out of bed so soon.'

'He'd be downstairs if the place was warmer. The new central-heating boiler should have been delivered by now...it's supposed to be fitted next week but I'll only believe that when I see it happening. Half the trouble is getting *anything* done efficiently and at the appointed time.' He gave a sudden deprecating grin. 'Showing my age, aren't I? Any minute now I'll be moaning that things ain't what they used to be!'

'Well they ain't.' Kate relaxed, glancing around appreciatively. 'That is a beautiful fireplace; a pity about the damage to the mantle.'

'Oh, I can deal with that.' She raised an eyebrow and he grinned again. 'I'm not just a pretty face; I like working with my hands, especially in wood. But having the right eye for decoration, furniture, curtains and floor coverings isn't really my forte. You, on the other hand, give the impression it might be yours. That's why I asked if you wanted a job.'

She gave him a long, thoughtful look. No tingle while he was at that distance, but she'd need to be careful, any kind of involvement with this man was definitely a non-starter. Even leaving her own feelings and wishes out of the equation there must be a wife somewhere in all this, even if she wasn't immediately in evidence, and she didn't want any messy misunderstandings. On the other hand she *did* need a job.

Although what she knew about tarting up country houses could be carved on the head of a pin, there was something about Rosscannan that drew her; she felt instinctively that she could work here in this admittedly shabby but quite extraordinarily peaceful and tranquil place. She said honestly, 'I'm not sure how much use I'd be, or even how long I'll be around. Although I'm an ex, very ex, stage designer and pretty good with fabrics, a tin of emulsion and a paint brush, I'm not in any way qualified to advise anyone on interior decorating. You'd be much safer getting in an expert.'

He said with patient persistence, 'The only expert I'd get is likely to have their own preconceived ideas, but I need someone to share ideas *with*, who can help me see what needs to be done to bring Rosscannan to life again. As soon as you walked in I knew you had a feel for the place.' He spread his hands, 'So what about it?'

He wasn't at all sure why he was being so reckless when recklessness was not a part of his nature. He only knew that Kate Shaw, with her quick dry wit and sharp brain; the flying, "winged victory" look she had about her when she walked, was pretty good company to have around.

'Seems to me you are being very impulsive; how do you know I can be trusted around the silver?'

He answered mildly, 'We don't have any silver – none worth nicking anyway,' then asked without a change of expression, 'Would you mind telling me your present line of work, and why you've chosen to holiday in Cornwall in winter?'

Kate made a wry face. 'I should have seen that coming.'

He said flippantly, 'If you keep evading the question you'll have me suspecting you run a knocking-shop in Shepherds Bush.'

She held her hands up in mock surrender, 'Okay, here's the potted version: I studied art, then spent around twelve years working in the theatre – ASM graduating to set-dressing, stage design, costume, that sort of thing, but for the last eight years I've travelled the world as a PA and kind of highbrow roadie to an orchestral conductor...' she grinned at his faint involuntary smile, 'and before you say "wash your mouth out and do an honest day's work in Shepherds Bush," you should know I was considered *very* good at my job, which was bloody hard work. Now I'm house-sitting for my elderly cousin once removed, who, for health reasons, is spending the winter in Italy.' She raised an eyebrow in mocking enquiry. 'So, what kind of soldier are *you*?'

He shrugged then smiled. 'I am,' he corrected himself, 'was, a Colonel with the Paras, latterly in Afghanistan.'

'Wow!' she was impressed. 'Looks like I'd better not ruffle your feathers too much then.'

'Nor I yours; I can see it was a bit of a cheek to offer a woman like you a job helping me to sort out Rosscannan. I'm sorry.'

'No need.' She hesitated and for a moment he caught a glimpse of uncertainty beneath the confident veneer. 'Just one thing, isn't this something you should first talk over with your wife?'

He crossed one relaxed ankle over the other. 'She won't leap out of the closets at you, if that's what you're worried about. Very soon, God willing, she'll be across the Atlantic and some other man's headache.'

He didn't sound too distressed at the thought. Mimicking his body language, Kate hooked her thumbs into her belt with studied nonchalance. 'In that case, if you promise to keep me in groceries, I'm all yours,' then aware of his deepening grin she closed her eyes in momentary despair. 'Dear God, I can't believe I actually said that; forget it, will you?'

He chuckled. 'You wish! Can you start Monday morning?'

'Monday's fine.'

'By the way,' he cleared his throat ostentatiously, 'as you noticed, my son has a crush on you, but I'm sure that's something you can cope with.'

She smiled in a way that made him feel he would quite like to slap her. 'I think that's rather sweet of him, don't you?'

His eyes glinted dangerously. 'No, I think it's damned presumptuous of him. But we'll leave that aside for now and talk about the cost of keeping you in groceries.'

This was one paradoxical woman he thought, as an hour or so later he watched her disappear through the door of Pendragon waving her new tax disc in farewell but, to use a transatlantic phrase, she sure was a class act.

*   *   *

Kate returned to her temporary home, her head filled with possibilities for the job that had been offered. Recalling her glimpses of attics filled with furniture, cases of fabrics, curtains, china, glass and pictures that had been stored safe behind padlocked doors for more than a quarter of a century, she realised what an immense, exciting and ultimately rewarding task it would be to help put the whole house to rights.

'I do hope our ex-colonel's pockets are deep enough for this, because it's going to be a long, expensive business.' She rubbed Heathcliffe's shaggy head as he leaned companionably against her knee. 'Even with the boss man doing his thing and me rolling up my sleeves and getting stuck in, it will still cost a packet. A pity *you* can't do something more useful than chuck yourself shamelessly at that randy little so-and-so up in the attic!'

I must be crazy, she thought as reality began to bite. She leaned her arms on the kitchen table and let her mind wander again through that fascinating house, with its twisting staircases, landings and square, no-nonsense rooms. Oblivious of time she dreamed on until at last Heathcliffe began to moan and push his head up under her elbow. Blinking and rubbing at her eyes she realised daylight was fading, she had by-passed lunch and her intestinal rumblings were rivalling Heathcliffe's groans.

Whilst she was making Heathcliffe's supper and thinking about her own, she remembered Sam was coming to lunch on Saturday. Leaving Heathcliffe wolfing his meal and temporarily postponing the nourishment her own stomach craved, she went out to retrieve the bag of clothes Andrew had put in the boot of Megan's car. A musty odour with an underlying whiff of fish invaded the kitchen as she tipped them onto the table.

'Holy God, Heathcliffe,' she grumbled, 'I can't have these things hanging around until the weekend; they're a bloody health hazard!' Shaking out the overcoat she hung it to air in the scullery then bundled the rest of the clothes into the washing machine. How on earth, she wondered, as she scrubbed her hands then cut bread and put a couple of eggs on to boil, could a man who looked and appeared reasonably clean possibly have clothes that smelled so awful? She supposed that working in a garden centre didn't call for Persil whiteness and a slug of lemon-fresh Comfort, but all the same…

She sat down to her scratch meal, letting her thoughts drift from Rosscannan to its owner. It was näive to pretend he didn't stir something in her; if she was honest she'd have to admit he had rather got under her skin. She thought about that stubborn chin; the long mouth that had more than a hint of humour about it. She knew he found her sexy, which was reassuring; in return, she thought him pretty sexy too, but had absolutely no intention of having more than a purely professional, friendly working partnership. She had just ended a long-term relationship and he, as she now knew, had just ended a marriage. She'd take a bet that despite his laid-back manner he had as many raw edges and as much unresolved anger inside as herself. Looked at logically, neither could afford to jump from frying pan to fire. When the time came, as it must, for her to leave Cornwall, there could be no messy emotions involved.

She yawned and stretched. This was turning out to be a funny kind of house-sit she thought, and wondered what Megan would make of it all.

'You sure you're not making a mistake?' George demanded when Andrew returned from taking Kate home. He rattled crockery in the sink and snorted in disgust, 'Bloody amateur; what you going to do if she cocks it up?'

'She's not going to tear down walls with her bare hands; just use her expertise to help get all the furnishings and what-have-you's right'

George waggled a knowing finger. 'You watch it. I don't like the look you got in your eye when she's around; first thing you know she'll be batting them long eyelashes right back at you like Lily Savage on a drag queen's night out – an' *you'll* be sniffing around her like some old bloodhound.'

Andrew chuckled, 'Somehow I don't think she's the eyelash-batting type.'

George muttered, 'No, more the ball-breaking type,' not quite beneath his breath. He rattled some more crockery.

'For God's sake,' Andrew rapped, 'use the dishwasher will you, and vent your spleen on something that won't break.' He heaved himself out of his chair. 'I'm going up to see Toby. We'll have lunch in the sitting room and he can come down for an hour or two.'

'First you want to brain him, now you're mollycoddling the little devil – an' what is he supposed to be doing while all this argy-bargy with the house is going on? Get under my feet I expect…'

Andrew left him muttering to himself and climbed to the attic. If anybody was doing the mollycoddling it was George; there was no doubt the boy had been in a bad way, both physically and mentally when he'd arrived, but George had been clucking over him like some old hen ever since. Just in time, he remembered to knock before opening his son's door.

Toby looked up, greeting him cautiously, 'Yo, dad.'

Andrew let his jaw hang slack and shambled across the room, hands dangling around his knees. 'Duh…how's it goin', man?' he asked vacantly. Toby laughed nervously and swivelled round in his chair.

'Not bad,' he said.

'But so-o-o not-brilliant!' Andrew sat on the edge of the bed, 'Thought you might like to come down for lunch.'

'Ace; I've already had these four walls.' Toby gave a sideways look. 'Uh, is thing – Kate – still here?'

'No. She had some business in the town; I drove her there then took her home.'

'Is she really going to work here – in the house?'

'Yeah, is that a problem for you?'

'No,' he blushed, 'she's all right.'

'Isn't she just?' Andrew studied his fingernails; he said carelessly, 'Knocking on a bit though.'

'Yeah, a bit, I suppose.'

Andrew stood and moved towards the door. 'Put on some more warm clothes before you come down.'

'Oh, adolescence, adolescence…' he murmured, closing the door behind him. He went slowly back down the stairs. One hormone-ridden teenager, one grumpy old man, and one still reasonably randy middle-aged one who ought to know better; watch out, Kate Shaw: with you around this house it could turn out to be one steaming hotbed of passion – of one sort or another.

*　　　*　　　*

On Saturday, shortly after midday, Sam roared up to Pendragon on his battered Honda, giving a satirical salute to the departing Ena as he swept past her at the gates; in return, Ena tossed her head haughtily, causing her purple knit-hat to teeter dangerously over one ear. Kate, watching this exchange from the window swore aloud, setting Heathcliffe's tail thumping in anticipation of some action, as apart from the early run along the beach it had been a long and boring morning. A lot of mouth-watering smells had filled the kitchen, but that was about it; beneath all the facial hair he was registering as much disapproval of his morning as it was possible for a dog to do.

Just five more minutes thought Kate, and Ena would have been on the cliff path and out of sight; now she'd have to put up with her nit-picking disapproval from here to eternity. She sighed as she went to open the door, perhaps if she could bear to start Tuesday's morning run in the semi-dark she'd miss the worst of the fall out.

Sam fought off the expected assault upon his person by Heathcliffe. 'Hi, not too soon, am I?' He hauled the bike up on its stand and came towards her, Heathcliffe treading on his heels. Plunging a hand into the front of his padded jacket, he produced a bunch of tightly budded roses, offering them with the awkward flourish of a man unused to doing such things. 'Flowers for the lady,' he said solemnly,

More used to receiving elegant bouquets and the equally flowery compliments that tended to accompany them, Kate was touched by the gift and the gesture. Forgiving him the lousy timing that had furnished what she was sure would be hours of speculative and possibly libellous gossip between Ena and her cronies, she said, 'Thank you, they are lovely,' accepting them with a warm and genuine smile.

A faint flush lighted his face. He said gruffly, 'There were daisy things but these looked more you.' He stepped into the hallway, removing his helmet before pulling off a pair of worn, shabby gloves. 'Hey, man,' he looked around at the pale walls, gleaming paintwork and polished hall furniture, 'this is something else!'

Kate said dryly, 'Ena puts the gloss on everything. It is her one talent – apart from gossip that is.'

He looked embarrassed. 'Sorry. I forgot – I shouldn't have let her see me arrive, should I?'

'No, but I can always try earplugs at her next visitation.'

'Sorry,' he said again. He peeled off his jacket and hung it on the hallstand, then tugged off his boots to reveal a pair of socks bearing a faded Scooby-Doo cartoon on each ankle and a hole in one heel. Suppressing a smile, Kate led him through into the big warm kitchen where, after suffering another assault by Heathcliffe, he sank onto a roomy wheel-back chair and with a sigh of contentment stretched his legs under the table.

He looked very cold, she thought with sudden concern. While Megan's car was agony in this weather, a motorbike was pure hell. She could testify to that after riding pillion with him the day Toby had turned up on his doorstep. Any minute now I shall start mothering him, she thought, and smiled inwardly: now that really would be something new, mothering never having been high on her list of things to do with a man – or even with a child.

With hopeless ease came the sudden painful memory of those few agonizing weeks, when her future with Paul hung in the balance; his first utter disbelief when she told him she was pregnant, followed swiftly by an outburst of histrionics that would have had Maria Callas chewing the carpet with envy, followed swiftly by a ruthless sulk that had lasted for days, until finally she had accepted the impossibility of having a child when the one she already had was such a handful, even though that child was middle-aged, moody and an unpredictable genius. But then she was still so much in love that life without him was something not even to be contemplated.

So almost two years ago to the day, on a bright winter's morning, quite like this one, and all in the name of love, Kate had done the sensible thing and closed the door on her brief and only chance of motherhood. But the regret and the sadness had stayed deep within her, rendered even more painful by the need to keep her feelings hidden, not only from Paul, who had resolutely refused to even talk about her loss – presumably under the illusion that if a problem wasn't discussed it would eventually cease to exist – but also from her own family and friends. It was the old story, she thought sadly, you never knew how much you wanted something until you had lost it.

She busied herself opening and pouring wine into two glasses, unable for a few seconds to keep from playing the old, painful game: *By now he/she would be walking, talking; in a couple of years just starting nursery school…*

She dragged her mind away from dwelling on an episode in her life that was past and should, must, be forgotten. Moving the pan of prepared soup onto the Aga she forced herself, instead, to think of Sam's dank little cottage; the untidy jumble of the one poorly-heated living room, the cold kitchen with its *circa* nineteen-sixties green and white kitchen cabinet with drop-down shelf, the spindle-legged electric stove and chipped stone sink, the Spartan bedroom. It was a terrible way for a young man to live…or *was* he that young? She did a quick sum in her head and came up with a probable age somewhere around the late twenties. Thinking about his obvious poverty reminded her of the clothes now bagged up in her airing cupboard and, asking him to keep an eye on the soup, she went to retrieve them.

He was embarrassed all over again when she handed him the washed and ironed clothes.

'You shouldn't have gone to the trouble…I use them mostly for fishing and keep them in the lean-to – it's a bit damp there. I'd have given the kid something better, except that apart from these I only have a couple of everything – you know; one to wear and one for the wash.'

Kate wondered where he'd got that old-fashioned expression from, then almost as though he read her thoughts he added, 'One of my grandfather's sayings, except I never actually saw him wash anything, even himself.'

'I can imagine.' On a sudden impulse Kate told him about her one meeting with old Sam. 'You've no idea,' she said as he laughed uproariously, 'how I felt the other night when I was waiting for that door to open. Of course I didn't really expect him to appear; he'd have been over a hundred by now, but it still gave me the abdabs even to see the place again.'

'He wasn't all bad; looked after me when I was a kid – kept me out of trouble for quite a while; made sure I buckled down to the O-Levels and all that.' The speckled hazel eyes peering through his spectacles were very slightly unfocussed and Kate realised that what she had taken as reserve when they met for the first time was probably nothing more than extreme long-sightedness. He gave a little cough. 'I guess you've heard all the scandal about me from good old Ena: what a disgrace to my family I was; how, after the old man died, I moved into the cottage in order to seduce the village maidens.'

She demurred, 'Only one maiden, I understand.'

'Yeah, well, we were both randy little buggers and well up for it – and who ever thinks about the consequences at seventeen; we certainly didn't.' He shrugged, suddenly silent.

Kate stirred her leek and potato soup and added a dollop of soured cream and a grating of nutmeg. She said with casual interest, 'Why didn't you come back here when you got out of clink?'

He propped an elbow on the table and cupped his chin with his hand. 'When I got out my family didn't exactly hang out the welcome flags, so I thought I'd give London another whirl. A pal of mine found tenants for the cottage and I used the rent money to have a good time.' He gave a sudden disturbing and mirthless laugh, 'or what passed then for a good time. I graduated from pot to E's and from them to the hard stuff, until I was nicking and selling anything that wasn't actually screwed to the floor to buy the next fix… Hey,' he broke off with another laugh, 'why am I telling you all this – you're not some part-time shrink are you?'

'No, but I told you about wetting my knickers when your old Sam scared the daylights out of me, and I've never told anyone that before, so why shouldn't you tell me some of your dark and dirty past?'

'Yeah, well,' he repeated, 'but it gets dirtier. See, I really hit the wall: cardboard city, in and out of the magistrate's court, then back inside again…twice. You name it, I did it.'

'But you stopped, didn't you, or you wouldn't be sitting at Megan's kitchen table now.' Kate put a bowl of soup in front of him. 'Help yourself to bread', she said, 'and don't talk with your mouth full.'

He gave a lop-sided grin. 'Megan helped – a lot. You remind me of her. I like you.'

She said dryly, 'I can do with the Brownie points, but I think you must have chalked up a few. After all, you have a steady job now and work hard for a living.'

He picked up his spoon. 'It's no hardship. I enjoy the work.' He took up a spoonful, tasted it. 'Nice soup,' he said.

He ate his way with enthusiasm through lamb chops with rose-mary, sauté potatoes, creamed spinach and a dream of a crème brûlée, one of Kate's specialities. He really was stick thin and she thought he looked as though he'd never had a decent meal in his life; perhaps he hadn't. In his way he was every bit as intriguing as Andrew Parradine.

'That was great,' he said as she placed a cup of coffee before him. 'I don't cook much – get most of my meals at the café at the garden centre. The food's good and it fills a hole.' He gave his sudden grin. 'I didn't aim to end up this way, you know; living in a damn near derelict cottage and earning shit wages, but in a few months I'll be in agricultural college – and the cottage will be okay when I'm earning enough to do it up and put in all the mod. cons.' He drank his coffee in silence for a few moments. 'I've got a girl,' he confided. 'If everything goes well, I'd like to get it up to scratch for her.' He was silent again for a moment then asked, 'How did you get in with old brass hat, Parradine? I bet he's a first class control freak!'

Kate gave a splutter of laughter. 'He's really quite human once you get to know him –'

'Yeah, yeah,' Sam interrupted her, 'seen his picture in the papers; read all about it. So he's got himself a gong, so what? He's no more a hero than all those other misguided nutters – on both sides – who sign up to blow the hell out of other poor misguided nutters.'

'You've lost me,' Kate returned sarcastically, 'perhaps you'd get down off your soapbox for a minute and explain why he's a hero, or even a non-hero. What's he supposed to have done?'

'You must remember…back around July last year: in Afghanistan, when a half dozen army blokes were captured by terrorists – or freedom fighters, depending on which side you stand. Parradine planned and led the operation to get them out. Seems he went in solo as a negotiator until things started getting nasty and the waiting cavalry charged in. He got himself shot up and a load of terrorists/freedom fighters were killed – quite a few by him personally.' He gave a snort of disgust, 'and for that he's just collected a medal.'

'I should damn' well think he has,' Kate was scathing, 'or would you rather he'd stayed nice and safe and let the men be butchered like others before them?' She paused frowning slightly. 'We were in Europe and the US through last summer. When you're on tour you tend not to get past the review page – and no Brit ever watches American TV news; it drives you crazy after a while.'

'I wouldn't know about that. Still, I'd say you were the lucky one not to have Parradine's face leering at you each morning from out of every paper and telly screen.'

'Well, I may subconsciously have heard or seen *something* because I thought I recognised him when we first met, but couldn't actually place him.' Kate smiled when she remembered Andrew's tongue-in-cheek pose as a Hannibal Lecter-type murderer. 'Whatever your take on him, I'd say he was one very brave man.'

Sam was laconic. 'Whatever, but as we're never likely to be what you might term pals, I'd rather we didn't meet; wouldn't mind seeing young Toby again though.'

'Why?'

'Not sure,' he sipped thoughtfully at his coffee then gave his engaging grin. 'Probably because he reminds me of me at that age,' he said.

Kate finished her own coffee then sat with the empty cup clasped in her hands. Poor sod, she thought, and was quite disturbed to find herself meditating for the second time in an hour that Sam really could do with some mothering.

Sam on the other hand, was thinking about the other half of the 'we' in Kate's life, the lucky bastard, while appreciating what a really terrific pair of legs she had.

11

NOVEMBER

The weather really was taking a turn for the better, Kate thought, as she began her run the following morning. It was still cold, but the bone-chilling dampness that had hung around for days had gone from the air and the morning was crisp, with a bracing breeze from the sea.

Exhilarated by the freshness and brightness of the morning she ran on the hard damp sand left by the ebbing tide, while Heathcliffe splashed through the water and chased the occasional tidbit-hunting seagull.

In the short time she had been at Pendragon she had begun to feel better; more alive than she had been for months, even beginning to catch a glimmer of light ahead in what had appeared a dark and dismal future.

A warm rent-free house, a new job and sufficient money to live on; what more could I want? she communed silently with herself as she ran. *I miss the sex and I do still have to look after a hairy and rather smelly male, but hell, I can't have everything, can I?*

Although she still mourned for Paul and wept a little from time to time and the dreams were still unkind, she hadn't realised until it was all over how exacting and exhausting life with Paul had been. His professional life she had organised in every detail; the planning and travelling, the dinner parties, the smoothing of ruffled egos, the endless dealing with the media in every town or city the tours took them; the sacrifice of any kind of leisure time for herself. In private he had been equally demanding of her time and energy, taking for granted that she would always be ready: to make love, to shoulder the burden of his moods, his hypochondria and his obsession with order. It was humiliating to recall that she, who had always thought herself a strongly motivated, independent and freethinking woman, had, over the past few years, slowly relinquished her cherished and hard-won independence to become nurse, lover, friend and mother to a massively self-absorbed and selfish man.

'Serves me right,' she panted, 'I really should have seen it coming – falling head over heels in love for the first time when I was galloping towards forty just had to be a recipe for disaster!'

Contemplating the future honestly, she thought it unlikely she would fall head over heels in love again, or that anyone would do the same with her. She might be lonely, but at least life would be free of any further painful emotional entanglements, although the odd nice uncomplicated roll between the sheets might be welcome...

And there was a certain ambivalent pleasure in thinking about Alberta Opie cocking up all the arrangements for Paul's tour. She might be a first-rate harpist but what brain she had certainly stopped short of organising anything more taxing than her next appointment with her orthodontist.

*　　　*　　　*

Andrew whistled '*Lover Man*' between his teeth as he worked on the damaged skirting board in the drawing room. He let his gaze move for a moment from the skirting board to the wallpaper, wondering if there was any way the scuff marks might be dealt with and the delicate handmade paper saved; this had been his mother's favourite room and he would like to restore the paper, not change it.

His train of thought was interrupted by Toby, who lurched rather than walked through the open door, to lean against the wall, hands thrust into the back pockets of his jeans. He gave a disparaging glance around the room. 'Don't know why all the sweat over this dump. You should get in a JCB to knock it all down and start again!'

Secretly, he was impressed. This was one hell of a place; knocked spots off the house in Hampstead, even if that had sold for a couple of mil; pity some of that had been paid for with Ma's money. Although he guessed the old man hadn't come off too badly on the deal. If it had belonged to him outright though, he could be living it up like crazy anywhere in the world by now instead of working his arse off here.

Andrew paused, viewing his son with a faintly jaundiced eye. 'This was my home up until I was your age you know.'

'Gross,' Toby ventured further into the room to perch on the arm of the sofa. 'You must have been bored out of your skull living a zillion miles from civilization.'

'Fliss and I didn't have time to be bored; your grandfather saw to that.' Andrew ran a sandpaper block several times along a new section of skirting board until it merged imperceptibly with the old.

'Yeah, that figures.' Toby watched for a minute in silence. He said, 'I thought you told me my room had been kept locked, but someone's used a permanent marker and written a dead scuzzy

93

limerick on the inside wall of that cupboard – the one with the hot water tank.'

'Yes I know,' Andrew hunkered down and squinted along the skirting board. 'That was Fliss; one of her nice little convent friends told it her.' He grinned back at him over one shoulder. 'When Pa found it, he went ballistic, so she said it was me and I got one hell of a beating for it.'

'I bet you got your own back on Aunt Fliss.'

Andrew paused, wrinkling his brow in thought. 'Not sure; laid in wait and gave her a couple of Chinese burns, I think.'

'Why didn't you drop her in it, I would have.'

'I bet you would, but she was younger than me and in my day you didn't put a kid in the firing line of a man like my father, even a sister who asked for it.'

Toby gave a faint sneer, 'Yeah, noble and all that stuff.'

'Not a bad precept to live by.' Andrew grunted and levered to his feet. 'Think I'll take a break. You had breakfast?'

'Not yet.'

'Then you'll have to get your own. George is down in the orchard chopping wood; not that he should be doing anything of the kind in this cold snap but its one job I can't do myself yet.'

Toby coloured. 'I'm OK now; I could do that. I'm not completely useless you know.'

Andrew stood massaging his shoulder for a moment then gave his sudden smile, 'Then don't do quite such a good job of trying to convince me you are. Come on; you do the toast and I'll boil the eggs – its ten o'clock, for God's sake and I'm feeling peckish again myself.'

Toby followed him to the kitchen. Gawd, could the old man be human after all? He studied his father's broad shoulders and wondered what it was like to be shot. The Head had embarrassed the hell out of him at school when it happened – banging on about how proud he should be to have a hero for a father. Toby scowled at the memory. Of course he had been pretty chuffed at the hero bit and got a lot of cred from it, but what bloke wanted it rammed down his throat in front of everyone?

Thinking about school, his mind shot off on a tangent: he didn't want to go back; if he did he'd have to crawl to the Head and apologise – and for what – for being found out doing what half the school did anyway, then sent to the sanny like some little kid to wait for daddy to come and take him home?

He hated the bloody place; always had done, and he was sick of it;

sick of being shunted off out of the way so his mother could shag the boy friends without a kid hanging around to spoil her fun. *Bitch*, he thought savagely, bloody good job she'd gone...suddenly his eyes were smarting and there was an ache in his throat. It wasn't asking too much, was it, to want a half-way decent mother; one who might be around when you needed her? One who wouldn't turn up on sports day hanging around the neck of some bloke you'd never seen before?

They had reached the kitchen now and he put a block on his thoughts. 'Bread,' he said, his voice rough, 'where does George keep the bread?'

'In there,' Andrew indicated the large white enamelled bin on the kitchen dresser which had BREAD printed across the front in bold black letters. He took a swift glance at his son's set face and suspiciously bright eyes and thought he'd give a lot to know what he was thinking right now. He felt his heart sink a little. He couldn't just ignore what had happened to bring Toby from school before time; now he was back on his feet again he would have to talk to him and quite soon; amongst other things there was the little matter still to be resolved as to whether the school would allow him back next year without some form of guarantee of good behaviour, and he couldn't exactly see Toby meeting that sort of criterion. He took a pan and half-filled it at the tap; as if he didn't have enough on his plate with the house, he thought: George and his bronchitis, his own retirement a full five years earlier than he had expected, or wanted, Kate Shaw...

For a moment he allowed a fantasy picture to form in his mind, transporting himself away from Cornwall in winter, to sit at ease on the terrace of some mythical villa in Tuscany, while George served coffee and Kate lounged beside him wearing one of those long skirts slit right up to the thigh, ... he gave a silent, exasperated sigh and lowered four eggs into the pan. Not bloody likely. A dream was a dream was a dream, and he'd damned well better see it stayed that way.

*   *   *

On Monday morning Kate was greeted at the doors of Rosscannan by an exuberant Toby.

'Hi!' he ran down the steps, 'Oh, great, you've brought the pooch.' He opened the rear car door and Heathcliffe leaped for his shoulders. Toby staggered and collapsed onto the steps, the dog on top of him.

'You need to sit down *before* he says hello!' Kate reminded him helpfully.

'Yeah, right,' he grinned up at her over Heathcliffe's head. 'If you want dad he's upstairs banging on walls and swearing, and George is in the kitchen doing whatever he does there,' he rubbed the dog's ears. 'Now I'm allowed out, can I take him for a walk? This place is crap today.'

'Take him and welcome; he needs all the exercise he can get.'

'Me too,' Toby got to his feet and caught at Heathcliffe's collar, 'come on mate, I'm about as welcome around here this morning as Ozzy Osbourne at a vicar's tea party.'

Kate said, 'Like that, is it?'

'Yeah, the old man's got a real snitty on this morning!'

'Thanks for the warning.' She waved a hand. 'Go on then, get weaving.'

She's OK, he thought as he went down the drive at a brisk trot with Heathcliffe at his heels, but dad was right; she *was* knocking on a bit, tasty mind you, but more in the old man's league. He grinned, now that *would* be something else again…'Hey, hey!' suddenly exuberant he yelled aloud with the sheer exhilaration of being alive and out in the bright fresh morning; he jumped, Heathcliffe jumped with him and Toby laughed and began to run. *It wasn't bad being here; not bad at all; even if the house was in the middle of nowhere and dad a bit twitchy, it felt good like he'd always felt home ought to be…*

Kate watched boy and dog out of sight, then leaving her duffle and gloves on the hallstand, went in search of her new employer. Following the sound of dull thuds and audible muttering, she discovered him up a stepladder on the first landing, cursing monotonously while juggling with a six foot long section of picture rail. At the sound of her footsteps and without looking around he snarled, 'I thought I told you to take your useless carcass out of here.'

'Don't chuck a hissy fit at me; I've only just arrived and you *did* offer me a job.'

'Bugger!' he swivelled around on the ladder and looked down on her upturned face. He held a pencil clenched between his teeth, his hair was rumpled and his face smudged with dirt. Again her stomach did that sneaky little side step. He removed the pencil. 'Sorry, thought you were Toby. I'd like to keep the little tyke from under my feet and occupy him with some work, but he isn't really up to very much yet and I can't be arsed with him hanging around.'

'He's heading for the beach with Heathcliffe, which is probably what he needs after being cooped up for the past few days.'

Andrew propped the length of wood against the wall and came down the ladder. 'I'm not sure what I'll do with him when he *is* fit. God knows what I've been paying school fees for all these years; he appears to have no practical skills and not many intellectual ones either.'

'He seems bright enough to me,' she said mildly. 'He might surprise you, given the chance.'

'How d'you know I haven't given him a chance.'

She smiled, 'Just a hunch.'

He leaned back against the ladder and scowled. 'Don't you ever get sick of being a busybody?'

'No. It is a gift.'

'There's lucky now.' He was heavily sarcastic. 'OK, so what do you think I should do to motivate him?

Kate gave it some serious thought. 'Well you could start him off in a day or two on a not-too difficult job– say getting all that awful carpet off the stairs.' She grinned. 'Offer to pay him and I bet you he'd be onto it like a terrier down a rabbit hole.'

The scowl left his face and he grinned back, 'Might give it a try.' He began to walk along the landing. 'Come down into the drawing room. I've finished with the woodwork in there and I need to pick your brain about the wallpaper.'

At the head of the stairs he stood aside for her to go first. George, coming into the hallway at that moment gave a small derisive snort at the sight of the boss following three steps behind That Woman and eyeing her like a well-mannered panther contemplating its next meal.

*Trouble, that's what she's going to be; just plain bleedin' trouble...*George grumbled silently to himself and returned Kate's breezy morning greeting of 'Hi, how are you today George,' with a morose, 'I been alright so far miss, but I wouldn't take a bet I stay that way.'

'You know,' Kate murmured as he disappeared back in the direction of the kitchen, 'I think George and I are going to develop a really beautiful and meaningful friendship over the next few weeks... that's if he doesn't poison me and shove me down a well before today is out.'

Andrew said, 'We don't have a well.'

She looked at him over her shoulder. 'I detect some ambivalence in that remark; almost as though you think poisoning me a possibility.'

'Oh, I wouldn't go that far,' he was bland. 'George strikes me as more your friendly neighbourhood impulse murderer. I don't think he'd actually *plan* anything!'

'You can't think how that comforts me,' murmured Kate as she opened the door to the drawing room. 'Now, murder aside, let me tell you what *I* think might be done with this wallpaper.'

*   *   *

Half-way through the morning, Mr Dawlish, builder and decorator, with an impressive track record in the interior renovation and decoration of old buildings, arrived from Penzance. After a great deal of initial head-shaking he agreed to begin work, but not until after Christmas. 'You'll 'ave to wait until then,' he warned, 'my missus wants the spare room decorated before Christmas – the mother-in-law's coming to stay.' He sniffed, 'Festive Season my eye!'

Kate made soothing noises and a large pot of tea, then seating him at the kitchen table with a plate of George's gingerbread, went to work. An hour later Mr Dawlish left, bemusedly wondering just how he had been manoeuvred into agreeing to make a start early next week. *Bang goes the mother-in-law's bedroom – and my holiday nookie,* he thought gloomily. The wife would more than likely retaliate by wearing half a ton of ironmongery in her hair and going to bed in a passion-killer flannelette nightdress.

George watched his departure with a sympathetic eye while covertly admiring the Kate woman's technique. She was one to watch all right.

12

DECEMBER

A pattern of work was quickly and easily established between the three main participants. Andrew took on board Kate's suggestion for involving Toby and, spurred on by the prospect of reward, the boy ripped out the offending stair carpet and attacked the stairs and banisters with sugar soap and something approaching enthusiasm. Kate mixed paint in the drawing room until she achieved an almost perfect match, then with the softest of sable brushes blended the result into the pale and subtle pattern of the wallpaper, while Andrew tackled the grubby paintwork and sandpapered the wooden shutters, ready for Mr Dawlish and his magic paintbrush.

At regular intervals each day, they were summoned to the kitchen by George ringing a hand-bell that must easily have been heard in the nearby village. They came together from their various occupations, gathering around the pine table to eat, drink and chat. It was during these sessions that Kate gradually became aware that Andrew Parradine was showing an increasing reluctance to talk about the proposed sale of the house; that whenever that subject came up he quickly turned the conversation in another direction, leading her to wonder if he really didn't want it to be sold at all. Still, what he did with the place when the work was completed wasn't any of her business, was it? *She* was only there to help make it all happen.

It was the most fun, work-wise, she had had in years. Every evening found her reluctant to finish and return to Pendragon; every morning impatient to speed back to Rosscannan and pick up from where she had left off. There was something special about the house; something indefinable that she couldn't quite put her finger on. It drew her and when she was there she somehow felt different, fulfilled, as though by just being there her life was enhanced. Little wonder, she thought, that Andrew might have the desire to hang onto his family home.

*   *   *

When Megan telephoned from Florence that weekend she found her niece positively fizzing with life, all the wit and sparkle that had vanished following the break-up of her long and ultimately disastrous love affair with Maestro Verdassey, appeared to be back again and in full measure.

While Kate enthused about Rosscannan and the work she was doing in the house, the fabulous wealth of fabrics and furnishings she was able to retrieve from the attics, Megan was taking a wry look at the circumstances that had sent her niece to work alongside Andrew Parradine in Cornwall, whilst she herself was spending most of her days in the company of his father in Florence.

Her sharp ears caught a certain tone in Kate's voice that spoke of a particular type of buzz, the kind that generally spelled 'man', even if in only small letters, and she wondered if the son was as attractive as his father had been, and still was, as she could testify for all that James was nudging eighty.

She tried to bring the young Andrew to mind, but her memory of the small boy in short trousers she had known were vague. The child couldn't have been more than five at the time of that unfortunate incident at the New Year ball, when James had kissed her a little too passionately under the mistletoe and been caught doing it by his wife. Relations after that had been strained, and as Johnny hadn't been any too pleased either, that one indiscreet kiss had effectively ended any further social contact between the two families.

Never a woman to waste overmuch time in sentiment, when Kate paused for breath Megan interjected briskly, 'It sounds as though you are putting in a great deal of hard work; I hope your employer is paying you well.'

Kate answered coolly, 'He pays the going rate,' and Megan chuckled.

'Tell him you'll expect a bonus when the house is sold.'

'It will be months before that happens…Andrew doesn't seem to be in any great hurry. Sometimes I get the feeling he'd rather like to keep it in the family.'

'He'd better not let his father hear that; Rosscannan has always been a millstone about James Parradine's neck'

'And how would you know that?'

Megan explained. Well I'll be damned, thought Kate. By the sound of it, this James was not a man to have his plans thwarted…and what was Megan doing swanning around Italy with some old *roué* of a boy friend, who just happened to be Andrew's father? With a quiver in her voice, she said, 'I hope you are behaving yourself on all those evenings alone with him in his villa.'

'At my age, and his, what else would we be doing?'

'What about poor old Humph?'

'Probably having the time of his life with the tight-trouser brigade by now,' said Megan dryly, 'he isn't complaining anyway.'

'God,' said Kate, 'your generation really is the pits. Anything else I ought to know while we're at it?'

When Megan finally ended the call, Kate sat for a long time with her elbows on the kitchen table, her chin cupped in her hands, puzzling over what appeared to be the opposing expectations of father and son. If push came to shove between them, who would win, she wondered.

*   *   *

Andrew finished stacking the supper things in the dishwasher then looked over his shoulder at Toby, who was about to escape while the going was good.

'Hang on a minute; I thought we might take a walk.'

Toby was immediately suspicious. 'Why?'

'Why not?'

He protested. 'Hell, dad, its dark and freezing out there.'

'On the contrary, it is bright moonlight and hanging in the hall is a large selection of coats, working men for the use of.'

George cackled. 'Go on, yer big Jessie,' he jeered. 'Call this cold? You should try the Khyber Pass in winter; near froze me bollocks off that did!'

'Thank you for sharing the state of your gonads with us, George,' Andrew rebuked him mildly. 'Come on Toby, before you hear anything else unsuitable for your tender years.'

Grumbling beneath his breath, Toby slouched after him, only slightly mollified when his father handed him his own overcoat; it had a dark red silk lining, reached almost to his feet, and was definitely cool enough to make even lard-arse Collins with his designer jeans look pretty crap…

The full moon was a perfect circle in a sky studded with stars, the air cold enough to condense the breath. They walked in silence for a few minutes, Andrew setting a circular tour of the grounds on the pathway that wound around the small lake and skirted a belt of woodland. Determinedly he tramped the frosty ground, trailed by a reluctant and disgruntled Toby.

'I've been thinking; about your school and what happens next year.' Andrew eventually broke the silence. 'Tell me, because I'm curious: just what *do* you think you've been at ever since you started there? Three years is one hell of a long time to be playing silly buggers and cannoning from one disaster to another.'

Toby shrugged, a gesture largely lost in the folds of Andrew's Crombie. 'Dunno,' he mumbled.

'Is that all you can come up with: "Dunno?"' Andrew didn't turn to look at him. One of the advantages of having a conversation whilst driving a car, or walking with someone was that you didn't have to keep eye contact, always an asset when you were batting on a sticky wicket.

Toby said grudgingly, 'I just can't stand the place; I've always hated it – the only reason I was sent there was to get me out of everyone's way.' His voice took on a bitter I-know-you-won't-understand whine. 'Prep school was bad enough, but at least it was near home, but this dump stinks.'

Andrew slowed his pace a little. Somewhere in the dim and distant past, he remembered, he'd had something like this conversation with his own father, but without the slang. Remembered, too, how it had felt after every holiday on returning to the barren existence of form room and dormitory; how bloody awful it had felt to be fifteen, with zits, exams, sex invading every waking moment and some of your dreams as well, and three whole months before the end of term and an all too brief escape from hell...

But his father's unexpected move to Italy had scuppered all Andrew's own plans to get away from boarding school at sixteen and live like a human being; James had held firm and Andrew had had to see out every dreary moment in the place until he hit eighteen and could escape to university. Even spending all those school vacations in Italy hadn't made up for the misery of feeling he had prison walls around him.

Suddenly he made up his mind. He stopped and putting a hand on his son's shoulder turned him, so that they stood face to face. He said quietly, 'You've several months to go before your GCSEs, and supposing they are good enough and that any halfway decent Sixth Form College would take you, you could leave then. You don't *have* to stay at the place for the whole whack, but...' he paused momentarily, giving emphasis to his words, 'I think you *should* go back, at least for those final few months. Not to do so would be the easiest, but not necessarily the best, way out. However, the decision is yours; I'm not going to play the heavy father and make you, all I ask is that you think it through carefully, because the only alternative is to stay here with me and spend the final couple of terms before college at the Comprehensive in Penzance. There you would be without the friends you already have, in a new environment in which you would have no standing and no knowledge of what's expected of you. You'll find that tough enough when you start Sixth Form College; spending time, however short, in a strange school where everyone already has his own friends and knows how the system works – hell, you'd stick out like a ham sandwich at a Bar Mitzvah.' He gave Toby's shoulder a squeeze. 'Think about it, and when you're ready, let me know what you've decided. Just don't leave it until the last minute to make up your mind.' He gave a faint smile, 'Deal?'

Toby averted his face. 'Yeah, OK; Deal.'

'Good.' Andrew started walking, his hand still on Toby's shoulder. He could feel his son begin to shiver, and quickening his pace demanded, 'Who's damn fool idea was it anyway to take a walk at this time of night? Let's get back indoors before I bloody freeze to death.'

*   *   *

Kate and Andrew stood together on a late evening at the end of the third week to survey with pride, and a certain sense of smug achievement, the restoration of the drawing room to its former glory. Andrew's renovation of the woodwork was complete; the ceiling-high window shutters and recessed seats freshly painted by Mr Dawlish so skilfully that no sign of his brushwork sullied their satin smoothness. Kate had worked a near miracle on the wallpaper and Toby, teetering dangerously on top of a step ladder, had, that morning, hung the curtains rescued from the attic by Kate, after she had stood for hours patiently steaming out the creases from the heavy damask, even coercing George into polishing the brass rods from which they now hung.

'Pretty impressive,' observed Andrew, and Kate smiled.

'You still have quite a way to go.'

He cleared his throat and asked quickly, 'Will you stay and see it out with us, Kate?'

'I'd like to. I have to return to London sometime and attend to some unfinished business, but I'll be happy to continue the work as long as I'm needed.'

'Is the unfinished business pleasant or unpleasant?' he asked.

'More tedious than anything else, but it has to be dealt with.'

'Hmm.' He gazed at her for a moment then said, 'George has taken to his bed wheezing like a grampus – not that I'm sure what a grampus is exactly. '

'It's a dolphin,' Kate supplied helpfully.

'Well, whatever it is, he's wheezing like one. Toby has retreated into zombie mode with his latest Playstation and *you* have slaved long past your agreed working day to finish this room. As we last ate at around five o'clock why don't I take you out to dinner...' he looked at his watch, 'or rather supper, tonight?'

She wrinkled her nose, 'Is that an invitation or a rhetorical question?'

Andrew sighed. 'Okay, so be pedantic if that's what turns you on. Now, in words of one syllable,' he enunciated carefully, 'may-I-take-you-out-to-supper-tonight?'

She corrected him, 'supper and tonight have two syllables – each; and we'll have to take Heathcliffe or he'll bark and wake everyone when we get back.'

He said wearily, 'Oh, just shut up will you and get your coat.'

'God, but you know how to get round a girl, don't you?' She gestured at their grubby jeans and shirts. 'We can't go into any restaurant as we are. I should think we'd even get thrown out of a McDonalds!'

'We go to a pub, woman, and sit in a dark corner.'

She fluttered her lashes, 'La, Mr Darcy, but you've quite won me over with your silver tongue...'

He caught her elbow and steered her towards the door. He said, 'George said you'd do that.'

'What did George say I'd do?'

'Flutter your eyelashes at me.'

Kate fluttered her lashes some more. 'Don't get all excited now,' she said, 'I do that to all the boys.'

*　　　*　　　*

As Kate heaved Heathcliffe over the tailgate then settled into her seat in the Land Rover, Andrew said, 'I thought we might try the pub in Maunsley as it's nearest. Will that do you?'

'Anything will do me, as long as it serves food.' As though lending weight to her words, Kate's stomach gave a faint protesting grumble. 'You see? I've usually eaten by now, but I did want to get everything in that room finished before the weekend. It does look good doesn't it?'

'It looks superb, and just as I remember it.'

She wondered once more about his reason for working so hard to

104

make it his home again if he knew quite well that his father intended to sell. Tentatively she asked, 'Why have you taken on all the work and the hassle that comes with it? I can see for myself, even without listening to George nagging you, that you obviously aren't really fit enough to be doing any kind of manual work, so why not turn all of it over to someone else?'

'Because that isn't the way I do things.' He gave a wry little shrug of the shoulders. 'Rosscannan is my home and I want to have a hand in restoring the place to how I remember it.'

Kate hesitated again then decided she really wasn't any good at this dissembling and she might as well make him aware she knew the score. 'Megan rang me a few days ago,' she said abruptly, 'she told me when the work was finished your father will put the house on the market.'

He scowled. 'And how would your aunt know what my father does, or does not intend doing?'

'They met in Florence; they are apparently old buddies. He told her all about his plans for the house – oh, and yes,' she grinned, 'she says she remembers you when you were in short pants.'

'Does she? Well, I don't remember her,' he gave a grim smile. 'That the house will be sold when the work is finished may be what my father wants, but not necessarily what will happen. I might have my own plans for Rosscannan.'

'Well unless your pa either shuffles off this mortal coil or you get to have power of attorney *before* he goes ga-ga, I don't see you can help doing as he wants.'

He said, 'Wait until we get to the Red Lion and I'll tell you.'

He chose one of the booths at the side of the bar, then after they each had a glass of draught cider on the table and were waiting for their order of beer-battered cod and chips and forget-the-mushy peas, briefly outlined the plans he had been forming over the past weeks to turn the stables and coach house into five, or possibly six, apartments for rental. 'You see,' he finished, 'while Pa may be paying for the main work on the house, I'd fund the work for creating the apartments out of my own pocket and offer to pay him a share of the profits. I know my father, if there's one thing he can't resist it's a possibility of seeing a return on investment – any investment.'

Kate pondered his words in silence for a while before answering cautiously, 'I doubt that converting just those buildings into a half dozen permanent lets would show enough profit to tempt your father. It might if you were offering property for rental in London, yes, but in Cornwall? I don't think so. However...' she leaned forward across the table, a mischievous glint in her eye. 'How about hosting regular Murder week-ends? Very popular at the moment and profitable, but a load of arty-farty actors and enthusiastic Poirots and Miss Marples might be a bit intrusive on your personal space. Or you *could* turn the grounds over every weekend as a venue for rich nutters to spend a day playing soldiers and paintballing each other to the death?'

'Oh, very funny!' Andrew gave a loud derisive snort and she laughed.

'OK, but *if* money was no object you *could* convert the whole lot – the stables, the coach house, the office *and* the barn into luxury holiday apartments, the place is only minutes from a secluded beach and has some of the best tourist spots in Cornwall within spitting distance. Make them luxurious enough, with central heating and open log fires and you might start making a profit in two or three years.'

'I couldn't find that kind of money – nor wait that long to see any returns.' He rolled his glass moodily between his hands. 'To be honest, it isn't only the need to make some kind of a deal with my father over the house; I *need* to work. I can't just sit around. I've never been a desk soldier; my life has been spent on the move and in trouble spots all over the world. Retirement just doesn't figure. The thought of giving up work altogether and vegetating is anathema to me.'

Kate sighed. 'I'm sorry to be such a damp sponge. What happens if you can't persuade your father to change his mind about selling? He sounds a pretty tough nut to me.'

'He is; but I'm here and he's there – and possession is nine tenths of the Law. Rosscannan is part of my inheritance. It might suit him to sell and give me a share and the rest when he pops his clogs, but it doesn't suit *me*. I don't want his money now; I have more than enough from my pension and my share of the Hampstead house and I'd rather work my ass off to pay what he expects for Rosscannan and have it all.'

Kate cupped her chin in one hand and asked innocently, 'So when Andrew Parradine wants something, he gets it; is that the drill?'

'Well, that depends on the circumstances and with whom I might be dealing, but yes, generally speaking, I do.'

Their eyes met; in his lurked an expression that made Kate pause and take a deep breath. She had looked into a lot of eyes in her time and read a lot of different and sometimes confusing messages in them, but the one in this particular pair was loud and clear…

She said, 'Speaking personally, I don't think you have a prayer.'

'Speaking personally,' he returned softly, 'I think I do.'

'Well, we are each entitled to our own opinion, aren't we?'

He nodded in grave agreement. 'Time,' he said, 'will undoubtedly sort things out, one way or another.'

There was definitely something about his tone as well as his look that told her it was time for a complete change of subject. She asked, 'So did you always want to be a soldier?'

'No,' he said, unfazed by the sudden sideways leap in their conversation, 'what I wanted was to be able to play sax like Charlie Parker and become rich and famous. What about you; what was *your* secret ambition?'

'An equally modest one; I wanted to paint like David Hockney, only I hadn't the gift; instead I became very good at creating a background for those fortunate people who had a "talent to amuse."'

He took a long pull at his drink then set down the glass. 'Would you like to go back to that life?'

She shrugged. 'It's what I did for over twelve years, until I changed course rather drastically eight years ago. Perhaps I'm a touch too old to backtrack now.' She saw the quizzical look in his eyes and gave her sudden smile, 'Forty-three years too old – how about you?'

'Oh, I *have* to change course – and I can beat you by six...' he broke off, as the barman arrived with their supper and Heathcliffe, roused by the smell of food, stirred from his snooze beneath the table and ran a hopeful snout up Kate's leg. She threw a disapproving look at Andrew; drawing her feet under her chair she ordered crisply, 'Watch it!'

For a moment he looked blank, then as Heathcliffe's great head appeared above her side of the table he grinned in sudden understanding. 'Not guilty,' he answered, and with no small degree of pleasurable malice watched her blush. 'Nice one Heathcliffe,' he said approvingly and, leaning across the table, fed him a chip.

*   *   *

Tired after the day's work, mellowed by good food and strong cider they drifted into the kind of easy, unforced companionship natural in people who shared a common interest and goal. Andrew was amusing and agreeable and Kate at her most amicable. While each was aware of danger in this new and growing rapport, each had confidence in their separate abilities to deal with a situation that appeared to be moving towards an even greater intimacy.

Taking advantage of the fact that he had offered to drive her home, Kate didn't stop, as he did, at one glass of cider, so that by the time they had finished their meal she was feeling delightfully mellow and relaxed.

'Just as well you are leaving your car at my place overnight,' he said as he held the tailgate for Heathcliffe to jump into the Land Rover, 'you're more than a touch over the limit for driving that mobile privy.'

'You could be right there,' Kate gazed dreamily up at the moon riding high in the starlit sky. 'I'll fetch it in the morning; I can do with the walk.'

'You will not; even across country 'the walk' is around three miles. Tomorrow, always supposing he's stopped wheezing, George can drive it over and I'll follow.'

'All right,' she yawned, 'I'm too tired to argue.'

He muttered, 'That has to be a first,' and helped her up into her seat.

She dozed on the way back to Pendragon, but came fully awake as he cruised to a halt at the front door. As she took her keys from her bag he lifted them gently from her fingers. 'Allow me,' he said, and much to his surprise, she did.

As he swung the door wide and stood clear to let Heathcliffe lumber for his favoured rug before the Aga; Kate stifled another yawn. 'Would you like a coffee? I have to make one for myself to be sure I'll stay awake long enough to crawl up to bed.'

He gave his deep chuckle, 'Perhaps you'd better let me make it,' he suggested but she smiled and shook her head then led the way to the kitchen. He followed her and taking off his coat hung it over a chair then sat, resting his arms on the table. 'The inside is certainly an improvement on the outside; warm too.' He stretched lazily. 'I'll be glad when the heating in my place is sorted; going to bed there alone has all the less attractive aspects of a polar expedition.'

An air of sexual tension began to invade the room; Kate tossed her keys on the kitchen table and keeping her back turned, swung the kettle onto the hotplate and taking down the tin of ground coffee began measuring it into the cafetière. In an effort to clear the air a little she asked, 'If you lose out and your father insists on selling, won't he baulk at the expense of having replaced all those old radiators – there are a hell of a lot of them, aren't there?'

Andrew shrugged. 'He can afford it. The landlord's insurance he took out against damage and wear and tear is paying up, and that, combined with his own loot, will more than cover it.'

'What does he do for a living,' she asked curiously, 'diamond smuggling?'

'Nothing so glamorous. The money his ancestors made out of tin he added to by importing wine from the Continent. He's a good businessman and after lugging us all off to Italy, he took his knowledge of wine a stage further and bought what is now a very productive vineyard near San Gimignano. Now he exports in an equally big way.'

She murmured, 'He doesn't by any chance need a good PA does he?'

'No, but I might when he discovers I intend hanging onto Rosscannan!'

'Why is the house so important to you?' she asked

'I've been asking myself that for almost thirty years. Perhaps because I always felt, even as a child, that the house was a living entity in its own right: full of memories, vibes – whatever you like to call them – they were good and made it a happy house. I'd like it to be that way again.' He looked up at her. 'When I walked through the door again after all those years I felt that intangible something. The first time I took you there I thought you felt it too.'

Kate said slowly, 'I did; still do. It draws me. I love being there: watching it come alive a little more each day.'

There was a long silence. He continued to hold her gaze; the vibes were going off the Richter scale now but she no longer cared. The lid of the kettle began to dance. Without looking away from him she reached back and moved it from the hotplate. She asked breathlessly, 'Are you reading my thoughts?'

'Yes. Are you reading mine?'

'I am; loud and clear.' She stood, and crossing the room opened the door into the garden. 'Heathcliffe: out!'

She waited by the open door for the hound's return, then after stooping to ruffle his head, turned again to Andrew and silently held out her hand. When he rose and took it she led him, still without speaking, up the broad carpeted staircase to her room.

*   *   *

She woke before dawn feeling warm and loose-limbed, like a woman who had been making very satisfactory love for most of the night, smiling as she came to full consciousness and remembered that was exactly what she had been doing.

The bedside lamp still burned, she turned and propping herself on one elbow looked down on Andrew where he still slept, head half-buried in the pillow, what could pass for designer stubble darkening his jaw. She pushed the sheet back carefully from his shoulder, touching the deep, livid scars with gentle fingers. Had the bullet struck a few inches lower and to the right, she thought, he wouldn't now be lying here beside her and sleeping the sleep of a tired and equally satisfied lover.

'You flew,' he had said when they were at last quiet. 'You bloody marvellous woman, you flew!' and she'd smiled, answering: 'and you flew with me.'

'So I did,' he'd said, 'so I did.'

Now, as if he sensed her watching him, he sighed, and opening his eyes focused slowly on her face. 'Ah,' he rolled onto his back, 'So glad it wasn't just another very erotic dream!'

'You have a lot of those, do you?'

'Not half as many as I'd like.'

Kate chuckled. 'I hate to tell you, but Ena the cleaner is due in about an hour – she comes with the dawn and sings "Jerusalem" very loudly. If she finds you in my bed she'll very likely change it to "Great God What Do I See And Hear..." then rush out screaming and tell the entire village she always knew I was a tart.'

'I take your point,' he sighed and sat up, rubbing at his bristly jaw, 'OK, I can fold my tent as well as the next Arab.'

She teased, 'If I'd known that I'd have put on my veil, stuck a ruby in my belly button and dug out the Turkish Delight.'

He laughed and asked, 'What will you be doing today?'

Kate lay back, clasping her hands behind her head. 'I think I'll give running a miss this morning, hide in my room while Ena does her worst, then whenever George appears with my car I may have the strength to spend another exciting morning in the town.'

Lowering his head, he brushed his lips over hers. 'I could come with you.'

'No, you'd distract me – just as you are right now,' gently she pushed him away, 'besides,' her mouth quirked, 'you have quality time with Toby to think about.'

He nipped her collarbone with his teeth. 'And you don't want me taking what happened last night for granted,' he said shrewdly.

'Umm, something along those lines.'

He said, 'I think you should know I don't go in for one night stands.'

'Neither do I,' she smiled up at him, 'but I don't buy any kind of commitment on the strength of one night...or even a whole string of nights.'

'Seems we suit each other then: one plunge into the matrimonial swamp was quite enough for me,' he said with careful detachment, aware that despite his unequivocal statement of non-commitment, somewhere in the recess of his mind a small sly voice added: '*for the time being anyway...*'

'We'll play it by ear and see what happens.' She sat up. 'Until the next time, then...' She raised an eyebrow. 'That is if you want....'

He grinned.

'I'd be a fool not to,' he said.

*   *   *

When he left, Kate wrapped herself in Megan's dressing gown and schlepping to the kitchen made a cup of tea, added a splash of whisky then pulled a chair over to the Aga and sat back, resting her feet on Heathcliffe's hairy flank.

Her body was beautifully languorously tired and still tingling with the remembrance of their night together. She had been surprised and touched by his gentle, unhurried, almost lazy lovemaking; moved by a tenderness that had overwhelmed her, and against all her reasoning, swept her into total impassioned surrender. She smiled and gave a contented sigh. Why, she wondered sleepily, if all she had needed was a little light dalliance, did she feel as though she had just discovered The Meaning of Life?

*   *   *

Andrew hummed *It's Been a Hard Day's Night* all the way back to Rosscannan. Although his night with Kate had turned all his emotions upside down and arse about, he was relieved she was content to play it cool. These were early days and she was obviously still carrying one hell of a lot of baggage from the recent past.

He keyed in his code then drove through the gates and slowly and carefully over the gravel, cutting the engine well before he reached the house to cruise the last few yards, but the blaze of the security lights woke both George and Toby from their slumbers. George muttered 'Randy bugger,' and pulling his pillow over his head went back to sleep, while Toby shot out of bed and padded barefoot to his window. By craning his neck he could see the Land Rover glide to a stop and his father jumping down from it and running toward the steps on his toes.

'Huh!' Toby scowled at the sight of the old man making like he was the head choir boy who'd just pulled the vicar's daughter. He trailed despondently back to his bed and lay thinking about the rottenness of life, when a bloke had to stand on the sidelines and watch an old geezer like his father get all the goodies.

The old geezer meanwhile had raided the fridge and was seated before the kitchen range with a bottle of Peroni in one hand, a leg of cold roast chicken in the other, feeling a contentment of mind and blissful weariness of body that any middle aged man would give his eye teeth for.

13

Next morning Toby took advantage of Andrew's unusually benevolent mood to ask if he might have a bike – 'Just to get around on, you know,' this said with great casualness, 'I don't want to be stuck here all the time.'

'Said with all your usual grace and charm,' Andrew looked up from his morning paper to study him in silence for a moment. 'I don't see why not. George and I have to take Kate's car over to her sometime this morning; if you come with us we could go on into Penzance afterward and see what's on offer.'

Toby eyed him back. 'Why's her car *here* then?'

'As we worked on after you and George had pushed off to your individual pads we went for a pub supper and I drove her back to Pendragon afterward.' He cocked an eyebrow. 'Anything else you'd like to know?'

Toby hunched his shoulders, 'Nah, s'nothing to do with me.'

'That's right; it isn't.' With an air of finality Andrew snapped the paper onto the next page. Nine-thirty in the morning was too early for verbal sparring with the nosy little bastard.

George appeared on cue, like an aged jack-in-the-box. He sucked his teeth. 'Pub must have closed bloody late. Security light woke me at six-thirty.'

'Foxes,' Andrew said.

'If it was foxes then what was they doing driving your Land Rover?'

He shrugged. 'Try asking the foxes.'

'Probably get more bloody sense out of them than you.' George sucked his teeth again and Andrew gave him a quelling glare over his newspaper.

'You make that disgusting noise just once more this morning and you'll very likely find yourself in need of a full set of National Health dentures,' he snapped.

George smirked and winked at Toby. ''Ope he don't get this arsey every time he has a night out on the tiles, or I'll be giving in me notice.' Scooping up the used breakfast dishes with an ostentatious flourish he made a dignified exit to the scullery.

*   *   *

Kate was ready and waiting on the steps as the Land Rover, followed by the Triumph, drew up before Pendragon.

'Good morning, Kate,' Andrew greeted, 'Get enough beauty sleep did you?'

'Good morning – as much as you, I guess,' she returned, as though the events of the previous evening had never occurred. She blew a kiss to Toby and gave George her very nicest smile as he climbed from Megan's car. 'Thank you George, I hope the journey hasn't taken your bronchitis up another notch.'

George made a great show of shivering and wrapping his scarf more tightly about his neck. 'I wouldn't know, Miss, I'm too ruddy cold to feel if it has.' He hauled himself into the passenger seat of the Land Rover, urging, 'Come on, guv'nor, before all the 'eat goes out of this thing.'

Andrew rolled his eyes heavenward. 'Enjoy your day off, Kate.'

She said, 'A very chirpy newsreader informed me this morning that there are precisely ten more shopping days to Christmas. As I hate leaving things to the last minute, I think I'll make a start on my festive shopping today – I have to find my father the really crap tie I promised him, and something for my mother that she won't think has come from Oxfam.'

Andrew said airily, 'Plenty of time for all that.'

Kate grinned. 'Don't tell me – you're the sort that does all their shopping on Christmas Eve.'

'How did you guess?' He put the Land Rover into gear. 'Happy hunting then – see you on Monday.'

*   *   *

She shopped diligently: a fire-engine-red silk tie decorated with vulgar-looking cats washing every conceivable part of the anatomy for her father, and soft leather gloves she couldn't really afford for her mother, overcompensating as usual for not loving her as much as she felt she should.

She felt a quick stab of guilt that she had made them promise on pain of death not to give away her whereabouts to any of her friends and closer acquaintances, but the last thing she wanted was people ringing to commiserate with her and pick over the details of her split from Paul.

She wandered through the streets, stopping to look in the windows of the gift and antique shops that jostled for space in the old part of the town, finally reaching one that simply defied classification where everything, from battered old dolls and tarnished silver cutlery to a full-size stuffed black bear, were crammed into a space no larger than the living room of a nineteen-thirties semi. Intrigued, she stepped inside and began threading her way through the narrow passageways between the piled-high junk, thinking that all it needed to complete the picture of an elaborate set for a TV series was for Auntie Wainwright to appear and flog her that rusty hip bath at present leaning drunkenly against a battered Victorian commode...

She completed her tour of the shop, then stopped to stroke the bear, which was actually quite a small one. She had a sudden mischievous vision of Andrew finding it at the end of his bed on Christmas morning...but no, she really couldn't do that!

Her arm brushed against a roll of cloth wrapped loosely in dusty brown paper, it fell to the ground and partially unrolled, revealing a small tapestry, very old and dirty, of what appeared to be a late eighteenth century hunting scene. The whole piece measured some three feet across and around two deep. Picking it up she unrolled it completely and immediately in her mind's eye could imagine it cleaned and hung above the stone fireplace in the dining hall at Rosscannan...

'Cracking piece of work, isn't it, m'dear?'

Kate turned around to meet a pair of shrewd rheumy eyes above a beaky nose: Uncle, not Auntie Wainwright, she deduced, but equally crafty. She gave a derisive snort. 'It's a disaster and would need one hell of a lot of work to make it even passable.'

'Wouldn't take more'n an hour or two wi' a spot of turps an' a cloth.'

Kate looked at him coldly. Damned Philistine; she gave a dismissive shrug. 'Rather more than that, but someone might take pot luck with it I suppose, if the price was right.'

'I can see you've got a fancy for it m'dear, so I'll let you have it for forty.'

Kate didn't even blink. 'Do I look like I've just arrived from the planet Zog?'

The proprietor eyed her up and down, assessing the probable price of her coat. 'Thirty-five – and I'm cutting my own throat selling it for that.'

She flicked a disparaging finger at the tapestry, 'Try cutting it just a little more and you might get lucky.'

'Thirty, then.'

'Twenty.'

He sucked his teeth, *à la* George. 'Twenty-five and that's my last word.'

She gave a seraphic smile. 'Done,' she said. There were still a few presents yet to go and she couldn't really afford twenty-five quid, but she loved giving, particularly she loved giving at Christmas, and it was hard to accept that for the first time in many years she couldn't shop with her accustomed generosity.

She cast a glance around the rest of the shop and the proprietor gave her a nervous look, 'You seen something else?' he enquired.

Pointing to a guitar case she enquired. 'Does that have an instrument inside or do you just keep your Kalashnikov in it?'

'It's a guitar all right,' he said spiritedly, 'but it don't come with Marilyn Monroe – and it's ten quid and no bargaining.'

'She played a ukulele, not the guitar,' Kate corrected, 'and I'll give you six.'

It would do nicely for Toby, she thought as she left with her spoils; he'd be a strange teenager if he could resist trying to coax a few recognizable cords from a guitar; it was in good condition and needed only a new set of strings from the music shop in the High Street. Now all she needed to complete her shopping was one of those man-sized fleece scarves from M & S for George and a pair of motorbike gauntlets for Sam. As he'd only worn thick knitted gloves on that damned bike she wouldn't wait for Christmas, but would slip them through his door in the next day or so while he was out flogging Christmas trees at his garden centre. She drove to the Supermarket in high spirits, with the indestructible Noddy Holder belting out *Happy Christmas Everyone* on the car radio, as he had been doing for more than twenty years.

*   *   *

Toby looked at George in some disbelief.

'Are you sure that's what he'd like?'

It was later that day and they were seated either side of the kitchen table, George stringing beans for their evening meal whilst Toby frowned in concentration over his Christmas list.

'Course I'm sure.' George flourished his knife. 'Always made a big fuss of the barracks moggies, he did.'

'Bloody hell.' Toby scratched his head, 'I was going to give him one of his naff old Jazz CDs.'

George gave a contemptuous sniff. 'He's already got bleedin' dozens of *them*.'

'So where do I get it from?'

'We,' George gave his fearsome grin, 'where do *we* get it from – you don't get them for nothing these days yer know; this is from you an' me both. We don't want to do nothin' yet – not until Christmas Eve, then you an' me'll borrow the Land Rover and get down to that rescue place in Penzance – they got dozens there to choose from. I'll just tell the guv'nor I 'as to do some last-minute shopping and takin' you along fer the ride. We can keep it in my room overnight.'

'I don't know how much dosh I'll have left. Ma hasn't sent a cheque or anything yet. She's usually coughed up by now; too busy with muscle man, I suppose, to think about me.' Toby looked down at his list, the tips of his ears reddening. 'I want to get Kate something but I'll just have to send a card and write something clever on it.'

'Know what my old man used ter say?' George grinned and quoted: '"Do right, an' fear no man. Don't write, an' fear no woman."'

Toby was puzzled, 'What's that supposed to mean?'

George guffawed, 'That where wimmin are concerned, you don't put *nothin'* down in writing!'

*   *   *

Andrew became aware that George was standing behind him; from time to time the man had a habit of silently materialising like some kind of sinister ectoplasm, his actual presence following a beat or two behind; a habit that might have worried someone of a less nervous disposition than Andrew.

'What is it now?' he turned from his computer, 'I'm *trying* to do the accounts, so make it quick.'

'All right, keep your hair on.' George matched him scowl for scowl, 'Like your girl friend said: Christmas is comin'. The boy's goin' to need some money soon; he won't ask but I will.'

Andrew said irritably, 'I've already paid him for the work he's done and bought him that bike he wanted; in any case Van always sends him a damned great cheque weeks before end of term, so what's he done with it all?'

'Nothing, cause she ain't sent it: so why don't you stop being such a tight wad an' make him a proper allowance.'

Andrew grunted. 'Why can't he come and ask for it himself.'

George gave a sarcastic snort, 'Think about it; if you was him, would *you*?'

Andrew squinted at the screen. 'Do we really spend that much in food?' He sighed. 'OK, I'll have a word with him now; tell him to come here, will you?'

'Can't do that, boss,' George was slyly triumphant. 'He's out on that bike and gone gawd knows where – took 'alf a loaf of sandwiches with 'im he did.'

'It would be quite in order,' Andrew answered tersely, 'if *I* might be allowed some knowledge of what my son proposes to do *before* he actually does it.'

George met this with a stony silence and Andrew sighed, aware that conscience was making him tetchy. As there was little practical help Toby could give him that morning, he had had actually told him to make himself scarce – and he hadn't paid him all that well for the work he'd already done. Knowing Vanessa's careless habit of handing out large cheques, particularly before the end of the Christmas term, and still suspicious of what the boy might be spending his money on, Andrew had intended that he at least would keep him on a tight financial reign.

He gave a shrug and wry smile. 'OK George, I'm the one out of order this time. When he does show up I'll see if I can mend a few bridges.'

Mollified George said, 'You gotta trust the little bleeder; else he won't think its worth trying – and 'e is trying, you know.'

'Yeah,' Andrew was laconic, 'he always has been – very!'

George eyed his back for a minute in silence before observing 'Good job it's Monday tomorrow an' your plasterer's mate 'ul be back, cause you ain't fit ter live with when she's at 'ome.'

Before Andrew could turn around, George had done his ectoplasm in reverse act and disappeared. Andrew sighed and turned back to the accounts. Oh well, soon be Monday then Kate would be at Rosscannan again.

But he couldn't settle. He tried to analyse his feelings. It wasn't just wanting to make love to her again as soon as possible, which he did; he simply wanted, needed, to be with her, to watch that expressive face, to see the laughter start behind her eyes; to know the reason for the baffling sadness and hurt that occasionally, very occasionally, showed through what appeared at times to be a precarious sophistication. On Monday they would have to behave as though Friday evening had never happened. He almost groaned aloud. He really, *really* didn't need any such complications in his life...

Oh, sod it.

He left his desk, closed the half-open door quietly, returned to his seat and lifting the handset on his desk phoned Pendragon. The bell rang a half dozen times before Kate answered with a breezy: 'Kate Shaw here.'

He didn't even try for either casual or subtle.

'Hi, is that the woman who gave me a bed on Friday night and no breakfast next morning?'

Kate turned away from the PC and settled back in Megan's creaking swivel chair. 'If you need a boarding house, try Yellow Pages.' He could hear the smile in her voice. 'What are you doing this morning?'

'The household accounts.'

'Steady. All work and no play and all that jazz...'

He said obliquely, 'It helps keep my mind off other things. What are *you* doing?'

She was silent for a moment or two then said, 'Job hunting on the internet.'

'For what? PA, interior decorator, or soldier's friend?'

'PA, I guess; a gal's gotta do what a gal's gotta do.'

'I think you should stick to wielding a mean paintbrush and being a soldier's friend...' he took the plunge. 'I'd like to see you tonight.'

'You don't exactly hang about, do you?'

He said reasonably. 'If I remember correctly, before I left last night you made a sort of suggestion and I gave you a sort of answer.'

'So you did.'

'OK...eight o'clock all right with you?'

'Well now,' he heard the underlying laughter in her voice, 'that sounds just the tiniest bit like: "I'm only coming for the sex, sweetie."'

'I'm coming for a lot more than that – I was figuring on taking you out to dinner and chatting you up.'

'Then make it seven and I'll give you dinner here.'

'In that case make it six,' he countered, 'then we can talk before and after dinner and maybe find time for the sex later.'

'Put like that, how can I refuse? Six it is.'

*   *   *

Kate put the phone back on its rest, amazed that even at a distance the sound of his voice could make her heart beat faster. What on earth was she getting herself into? With a cross between a sigh and a groan she leaned back and closed her eyes.

She had to face facts, however painful. When this precarious, wonderful interlude of romance and dilettante faffing around with paint and fabrics and furniture was done with, she must, in the fullness of time, leave Cornwall and Rosscannan and all therein, return to London and start all over again.

But she knew she wanted no job other than the one she had right now and the idea of a return to London had lost whatever charm it might once have possessed; all because on one particular day in October, Andrew Parradine had catapulted through a train door and into her life. Working alongside, or at least near him all these weeks, always with George or Toby close at hand, she had been able to mentally distance herself from his presence, but Friday's episode had put their relationship onto a whole new footing. Andrew's intentions apart, she wasn't at all sure of her own feelings, or even in which direction they were heading.

'You are forty-three,' she reminded herself aloud, 'and that man has only just got shot of one woman, so what makes your tiny, feeble little mind think he might have more than a passing interest in *you* when the world is full of considerably younger young things? Just paint his walls and hang his curtains, enjoy a little light dalliance on the side, and when it's all over, run for your life...'

Heathcliffe opened one eye at this diatribe and farted delicately. Kate glared at him. 'I hold you responsible, Heathcliffe, you disgusting hound. This is all your fault – if it wasn't for you I'd never have ended up in this mess. Without you, Megan could just have gone away leaving Ena to keep an eye on the house; I could have stayed in London and begun getting my life together again.'

She closed down the PC and sat staring moodily at the blank screen. Who was she kidding? When it *was* all over she was pretty damn sure she wouldn't want to run anywhere – certainly not back to London to become an overworked PA to yet another egocentric male too busy making money, or being famous, to manage his own affairs.

*   *   *

Andrew stood looking down at the phone still clutched in his hand, waited for his blood pressure to return to normal, and thought he would give a great deal to know what was going on in Kate Shaw's head. That she was job-hunting was bad news; it could only mean she still intended to leave Cornwall when the absent Megan showed again at Pendragon. Perhaps he'd been wrong in thinking of her as a refugee from some recent trauma in her love life. It might well be there was someone waiting for her back in London. But if that were so, why the hell had she let him into her bed, and why agree to his suggestion of another evening together so soon?

He rubbed a hand over his face. He must be a glutton for punishment if he could even think of looking for more than a passing affair with such a complex and unreadable woman as Kate Shaw, but with all that sensual passion lurking behind the cool, throwaway manner, she had damned well got under his skin...

*   *   *

Toby pedalled head down against the wind; although three miles and a bit hadn't looked much on paper, it seemed a very long way on a bike. Still, he'd made up his mind to do it today; he only hoped the guy was home.

The itch to return to Sam's cottage had been with him ever since that first day; he didn't know why both the place and the man attracted him, any more than he could figure why being around his father was gradually becoming less of a pain and more of a pleasure. Working on the house had helped, of course; there was something about the place that felt good, he even liked being in the old nursery, tucked up there away from everyone. It was almost like having his own pad.

But principally he wanted to see Sam because he was like no one else he'd ever met. Because he hadn't really been with it the first time they met, he felt a need to put things in some kind of perspective. Toby, who seldom took anyone at face value, knew somehow that he could trust Sam; although there was a big difference in age, he felt they spoke the same kind of language.

When he arrived at Hawthorne Cottage and saw smoke rising from a chimney and the glow of lamplight in the window, he let his breath go in a huge sigh of relief. After the long ride he was almost as cold as on his first visit and didn't fancy a return home without the chance to at least thaw out his hands and feet. He fumbled at the knocker with numbed fingers, then as footsteps began to approach the door, propped his cycle against the porch and nervously got ready to deliver his rehearsed speech.

Sam Trevene forestalled him.

'Well, you look a sight better than the last time I saw you.' His eyes behind the Lennon spectacles glinted with amusement. He held the door wide, 'come in mate and de-frost!'

'Thanks,'

Toby stepped inside, rubbing his gloved hands together. Sam closed the door against the wind and nodded towards the fire. 'Sit down – fancy a beer?' The eyes glinted again, 'or maybe that's not such a good idea for a guy on a bicycle; how about coffee?'

'Fine, yeah. Great.' Toby sat and, taking off his gloves, reached his hands out to the flames.

Sam opened the door to the kitchen. 'Won't be a tick; make yourself at home.' He grinned. 'Have a look around and see what you might have missed the first time!'

Toby wriggled his shoulders back into the uncut moquette of the sagging old armchair and, stretching his legs to the fire, allowed his gaze to drift around the room. He eyed the fishing gear enviously for a few moments then got up to move a pair of jeans and an old Guernsey across the table and leaf through a meagre pile of CDs: James Blunt, Red Hot Chili Peppers, Rilo Kiley...he gave a grunt of approval and returned to his seat by the fire.

This was some place; a bloke could really chill out here.

In the kitchen Sam spooned coffee into the mugs and waited for the kettle to boil. Now this was something to think about. Parradine's kid was in the next room sitting by his fire, and he doubted if his old man had the fainted idea he was there – and what on earth had brought the boy back anyway – gratitude, curiosity? Probably a mixture of both, Sam grinned and scratched his head. Whatever; it did have its funny side.

'I was going to have something to eat before I went into work – I'm on lunch time till late today,' he said as he carried the mugs of coffee back into the living room and set them down on the hearth.

'Shit – you work Sundays too?'

'Sure. Week-ends are when most people get to visit a Garden Centre.' Sam grinned. 'Lunch is only soup out of a can, but you're welcome to stay and share it, if you've the time to spare.'

'I brought sandwiches,' Toby blushed at Sam's lifted eyebrow. 'Couldn't do much for dad today and as I had the bike...' his voice faded and he shrugged.

Sam gave another grin. 'So you took off for a few hours.'

'Yeah,' Toby's blush deepened. 'If you were out, I was going to go back home and eat – you could have some of the sandwiches if you like; me and George did loads. They're out on the bike.'

'Better get them in then else they'll likely be frozen stiff. Tell you what,' Sam started in on his coffee, 'you supply the sandwiches and I'll make with the soup.'

'OK. I'll fetch them now.' Toby jumped up and made for the door. This was getting better by the minute, he thought, in a daze of pleasure. He felt like hugging himself. If he hung around when Sam had more time, maybe he might let him try a run on that motorbike.

They ate the soup and sandwiches before the fire, plates balanced on their knees. Toby mopped the last of his soup with an end of sandwich and sat back content. 'Thanks, that was great. Do you usually eat at work?'

'Mostly, or the pub around the corner.'

Toby asked curiously, 'What do you do there all the time?'

'Look after the plants; potting and all that. Serve customers, listen to them. Help them find the thing they want. Advise them what to plant if they're not sure.'

'Why?' Toby asked simply. 'I mean, I bet it doesn't pay much.'

'It doesn't, but that's not the point.' He looked straight into Toby's eyes, 'See, when I was a bit older than you, I didn't give a rat's arse about anything; didn't bother with a little thing like work; I thought the world owed me a living. I was in and out of prison until I did my last stretch in the kind that still ran a sort of mini-farm; kept hens; grew all its own veg. There was an orchard – even a flower garden. I learned a lot there and it turned my life around. Now let's just say I'm looking to return the favour.' As Toby still looked puzzled he added, 'Sometimes you have to stop taking and put something back.'

'Bloody hell,' said Toby, 'are you for real?'

Sam smiled, 'Mate, you'd better believe it, because you don't get any more real than me!'

*   *   *

Andrew looked up as Toby crossed the room with all the energy of drugged sloth and crouched shivering before the fire.

'Cold out on that bike, was it?' he asked and Toby gave an indifferent shrug; the gesture somewhat marred by another violent shiver.

'Yeah.'

'How far did you go?'

He went for another shrug, a silent one this time. Andrew lowered his head and stared at him over his reading glasses until Toby reddened and mumbled, 'Over to Godolphin Point; thought I'd say thanks to that bloke at the cottage.'

'There now,' Andrew returned to his book, 'that wasn't difficult, was it?'

Toby looked baffled. 'What wasn't?'

Andrew glanced up again, 'Giving a straight answer to a straight question. You should try it more often; saves all that faffing around,' he gave another long stare at his son's pinched face. 'You've overdone it, haven't you?'

'A bit,' Toby admitted it grudgingly, 'didn't realise it would take so long; it didn't seem all that far when Kate brought me here.'

'Well, here's something to brighten up your day.' Andrew dove into his jeans pocket and held out a substantial fold of notes. 'Your bonus; you've earned it.'

Toby couldn't help the delighted smile that burst over his face. *If this wasn't just the dog's bollocks...* he took the notes as though he thought they might explode or just simply vanish before his eyes. 'Thanks,' he swallowed hard, 'thanks, dad; I was, you know, getting a bit skint.'

'I know, but don't spend it all on booze and fast women. Keep some of it for Christmas – don't forget that lot up in Scotland.' Andrew poked a finger at Toby's hair, 'You could get a re-thatch job on that before it reaches your feet – or you could ask George to take the scissors to it instead and save the money!'

'Not likely. If he was in the wrong mood he might shave it.' He had a sudden vision of Sam Trevene, 'thought I might tie it back. '

'It could only be an improvement.'

*   *   *

That evening Kate relaxed in the luxury of a scented bath. Afterwards, avoiding any tendency to analyse "why", she dressed in her corduroy skirt, a navy silk shirt and Paul's cashmere sweater. It was no big deal and nothing to do with Andrew she reasoned, as she added chunky silver earrings and a matching bracelet. Since she had started work at Rosscannan she had practically lived in jeans and sweatshirts; now she was dressing well for her own pleasure, she told herself, not necessarily his.

All the same, Andrew, and the memory of their night together, was constantly at the forefront of her mind, causing her to swing erratically between a deep unease about the kind of involvement such a relationship might lead to and an impatient desire to be in his arms again and hang the consequences. Of course, there was always the possibility he may have decided it had all been a ghastly mistake and this evening would be at best an embarrassment, at worst a disaster. Her stomach did a little segue at the thought. What had happened to her resolution to cut men out of her life? she asked her reflection as she took a last inventory of herself in the long cheval mirror, and how come she had succumbed so easily to Andrew Parradine's charms? Blame it on the cider, she thought.

*   *   *

When he arrived bearing a bottle of very good French Cabernet Sauvignon, the lemon chicken was cooking gently, the duchesse potatoes ready to slip into the oven at the right moment, the spinach waiting for the pot. In the refrigerator a trifle rich in sherry and cream was chilling nicely.

Kate took the wine with a smile. 'How did you know to bring white?' she asked. 'I might have been roasting an ox, or serving jugged hare!'

'I've noticed that busy career women don't in general have time for roasting joints of beef with all the trimmings – or jugging hares. Fish or chicken was a pretty safe bet.'

She was unsure whether to be flattered or annoyed and wondered briefly just how many busy career women had cooked for him. But he was right of course; whipping up intimate dinner parties, very often at short notice, required ingenuity and simple ingredients, with chicken and fish generally heading the list. 'Very clever, full marks for the army intelligence service,' she murmured. She led the way into the sitting room and, gesturing towards the drinks cabinet, invited, 'As I've done the cooking, you can do the drinks. Mine's gin with very little tonic.'

*   *   *

They chatted companionably over the meal and later when they were settled before the fire with their coffee, he told her about Toby's visit to Sam Trevene. 'I was surprised to find him so keen to make a return call,' he finished and Kate laughed.

'I'm not. Sam's a nice guy and seemed to have the right touch with Toby; he was here to lunch the other day and I was quite impressed. As a reformed character I should think he'd be good for that boy.'

He pounced at once. 'Reformed? Reformed from what?'

Kate realised her mistake and covered quickly. 'Oh, you know, the usual things: hassle with parents, into bad company, dropping out of college.' She sent an innocent look at him over the rim of her cup and got a distinctly flinty stare in return. Damn, she thought, he

125

wasn't going to let it pass.

'So what does this reformed character do now?' he asked silkily, 'and what makes you so sure he might be good for my son.'

She shrugged as though the matter was of no great importance.

'Just that he's been through and come out the other side of all the teenage angst and young men's troubles and doesn't seem, like so many others, to have forgotten what it was all about. In fact, he's a most laudable character. He seems to have a steady girl friend and works, I imagine for very little salary, at a garden centre just outside Penzance.'

'The Old Friary?'

'I've no idea what it's called. Why, do you know it?'

'Heard of it via George, who minds everybody's business but his own; quite up-market and the owner is a bit of a philanthropist – takes on difficult youngsters for work experience and I believe he's also willing to employ the odd ex-con or two.'

Kate felt as though some invisible finger had given her a short stab in her solar plexus. She saw what looked like another awkward question dawning in his eyes and dug into her considerable reserves of calm diplomacy.

'As I said, Sam's a nice guy.'

'Umm.' Unusually, Andrew let it ride. He didn't want anything to spoil this evening, least of all a battle of wills with Kate over Toby and Sam. 'How about a brandy?' he asked to cover what threatened to be an awkward pause.

'Please.'

Kate settled, feet tucked beneath her. OK, she thought, back to more immediate happenings: we've had the wine and the food and the coffee and got as far as the brandy…now it's your turn to set the pace Andrew.

Andrew took the fireside chair opposite in order to study her face, the memory of her lovemaking still warm and fresh. He could sense her faint aura of unease and wondered if she was feeling as unsure as he about this evening.

What a pair, he thought with a wry inward smile; he knew why he was slightly wary of taking the previous night's events onto the next step. He wanted her all right; he had for quite a while, but he didn't understand her, was only just beginning to know her, and already a gut feeling was telling him that she was different, and could be more important to him than any other woman he had ever met.

Some might, and would, think him crazy to go from a long and unhappy marriage, straight into the arms of a woman like Kate. A bloody good job he reasoned, that life had taught him to keep his feelings under wraps.

After a few minutes of his silent scrutiny, Kate smiled and looked directly at him. 'You know,' she said, 'you are one of the noisiest thinkers I've ever come across.'

'And you,' he answered promptly, 'are one of the most devious. Don't you *ever* let your real thoughts show?'

'Not if I can help it.'

He leaned forward, rolling his glass between his hands. 'I want to get to know you Kate; know what makes you tick; whether you like me as much as I like you – and who or what in your past hurt you so much that you need, even after Friday night, to still fence a little. It would be easier,' he said with a sudden smile, 'to open an oyster with a wooden toothpick than to get behind that façade. For God's sake, we've been to bed together; we both know what tonight is all about, I know damned well you want me to make love to you again, maybe even as much as I want you to make love to me. So for pity's sake will you just let go and tell me what it's all about?'

She raised an eyebrow. 'How long have you got?'

'All night, if that's what it takes.'

'There's rash. Honestly, it's all old news and I don't think it would help for me to tell, or for you to know. I like you Andrew, I like you very much; I find you attractive and sexy and I more than like making love with you, but I am not a fixture here; when the time comes to leave I'd like to do so in one piece and without regret – on either side.'

His grey eyes never wavered. Kate felt her whole body was about to melt and slip away through the floorboards. He stood suddenly and taking the glass from her hand lifted her to her feet. Pulling her against him he brought his mouth firmly down onto hers; her legs did the jelly bit again, then somehow her own arms were around his neck and she was hanging on for dear life. *How does he do that and why do I let him,* she wondered; then his arms wrapped more tightly around her, the kiss deepened, her whole body lit up and she ceased to care either one way or the other.

*   *   *

A bell was ringing very loudly. Andrew, surfacing from deep sleep automatically rolled toward the source and immediately met a resistant body. Kate said, "*Off*" and shoved him back with a strong forearm. 'Down boy,' she murmured, 'it's only the phone.'

He looked with bleary eyes at the luminous dial of his watch and hissed incredulously. 'What fucking lunatic is calling you at four-thirty in the morning?'

'How should I know; I'm not a mind reader.' She groped for the bedside lamp and snapped it on. Picking up the handset she snuggled it against her ear. 'Hello...yes, that's me...who, what...yeah, he's here...' she rolled her eyes and passed it to him. 'The fucking lunatic is called Fliss, and it's you she's after.'

'Christ, I'll bloody murder George...' he sat up. Snatching the phone from her he hissed, 'if she's just snowed-up in the frigging Highlands and wants me to bring a shovel, she can whistle for it!'

'I heard that – and I'm not *in* the Highlands,' indignation seared down the line, 'the boys and I are in the Range Rover just south of Spaghetti Junction and bloody freezing...and don't blame George,' she was acerbic, 'I've been badgering him since nine last night and only just managed to wring your number out of him...what *have* you been doing all these hours?'

'Use your imagination – no, on second thoughts, don't. What the hell are you doing in Birmingham?'

'I've left Duncan. The bastard has been shagging that tart at the local stables and I'm getting out before I have to spend Christmas snowed up with the two-timing dickhead...it's hell in Glenmoray... terrific snowstorm, then a freeze up; you must have seen it on the news.'

'Thanks. I don't have time to ogle the box.'

'It's been a real bummer.' Her voice began to quaver, 'We had one hell of a row and he roared out to stay with the Camerons, who think the sun shines out of his arse and are doubtless spreading the word that I must have driven him to look for a bit of extra-marital nooky...' she gulped on a sob. 'There isn't anyone but you I can turn to.'

'Okay, okay, don't go all weepy on me, Fliss,' his voice gentled, 'bloody good thing I haven't sent your prezzies yet!'

She sniffed, 'Isn't that just like you; you wouldn't have sent them in time for Christmas anyway.'

He was suddenly practical. 'Don't try to drive on now; book into a Travelodge or hotel and finish the journey when you've all had a few hours sleep and a decent breakfast. That'll give us time to sort out rooms and beds; I warn you, it's all pretty chaotic here and there will be at least one workman around about the place right up until Christmas. Ring me again when you hit the Cornish border and we'll hang out the flags ready for your arrival.'

'You're a darling, Andy.'

'I know.'

'Sorry I woke you.'

'That's all right.'

There was another sniff. 'Is she nice?'

He cocked an eye at Kate who laid back naked and unself-conscious, hands behind her head and a gleam he was beginning to recognise in those smoky eyes. 'Perhaps *nice* isn't quite the word I'd choose.'

'Umm. I can't wait to see her...dark or fair? Short or tall – give with the details, or is she breathing in your ear?'

'Fliss,' he said patiently, 'I can't be arsed to chat now so shut up and do as you're told: shelter, eat, bed, sleep, eat again. Okay?'

'Bully.'

'That's me. Goodnight, Fliss.'

'Good morning, Andy.'

He put down the phone and drew Kate into his arms. 'Now where were we,' he asked, 'before we fell asleep and were so rudely inter-rupted?'

'Don't ask me, I think my brain is fried.'

'And I thought I made the earth move for you.'

'You did. That's how my brain got fried.'

'So let's fry it some more.'

'Thank God,' she said. 'For a moment I thought you were going to explain all about that phone call right now.'

He slid his body over hers, 'when a naked woman looks at me the way you do, talking about my sister is the very last thing on my mind.'

*　　　*　　　*

Some four hours later Andrew, Kate and Heathcliffe returned to Ross-cannan. By the time George heard them and struggled out of bed to appear blear-eyed in the kitchen, a pan of bacon and tomatoes was sizzling on the hob and a mountain of toast keeping warm at the back of the Aga.

Clearly put out at being caught by Kate in his bedroom slippers and dressing-gown, George grumbled and glared fiercely at Andrew, 'Where's the fire then? I've 'ad Fliss bawling her bleedin' eyes out an' bending me ear 'alf the night – in the end I 'ad to tell her where you was to shut her up. In a right state she was.'

Andrew explained and George listened, shaking his head. 'S'what come of marrying landed gentry and livin' in the middle of bleedin' nowhere. Where are we going to put her and them boys then? We ain't got the rest of the beds down yet.'

'Fliss can have mine for now and we'll put the boys on mattresses in my dressing room. I'll kip down in the study. We can fetch more beds down and sort out the sleeping arrangements properly tomorrow when they've settled in.'

George muttered, 'Going to be a lot of work, innit?'

Kate grinned. 'Cheer up, George; I've come to give you a hand. I can make up beds and help with the cooking and do whatever's needed to get things ready.'

He glared at her suspiciously, 'You staying as well then?'

'No, just helping out. If you can forget I'm a woman and just look upon me as an extra pair of hands, we should get along fine.'

His face contorted into what might have been a smile. 'That's all right, then. I could do with some extra 'elp.'

He sounded even wheezier than she'd heard him before. Kate was reminded that, despite Andrew's best efforts to make him slow down, this awkward, bloody-minded old man still worked incredibly hard. She asked diplomatically, 'How would you feel about taking Toby off this morning to get a Christmas tree? I know it's a bit early but Andrew says there are boxes of decorations up in the attic; we could get them down when the boys arrive and you could turn them loose with Toby to dress the tree and generally jazz the place up.'

He darted a doubtful glance in her direction and pulled at his lower lip. 'I'd 'ave to supervise, else he'll egg them two onto doing all kinds of stuff.'

'Great, if you'll do that I can get on with the other bits and pieces.' *Like hauling linen, making beds, clearing cupboards and cleaning dust off the floors and every other available surface...* She watched him shuffle off to dress and felt her back begin aching in anticipation; there was nothing, she thought privately, like a bout or two, or even three or four, of good steamy sex for setting a girl up for a hard day's slog.

George grunted. 'Very 'andsome of you miss. Now I'll just get back to me kitchen an' whip up somethin' warming fer when that lot arrives.'

Andrew placed his hands on Kate's shoulders. 'Good work, Batman,' he murmured as George departed. 'I do believe you've found a chink in George's armour.'

'Umm,' She turned and put her arms about his neck, 'you could be right, but I have a nagging suspicion that it will take a lot more soft-soaping before the armour comes off completely.'

'Steady darling,' he said, 'stripping one man at a time is enough.'

She smiled and gave him a deep lingering kiss. It was rather nice to be called darling by a man who might possibly even mean it.

14

If Andrew was calm and restrained, his sister in comparison was a whirling Dervish. Kate halted on her way down the stairs from her final battle with the vacuum cleaner just as a small elegant figure in a long red coat erupted through the front door. An enormously long scarf of many colours was wound about her throat and a matching velvet hat squashed down over her forehead. Shoulder bag, magazines, comics and a half-full plastic bottle of Cola cascaded to the floor as she flung her arms first around George and then around her brother.

'Thank God some things never change,' her voice was deeply dramatic and charged with emotion. 'George my sweet, as full of *joie de vivre* as ever I see!' she landed a smacking kiss on his balding head, 'and Andy darling, as handsome as ever.' She gulped, 'What a lucky girl I am to be spending the festive season with the pair of you.'

Reeling slightly from the onslaught George began picking up the oddments littering the hall floor while Andrew kissed his sister on both cheeks, saying dryly, 'Think nothing of it; we need someone to wash the pans up after Christmas dinner,' then as two small boys appeared, dragging a large hold-all between them, added with heavy sarcasm, 'although I guess that's a vain hope as I see that, as usual, you've organised your poor offspring into doing the dirty work. You don't change, do you?'

He bent to grapple the pair as, squealing with delight, they leaped into his arms. Hugging them briefly he set them loose. 'Well done men, but you can leave the rest of the luggage to Toby and me.'

'Speak of the devil...' Felicity Carmichael waved a greeting as Toby, followed closely by Heathcliffe, joined them. 'Oh, hi, Toby, I hope you're ready to do your stuff with these two...and where in the name of God did you find *that*?' She pointed at Heathcliffe, who had howled and collapsed on his back as the two little boys launched themselves upon him.

'Hi, Aunt Fliss; this is Heathcliffe; he sort of belongs to Kate.' Toby ruffled each boy's hair in turn, 'C'mon, Heck 'n Gus,' he said commandingly, 'stop dribbling on Heathcliffe; we've got things to do that only men can do – shift it into the kitchen for some grub and then we'll start work.'

George held up an imperious hand. 'You two get them boots off

132

first, else I'll make you scrub the floor.' He glared ferociously and both boys giggled and nudged each other. Kate watched in fascinated disbelief as the black-haired blue-eyed pair shucked off coats and boots, then clutching George's hands dragged him towards the kitchen chanting, 'Food, food, glorious food...' while he grumbled, 'Alright, alright, be'ave yerselves now or I'll larrup yer arses.'

Toby grinned at his aunt. 'A dollop of George's chocolate cake should shut them up for a bit before we start on the tree.'

'God, you're welcome to that.' Fliss shuddered, 'Andy, you must remember how pa always made me stand on his shoulders to stick that bloody fairy on the top. It's a wonder I didn't end up with a troop of acrobats. I could have done a wonderful topping off for a human pyramid.'

Mad or what, thought Kate, and what kind of woman calls her kids Heck and Gus...and did she have to be *quite* so well turned out, despite all the panic and tears of a few hours ago? Kate was in her work jeans and one of Andrew's old shirts; acutely conscious of her hair sticking to her head in damp wisps; her hands and clothes grubby and creased from ferreting in the attic cupboards for bedding. Andrew was in a similar state, but on him the tousled work-stained look translated into rugged and manly, whereas she looked and felt like a hag. Given all these negatives she could only wish herself a million miles away from the exquisite Fliss. Cursing under her breath she completed her journey down the stairs.

Andrew turned, as though an invisible cord drew him to her and in an instant, all irritation and consciousness of her workaday appearance fled. Taking her hand and lacing his fingers in hers, he drew her to his side. 'Kate, this is my sister Felicity, known as Fliss.' He was mock solemn. 'She's an absolute pain in the neck but all right when you get to know her. Those two small creatures who have just kidnapped George are her sons Hector and Angus. Fliss, say 'Thank you' nicely to Kate for working like a slave to get everything ready for the three of you.' *Please,* he begged silently, *let them hit it off because either or both of them are quite capable of creating merry hell if they don't!*

*　　　*　　　*

He need not have worried; in the few seconds it took to exchange greetings, Kate and Fliss had sized each other up, seemingly liked what they saw and appeared instantly at ease; mostly, he acknowledged with an inward smile, because Kate had gone smoothly and automatically into a warm, flawless professional welcome that was almost as good as the real thing. Chalk and cheese, he thought, contrasting his sister's instant wide, if rather watery, grin with the smile that started in Kate's eyes and spread slowly to that long mobile mouth. He let go the breath he hadn't realised he'd been holding. Was it the season, or the family reunion that appeared suddenly to have brought everything and everyone together in this warm easy camaraderie? Kate and his sister were chatting as though they had known each other for years, Toby had been engagingly cheerful and displayed real grown-up authority with his two small cousins; even George, who had not quite managed to disguise his pleasure at being kissed, should now be in a good mood for at least a week.

He caught Kate's eye and was conscious of a nanosecond of suspended time then, as she continued to hold his gaze, he knew with a sudden swoop of his heart that nothing happened by chance; that whether either of them had realised it, or even wanted it, destiny had made Kate Shaw a part of this place; that she belonged in Rosscannan as surely as if she had been born here...

*   *   *

Much later that evening, when the tree had been set up in the long gallery and decorated, supper eaten around the big kitchen table and two very tired small boys put to bed, Kate and Heathcliffe returned alone to Pendragon.

'Stay,' Andrew had murmured as he kissed her in the shadows of the porch. 'I want you in my bed tonight, even if it is only the couch in the study.'

'I can't; not tonight.' She held his face between her hands. 'Tonight I need space and time to think,' she kissed him swiftly, 'until tomorrow.'

*   *   *

Back at Pendragon she made a large mug of coffee, kicked off her shoes and flopped onto a chair before the empty hearth, re-living the day that had begun with that early morning phone call; remembering in minute and precise detail the moment she had come down the stairs; when Andrew had taken her hand, his smile telling her without words that, despite the general deshabillé of her appearance, he thought her beautiful...that particular shining moment when she knew, without the shadow of a doubt that she was in love.

'Sod it Heathcliffe,' she gazed into his soulful eyes as he sat with his head on her knee, 'I didn't *like* the man overmuch when we first met; even when I found him attractive enough and sexy enough to go to bed with I didn't want *this* to happen. Now it has, I don't know what I'm supposed to do about it. Sex is one thing, but love, ah well, that's something else again: love hurts.'

Despite all her determination to the contrary she had crossed the line between plain uncommitted sex and hopelessly committed and complicated love. If it turned out that the object of that love had neither the desire, nor the intention, to cross that line with her, the heartache would begin all over again. Raking restless fingers through her hair she groaned aloud. How had all this come about; why had fate set her again on a path that would leave her so vulnerable and open to being hurt?

She leaned back in the chair, seeing again in her mind's eye Andrew's gaze as it held hers across the hallway, and knew that she was lost.

* * *

Too restless to sleep, or even read, she wandered into the kitchen to make a sandwich she didn't want and knew she wouldn't eat, poured another coffee, turned on the TV to cruise through a few stations but found nothing to hold her interest. Eventually, driven by the need to do something, anything, to keep her mind and hands occupied she went into the study and taking the tapestry from its paper cover carried it into the kitchen, Heathcliffe following a pace behind her, treading on her heels at every second step as though he understood her restlessness and was determined to show there was at least one creature who could be relied upon not to leave her.

Muttering to herself, she half-filled a bowl with warm water and hand-wash detergent then spread the tapestry out onto a clean piece of sheeting. 'A pox on all junk dealers; have nothing to do with them Heathcliffe my boy.' She took a wire whisk from a drawer and attacked the greenish liquid in the bowl, whipping furiously until the surface was covered with a satisfactory two inches of foam. 'I may not know much about cleaning delicate old tapestries but I know enough not to bloody try doing it with "a dab of turps – *m'dear*"!'

Taking up the soft baby hairbrush she had bought from the chemists in Penzance for her task, she began to work the foam lightly and carefully over the tapestry, one small area at a time, dabbing each cleaned section dry with a soft cloth, working slowly and methodically to the measured tick of Megan's old clock. Tomorrow

135

she must go into Penzance and find some small gifts for those two little boys. She hoped they would be the last unexpected guests to arrive; any more bodies around the place would make her life even more impossibly complicated.

*   *   *

After a short, restless night she was up early and out for her run before it was properly light, returning to the house to shower, eat a piece of toast and drink a mug of coffee before she left for Penzance. With her she had Sam's gloves, wrapped in suitably manly brown paper, intending to call at the cottage *en route* and leave them in the porch. In place of the old gloves, worn thin and holed in several places that were his only protection against the weather, she had chosen a pair of padded Belstaffs. However she didn't want him to think they were a Christmas present – she doubted he had money to spend on seasonal gifts so had slipped a note in to say, 'Just a "Thank You" for all the wood you chopped and for looking after Heathcliffe.' Rattling and bumping along the narrow cliff road that was little more than a cart track, she crossed her fingers superstitiously and hoped he would be out; she didn't want to embarrass him by handing them over like some Lady Bountiful distributing gifts to the poor and needy.

Weary from lack of sleep and the deliberately punishing run she had taken, she turned the corner into Maury's Lane and almost drove up a tree when Toby, muffled to the eyebrows and with a Hooray-Henry tweed cap pulled low over his forehead, came peddling furiously towards her in the middle of the road. Slamming on the brakes she brought the car to a skidding halt; Toby jammed on his own brakes, veered across the road, wobbled wildly for a moment then fell into the ditch, the bicycle on top of him.

On the back seat of the Triumph Heathcliffe went wild.

Covered in spit, ears ringing from the full decibel range of a dog in the throes of hysteria, Kate pushed open the car door, yelled, 'SHUT UP, YOU NOISY SOD!' and slamming it on a shocked-silent Heathcliffe, stalked menacingly to where Toby was seated in the ditch, his bike in his lap and a look of bemused disbelief on his face.

'Toby, what in the name of God do you think you are doing on that thing – training for the Tour de France?' she demanded.

He blinked and she could see his mind come slowly into gear. 'It's bloody cold on a bike in this weather; much warmer if you pedal fast.'

'You'd be a damned site colder on a mortuary slab.' She lifted the

136

cycle from off him and, leaning it against the hedge, held out her hand. Helping him to his feet she said: 'The bike looks okay; what about you?'

'I'm fine – got so many clothes on I didn't feel a thing.'

She laughed as he brushed his Barbour down with his hands. 'Where were you heading in such a hurry anyway?'

'I came to see Sam but he must have gone to work early. Thought I might get into Maunsley and catch the bus to Penzance. Have a look-see where he works.'

'I have to leave a parcel for him but then I'm heading for Penzance myself, so why don't you put your bike round the back of the cottage and I'll give you a lift. I'll be coming back around midday and we could pick it up then, if that's all right with you.'

'Yeah, great – thanks.'

'I'd better let Heathcliffe out before he pees himself with excitement,' Kate turned back to the car where Heathcliffe's face was flattened against the side window. She grinned over her shoulder at Toby. 'Go on; I'll give you a ten second start!'

He yelled, 'Watch me go!' jumped on the bike and raced back to the cottage, beating the dog by a short head. *What it is to be young and resilient,* Kate mused as Heathcliffe reached him and they both fell in a tangle of legs. *The boy escapes death by a cat's whisker and bounces right back. All I've had is a restless night after a hard day's work, and I'm feeling totally and utterly knackered. If Andrew was to appear right now and whisk me off to make mad passionate love, the way I feel he'd probably have to do it all by himself, with no input from me whatsoever...*

*　　　*　　　*

She left Toby at the entrance to the Friary and went straight to the DIY Centre, where she selected delicate wrought iron brackets and a pair of slender poles with twisted basket stops for hanging Andrew's tapestry. That completed, she browsed the toy section in the town's largest department store, conveniently braving a Sunday opening in expectation of the Christmas last minute rush, and filled her basket with a monster pack of Jumbo felt-tips, several packets of coloured sugar-paper, supposedly wash-off Kid's Stuff glue, tubes of glitter and enough paper scraps of cars, planes and automobiles to cover South West Cornwall. Although the amusement of small boys was not her *forte,* she guessed anything guaranteed to create the maximum of mess would be gratefully received, by the boys if not by George whose kitchen table would no doubt become the first casualty of felt-tip poisoning and a testing ground for the wash-off glue. She completed her purchases for Gus and Heck with two pots of something green labelled "Slime" and a half-dozen revolting and highly-coloured soft plastic bugs which, when thrown at windows and doors, descended slowly and sinuously by means of a kind of boneless somersault.

Buying for women was a lot easier than it was for men, she thought, as she added hand-made chocolates and a dramatic tie-dye raw silk scarf for Fliss to her basket; you knew where you were with women, with men you had mostly to play safe and stick with inoffensive and un-embarrassing things like socks and handkerchiefs, or if you knew them *very* well, Calvin Klein boxer knicks in macho black with advertising slogan all around the waistband.

She had coffee at the same café she had gone to on her first visit to the town. Seated at a small table by the window she flicked idly through the Sunday Mirror thoughtfully provided by the management. Since coming to Cornwall she hadn't bothered with a daily paper, catching all the news she wanted on TV or radio.

She noted now that Posh and Becks were back from Spain and having another party; the Queen had left Buck House for Sandringham; serious crime in the Capital was down; muggings and assaults were up, so presumably not considered serious, except to the mugged and assaulted; binge drinking and Yob culture was gaining the upper hand; thirty-three percent of Inner City school kids carried knives and a record number of teachers were on Prozac. So, she thought, putting the paper aside, things were going along pretty much as usual and London was surviving very nicely without her.

All the same…she sipped thoughtfully at her coffee: she still had to make a final visit to the Ealing house to remove the rest of her belongings before Paul's return in January if she was to avoid another encounter with the lovebirds. She groaned quietly to herself; she had no time to find and rent a room in which to store a dozen or more boxes, so would *have* to make the tedious journey into Essex and ask her parents to store those things she needed to keep…

A persistent sound, irritating as the buzzing of a fly, but sharper, brought her from her reverie. She looked up to find Sam grinning and scraping his fingernails down the window while beside him Toby contorted his face into a very good impression of Munch's "Scream".

Kate sighed and beckoned them in and they came, shuffling and rubbing their hands in exaggerated parody of a pair of Inuit gaining the shelter of their igloo after a strenuous morning's seal-bashing.

'Sam said women always stop for coffee,' Toby slid into a seat opposite Kate and Sam plumped down beside him. 'Do you *know* how many cafés there are in Penzance? We've been to about a dozen before this one.'

'Full marks for persistence then.' Kate raised an inquiring eyebrow. 'Do I sniff just the tiniest hint of collusion in the two of you seeking me out?'

'Yeah,' Sam grinned, stretching his long legs beneath the table. 'Toby's volunteered to spend the day helping out at the Friary and Bob Prothero, the owner, is chuffed because we're snowed under with orders. He's given us an hour's breather because we'll be working late.'

Kate looked Toby over with a thoughtful eye. 'I take it you *have* checked home that it's okay with everyone?'

Toby looked shifty, he mumbled, 'I thought you might tell dad – he doesn't really need me for anything right now. Sam'll give me a lift back on his motorbike when we finish for the day.'

Kate sighed. 'I'll stand you both coffee and we'll talk this through. I've no desire to have my ankles savaged by your father for aiding and abetting you – and just who do you think is going to keep those two kids amused until bedtime if you skive off?'

'George,' Toby answered promptly, 'he's brilliant with them. Anyway,' he was wheedling, 'I'll be there in time to help get them to bed and that's the really knackering bit.'

Amused, Kate asked, 'Where does your Aunt Fliss come into all this? Doesn't she get to do the bedtime shift?'

He gave his engaging grin. 'She loves them to bits, but seeing that Duncan's around most of the time he does a lot of the grot stuff. *She* likes to get them out of doors: riding or dragging them up mountains or yomping over the glens!'

Kate adjusted her mental picture of the exquisite Felicity to take in this new image, thinking privately that the Parradines were a pretty rum bunch altogether: expatriate wine-growing father; high-profile soldier and a female Sherpa who was happy to lug her kids up mountains but roped in the old man for the bed and bath time battles. A bit precipitate of her, Kate thought, to have left home. You didn't get many such useful spouses to the pound...she signalled to the waitress and when she came ordered two more coffees and double portions of buttered toast and jam. Toby licked his lips appreciatively. 'Stonking grub and just in time. I'm starving.'

She murmured, 'Why doesn't that surprise me,' and caught Sam's collusive wink. *Now you*, she thought with some asperity, *should know better than to encourage this adolescent delinquent without so much as a "do you mind" to his father.* She gave a repressive frown.

'I don't think Toby should be cycling back from your place after dark; he's lethal enough in daylight. However, *if* I smooth things over with Andrew and *if* he agrees, provided you take him back to Rosscannan...' she allowed herself a faint malicious smile at Sam's change of expression from conspiratorial to alarmed, 'I'll pick up his bike on my way home; that's if I can persuade Heathcliffe to pack his great backside onto the passenger seat.'

That should take the silly grin off Sam's face and teach him not to pull a fast one...

'Brilliant,' Toby said again, apparently unaware of any under-currents, 'I owe you one, Kate.'

'Hmm,' added Sam, not quite under his breath, 'so do I!'

*　　　*　　　*

Approaching the gates of Rosscannan, Kate began to feel uneasy about her part in Toby's visit to the Friary, realising rather too late in the day that he might just have landed her in a very tricky situation, *vis-à-vis* his father. Going on his previous track record, Andrew wasn't exactly a soft touch where his son was concerned and he hadn't, after all, been very enamoured of Sam, even sight unseen. What he might make of that young man in the flesh, with his general air of being a left-over hippie and his previous acquaintance with the law, she had no idea. But she could make a very good guess.

Oh, well...pushing Heathcliffe away from one shoulder and a bike handle from the other, she hopped from the car to key in the code; better get it over as quickly as possible then she could return to Pendragon and wrap the rest of her presents. She felt a warm, satisfied glow when she thought about the tapestry; it really was looking rather fine...

Heaving the bike from her back seat she leaned it against the low stone wall and ran up the steps to pull on the bell, Heathcliffe bouncing at her heels. 'Hi, George,' she greeted him at the door, 'is Andrew around?'

'In the drawing room with 'er 'ighness; they've just had tea. I'll bring another cup for you.'

Gosh, thought Kate, he *is* mellowing.

Pleased that Fliss would be present to act as a buffer if the going got rough; Kate pulled all her mental faculties together and opened the door to the drawing room.

140

*　　　*　　　*

'Let me get this straight,' Andrew seemed to have grown in size while Kate was speaking. 'Do I understand that my son has taken off – without first asking permission, or saying where he was going – to see your supposedly reformed character Sam,' his voice rose, 'and that you not only helped him on his way but also agreed on my behalf that he can spend the day with him.'

Fliss jumped up from her seat by the fire and put her hands over her ears. 'If you are going to blow then I'm out of it…' she rolled her eyes at Kate. 'If you need any bandages they're in the kitchen – last wall cupboard on the left!'

'Traitor!' Kate flung after her before turning back ready to do battle, confident that her wits and repartee had been finely honed by Paul, an opponent far more temperamentally bloody-minded than any Andrew Parradine.

'Taking your objections one at a time;' she answered with icy restraint, 'if he took off without consulting you, I can't say I blame him; you are not the most amenable bloke under the sun where Toby is concerned, are you? As for Sam, although he *is* a reformed character, he isn't mine, although I'm happy to call him a friend.'

'Now that does comfort me!'

She ignored him and continued relentlessly, 'I saw no harm in my giving Toby a lift to Sam's workplace – and in my book, anything that makes a member of this present-day lazy, self-absorbed generation actually volunteer to do a day's hard graft has to be a bonus.'

'Ah, I do apologise,' he returned with silky menace, 'I didn't realise you had a degree in child psychology.'

'As you have, I suppose?'

He showed his teeth, like a dog about to take his first bite. 'I don't need one. Toby is my son.'

'Oh I *see*,' Kate's voice positively dripped honeyed sarcasm, 'he's your *son* so that's how you know what he thinks and feels and needs? I must have heard you wrong the other week when you were sounding off: I thought he was the chap you told me you didn't understand; the one you'd scarcely laid eyes on for the past couple of years; the one you were only called on to sort out when he'd been a naughty boy.'

'None of that is relevant to the present situation.'

'Well, you would say that, wouldn't you? What has or hasn't happened in the past between the two of you has nothing to do with the present problem. Is that it?'

'If I say it is, yes, and as I hold you entirely responsible for his

141

latest escapade you can take your half-baked act as a social worker a stage further and bloody well fetch him back. Like as of *now*.'

By God, thought Kate in grudging admiration, he was quite something when he was boiling under all that calm. Knowing quite well that she was adding to his fury she snapped. 'I shall do nothing of the sort; you want him back, you fetch him yourself. Turning up at that place with steam coming out of your ears to haul him home should confirm you are the overbearing, intolerant *professional* ball-breaker he already thinks you are.'

He took a step towards her. Through gritted teeth and without raising his voice, he let rip a string of profanity that made even Kate blink. Suddenly she was all too well aware that Andrew Parradine was not the kind of apoplectic raging prima donna she was used to, one who yelled and threw things and at whom she could yell and throw things back, but the kind of man who stood toe to toe and eyeball to eyeball and slugged it out with relentless controlled determination. If she didn't want to be flattened by him she would need to hold fast and fight dirty. She took a deep breath.

'Don't you swear at *me* like that; I thought an officer and gentleman is supposed to keep cool at all times and not indulge in verbal abuse of a lady.'

He took another step forward. 'Then you thought wrong. I haven't even started yet.'

Kate held her ground. 'Don't you think you should get back on the subject of Toby, rather than waste time threatening me?'

'I'm not threatening you; I'm telling you. You had no right to collude with him as you did.' His eyes, dark with anger bored into hers. 'I don't *mind* that he wants to spend time at the Friary; he should however, be straight with me and not hide behind your skirts. When he returns this afternoon I shall deal with him in my own way and without interference from you, George, Fliss or anyone else. My son may not love me, he may not trust or respect me, but by God, in future he's going to be honest with me, or I'll take him to pieces, one limb at a time!'

Kate repressed the impulse to scream with frustration. How could any apparently sane and reasonable a man be so sure he was always right – and let you know he was in such an uncompromising manner? God help Toby when he does come home, she thought, and she prayed Andrew wouldn't go hurtling down into Penzance to create hell at Sam's place of work. That would almost certainly screw up any chance of a reasonable father/son relationship for life…

They stood glaring at each other, the air between them positively quivering with tension; Andrew, impassive and unmovable as a rock but boiling with temper beneath; Kate, seething with her own brand of fury and determined not to give an inch. Eventually, when she had her voice and temper under control she broke the silence.

'I rather think I'll leave now because, believe me, I'm more than capable of taking *you* to pieces if you take this one step further.' She turned and walked towards the door, snapping her fingers at Heathcliffe, who at the first signs of battle had hidden behind the couch. Reaching the door, she paused for a moment and without turning her head added, 'Have a nice time playing Happy Families at Christmas, won't you,' and walked out of the room, her back ramrod straight and eyes flinty as steel filings.

Stony-faced, Andrew watched her go, heard her call a goodbye to George and Fliss in the kitchen; listened to the slam of first the front, and then the car door, and the fading rev of her engine as she took off down the drive. Very slowly, he banged his head three times against the wall. 'Bugger, bugger, and bugger again!

'Yeah,' George stood in the doorway, his eyes glittering, a tea cup and saucer in one hand, a plate of biscuits in the other. 'That told 'er alright, didn't it – *now* what you going to do, you daft 'a'porth?'

'Do?' Andrew turned with a snarl, 'I'll tell you what I'm going to *do*. Nobody walks out on me like that; I'm going after the bloody woman.'

*   *   *

Kate swept out through the gates, but instead of taking the road to Penmaric, turned in the opposite direction towards Porthcledra Cove, where a few small boats bobbed at their moorings. Stopping the car at the head of the slipway she let Heathcliffe out. Keeping one eye on the incoming tide she walked down the concrete slope and began pacing to and fro along the short pebbled beach, quite unaware that Andrew was now hurtling the Land Rover in the opposite direction towards Pendragon.

She raged, letting her feelings have full reign; he really was an impossible bastard. Even at the height of one of their many noisy rows she had never let Paul get to her that way. She gave a short mirthless laugh; 'I was actually falling for that bloody-minded monster,' she informed the unheeding Heathcliffe, 'can you believe it? A couple of nights of roaring good sex and I really thought I was in love…'

You still are, said a voice deep inside her head, 'I am not,' she yelled aloud, and cursed the wind for the tears that stung her eyes.

Finally, exhausted by anger, she sat on a rock and tried to rationalise the events of the morning, eventually having to admit, however unwillingly, that Andrew might have a point; several points in fact; that while everyone concerned was in his own way culpable, some were more so than others. In a nutshell, Toby should have said where he was going and done his own dirty work; she should not have agreed so quickly to intercede on his behalf, and Sam should have know better than to collude with a fifteen year-old to effectively pull off a *fait accompli* against his father.

In fact, the only one who was even remotely in the right was the man she had just walked out on, his major weakness that of being unable to turn the occasional blind eye to the doings of his particular teenage rebel.

*   *   *

She stayed, sitting on the same rock, growing slowly colder and more wretched, the tide threatening at any minute to wash around her feet. Andrew, drawing a blank at Pendragon and guessing how she had given him the slip, returned and found her there. For a while he watched her, his heart stirred by that lone figure hunched on the rock, the watchful dog at her side; knew, even without the cooling of his temper on the drive to and from Pendragon, that he couldn't have maintained his anger once he saw her again.

Slipping out of the Land Rover he walked slowly down to the beach, watched all the way by Heathcliffe, who didn't move from Kate's side but gave a low threatening growl at his approach. Andrew smiled, put a finger to his lips and the dog quietened, moving his tail fractionally in greeting.

Kate heard the approaching footsteps crunch over the shingle but kept her head turned away, her muscles tensing in anticipation of a continuation of their row, but he stopped a few steps away to ask in a reasonable tone, 'Are you having a private snit, or can anyone join in?'

She shrugged. 'Feel free; it's Groundhog Day so far as my ability to reason is concerned. I keep trying to put things in their proper perspective, but find I've thought myself back to the beginning again.'

'God Almighty,' he sounded awed, 'if, as I suspect, that gobbledygook is PR speak, you should think seriously about going into therapy.'

'Been there; done it.'

She didn't turn her head, even when he put his hands on her

shoulders and began to massage the base of her neck with his thumbs, 'When? Why?' he asked and felt her shoulder muscles tense and tighten beneath his hands.

'Too long ago to bother about,' she was curt and dismissive.

'Not if the thought of it sends your muscles into spasm like this, it isn't. For God's sake relax, will you.'

'I don't do relax today.'

'I'd noticed.' He moved and, squatting down, took her cold hands to chaff them between his. 'I could murder one of George's hot toddies; how about you?'

She almost smiled, 'Make a change from wanting to murder George, I suppose.'

'Come on back to the house then.'

'Not a good idea. George will be gunning for me, your sister will be embarrassed, and right now I'm too totally pissed off with you to want your company.'

'Why? Is it because I swore at you? If so I apologise.'

'No. I've heard worse: I just can't do with a man who gets in a strop because everyone doesn't dance to his tune. Besides, you threatened to tear your son's ears off.'

'I don't think I put it that graphically; besides, I wouldn't really. He has rather nice ears.'

'That's beside the point.'

As he continued to rub her hands in silence, she began to feel the faint, treacherous stirrings of…what…love, lust; exasperated affection? Whatever it was, she'd a nasty feeling he was going to win this one. Worse, she really didn't care…

'Kate…'

She feigned surprise. 'Are you still here?'

His mouth twitched at the corners – he said mildly. 'For someone who has charm in spades, you can be just about the most awkward, aggravating, cussed bloody woman I've ever come across, and do you know…' he lifted her fingers to his lips, 'I think I am in it for more than the sex, sweetie.'

She answered shortly. 'You hardly know me.'

'Anthony hardly knew Cleopatra, but that didn't stop him and it won't stop me. Once something like this starts it's like a roller-coaster; very difficult to get off without doing an awful lot of damage.'

'I know. I've been thrown off before, and I warn you, I'm not getting on again.'

'We'll see.' He stood and pulled her to her feet. 'Better move before we get our feet wet.' He took her hand. 'Lead the way, Heathcliffe, we're going back to Rosscannan.'

Kate took a deep steadying breath. '*We* are not. *I* am going home.'

'That's what I said. Come on, we can fetch your car later.'

Sod it, she thought. Let him steamroller away. Another hour or so wouldn't make much difference. Muttering beneath her breath, she let him pull her up the slipway to where the Land Rover waited on the headland.

*   *   *

George was hovering at the open door as they climbed the steps then crossed the hall, Andrew towing Kate in his wake followed closely by Heathcliffe. George gave a knowing smirk.

'Want me to fix a n'ot toddy, do yer?'

'Make it two,' Andrew answered him shortly, 'Kate needs to rest for a while and thaw out, so try and keep the kids away from the study, will you.'

Kate ground her teeth as he pushed open the study door and drew her inside. 'I do not need to rest. I need to go home.'

'We've already been through that.' He eased her coat from her shoulders, walked her backward to the long couch until her legs hit the edge and she overbalanced and sat down hard. Ignoring her hiss of fury, he tugged off her boots and, pulling a rug from the back of the couch, ordered, 'Put your feet up. I don't know how long you were sitting on that blasted rock but I imagine even your bones are freezing.' When she didn't move, he shoved her legs up on the couch, tucked the rug around her then stood up. Wagging an admonitory finger at Heathcliffe he warned, 'I'm going to collect the drinks. If she moves, bite her!'

He went out, shutting the door behind him. Kate closed her eyes against the leaping flames from the fire. She was so cold she doubted blood would ever flow normally in her veins again. It couldn't possibly hurt to lie here and warm up before driving home, but this old, battered but very comfortable couch was where Andrew had slept while Fliss was occupying his own bed, and she couldn't help imagining him lying beside her, his hair all rumpled and his face unshaven...

But she was not going down that path again, or indeed any path with Andrew Parradine, she was resolute about that. She couldn't let him shake the nice safe world she was only just beginning to burrow into. Once back at Pendragon she would pull up the drawbridge and stay there, safe and immune from the illusion of love until Megan came home.

But in spite of this eminently sensible and sane decision she felt an actual physical ache around her heart at the mere thought that Rosscannan would inevitably be lost to her; that she would no longer be a part of its regeneration; would never see it finished; never again feel Andrew's arms around her. Her head began to ache with the effort to detach herself from the all too seductive lure of Rosscannan and the man who had made her feel like a whole woman again.

But what else could she do? He wasn't the first man she'd loved and believed might love her. But time had always proved otherwise: with Paul it had taken years for the scales to fall from her eyes and know she'd got it wrong – again. "I love you" was easy to say, much harder to maintain as a lodestar for living.

She gave a deep, audible sigh and hunched under the rug. No, better salvage what was left of her pride and go it alone.

*   *   *

When she surfaced again she felt rested and refreshed, as though during sleep some unseen hand had passed soothing fingers over her aching head, smoothing away the confusion of thoughts and feelings that filled it. 'Lovely,' she murmured in drowsy content. Stretching luxuriously she opened her eyes to find Andrew seated beside her, Fliss was perched at the end of the couch and George busy pouring tea into satisfyingly large mugs.

'Hi, there,' Fliss fluttered her fingers. 'We thought you were going to sleep for *ever*, but Andy wouldn't let me wake you. Missed your toddy, though; I drank that.' She grinned. 'Hey, how come you can wake up looking so great? If I nap during the day I'm a hag for hours.'

Kate sat up, hugging her knees. 'Me too, and I usually feel like hell with it. I must have been having a good dream.'

She gave a sleepy smile that had Andrew's senses thrumming, but before he could speak, the throttled-down putter of an approaching motor bike engine made everyone stop what they were saying and doing to look at each other. Andrew was the first to move. Rising to his feet he made swiftly for the door with George close on his heels.

'Sounds like the prodigal's return,' commented Fliss.

With a reprise of Andrew's furious words running through her head Kate made to follow, but Fliss shook her head. 'Better not. Let Andy sort it.'

'That's what I'm afraid of.' Reluctantly Kate subsided back onto the couch, noticing for first time that the shutters were closed. 'What time is it?'

Fliss looked at her watch, 'Just after six- thirty.'

'Hell, I'd no idea I'd been asleep that long.' Kate was startled. 'Where are the boys?'

'Across the passageway in the snug; they're fighting over Toby's Playstation. Keeps them occupied at the odd times when it's a case of "not in front of the children".' Fliss returned their cups to the tray then came back to sit beside Kate. Curling her legs under her and settling against the cushions, she asked, 'Are you as potty about Andrew as he is about you?'

Kate was too old a hand to be caught completely off guard, but even she blinked slightly at the blunt question. The Parradines were nothing if not direct, she thought. She considered the matter carefully. 'Not sure about that,' she said at last, 'and I can't vouch for him.'

'I can, and I tell you he's got it badly.'

'It wouldn't work.' Kate said flatly, 'I've a lousy track record where love is concerned.'

'Bollocks; chances are you've just not tried it with the right man.'

'Look, we couldn't be more opposite and we piss each other off on a regular basis, which hardly seems the best foundation for a meaningful relationship.'

'George reckons you were made for each other, seeing the pair of you are opinionated, stubborn, edgy, know you're always right, and are ripe for a slanging match the minute you think the other might win a point.'

Kate narrowed her eyes. 'I always knew that ratchet-mouthed troll loved me.'

Fliss laughed out loud. 'He likes you well enough; you wouldn't have lasted otherwise. He'd have found some way to freeze you out.'

Kate thought back to her first few encounters with George. 'He tried,' she said feelingly, 'oh, he tried.'

'Yeah, but I guess not very hard. Anyway, what are you going to do about Andy?'

Kate was silent, staring into the fire with blank unfocussed eyes. What *was* she going to do about Andrew? She thought about his mouth and the depth and sweetness of his kisses, the tenderness in his eyes when they made love, the gentle hands; the hard-muscled body that could be both artfully seductive and impossibly demanding in turn, taking her over the mountain tops and beyond...

'Nothing at the moment,' she sighed. 'I think I need a little

148

simmering down time. We both do. I've only just made it clear of one man I loved, and thought loved me. I really don't want to walk hand in hand into the sunset with another. Andrew doesn't know me, and I don't know him; there may be as much unfinished business in his head as in mine – things which, like me, he may find it almost impossible to talk about.' She hesitated then went on rapidly, 'I've no real idea how he feels about the break-up of his marriage for instance, or how much that matters to him. I know little or nothing about his life; what he's done, where he's been, whether he was a good or bad husband. I don't even know why I find him so attractive. For all I know he might be another Bluebeard with a cupboard full of murdered wives.'

His sister gave a loud hoot of laughter. 'Only one wife, with whom he's been mega hacked-off for years, and from time to time would no doubt quite like to have murdered. It was a lousy marriage anyway and, knowing him, I'd say the last thing he needs is simmering down time. What he *needs* is you, and preferably right now. Bloody hell, Kate, it's screamingly obvious. He can't keep his eyes off you – or his hands either.'

Kate said crossly, 'It seems to me your whole family runs on high octane optimism; what happens if it all fizzles out? Andrew would have you and George to help pick up the pieces. I've just had to pick up an awful lot of them on my own. Frankly I'm not in the market for doing it again.'

'Nothing ventured, nothing gained,' Fliss waved a dismissive hand. 'Go for it, I say, because he's not playing games. He wouldn't admit it in a million years but he's the marrying kind.' She was suddenly pensive, sad. 'Some men never learn.'

'What makes you think I'd want to get married?' Kate was heavily sarcastic, 'I've managed to avoid it so far.'

'Balls,' said Felicity vulgarly, 'when a girl hits forty she needs to know she'll wake up with the same bloke every morning, even if he isn't always Prince Charming. You love him: you can deal with having him get on your tits from time to time. I'm sure you'll get on his!'

Kate had the feeling she was being backed into a corner. 'Thanks, but I think I'll spare him the hassle...and talking of hassle...' she stood up, brushing down her slacks, 'I'm going to sneak off back home before George starts looking for a dustpan and brush to sweep up what your dear brother has left of Sam and Toby.'

Fliss cocked her head. 'I wonder where they've all gone; I can't hear a thing. If Andy's losing his rag, he's doing it very quietly. Me,

149

when I get in a strop with Duncan I like a good old slanging match, with all the trimmings…Oh, damn…' she wailed, reaching for her handkerchief, 'There I go again: bloody men!'

Kate grimaced and gave a crooked little smile.

'Join the sisterhood,' she said. 'Would you like to tell me about it?'

*   *   *

But Andrew wasn't losing his rag, quietly or otherwise. One look at Toby's glowing if slightly apprehensive face, and Sam's closed expression as they came up the steps, side by side, had him reining in his annoyance and irritation. Where once he would have gone straight for the jugular, recent events and Kate's commonsense attitude towards his son had him take a firm grip on his temper.

'Sorry we're late-ish.' Sam spoke first, 'Last minute rush on Christmas trees.'

'Yeah, it all got a bit busy,' Toby interjected quickly,

'The study and the snug are occupied,' Andrew kept his voice neutral. Turning on his heel he walked across the hall. 'Better come into the drawing room.'

They made to follow, but George stepped forward, barring their way. 'I'll 'ave yer boots and them 'elmets first,' he said, and watched grimly as they each sheepishly put down the helmets and heeled off their boots before padding silently in Andrew's wake. George gathered the offending items and, holding them fastidiously at arm's length, marched slowly to deposit them in the scullery.

Arrived in the drawing room where Andrew stood waiting, his back to the fire, Toby said quickly, 'It wasn't Sam's fault. He didn't know I was going to turn up.'

'I can believe that. You didn't even bother to inform *me* where you were going.' Andrew looked past Toby to his companion, 'and you didn't exactly dissuade him from staying when he did appear, did you?'

'He wanted to give a hand and we were grateful,' Sam answered him mildly.

'And I want to go back again,' Toby did his best to copy Sam's relaxed tone and manner. 'They're always short of helpers and I like it.'

'Why, what's the attraction?'

Toby frowned in thought. 'The money's crap – only two quid an hour for me 'cause I'm only helping out. I dunno; it's hard to explain.'

'Try,' Andrew encouraged.

Toby's frown deepened. 'Well, apart from the shop, it's all out of doors; no one hanging over your shoulder – no stress, know what I mean?' He struggled with the novelty of actually giving voice to his feelings. It was naff and the blokes he knew didn't do that sort of thing.

Andrew looked at Sam, who met his eyes steadily with his sardonic gaze. 'It seems to me,' he said carefully, 'that if Toby is going to make a habit of this, it might be a good idea if George or I were to provide the transport, then he wouldn't knock himself out cycling around the countryside and *you* wouldn't feel obliged to bring him home.'

Toby blushed. 'I only biked it as far as Sam's cottage. Kate took me the rest of the way and –'

'Brought your bike back and played defence lawyer with me,' finished Andrew. 'I know; we had quite a ruck about that.'

Toby mumbled, 'Sorry,' and blushed some more.

'The great thing about Kate,' put in Sam unexpectedly, 'is that she doesn't arse around; she tells it as it is.'

'So do I,' answered Andrew, 'that's why we had the ruck!'

*   *   *

After Andrew had agreed for Toby to work a part of each day at the garden centre, Sam left. Politely refusing a drink, alcoholic or otherwise, he collected his boots and the helmets from George and disappeared back into the night. When Toby returned to the drawing room from seeing him off, he found his father stretched out in an armchair, his feet resting on the leather-top of the low fire surround; looking so patently relaxed and non-combative that the boy felt safe enough to take up a similar position on the other side of the hearth.

For the space of several minutes there was silence; eventually Toby cleared his throat. 'I've been thinking. When school starts again, I'll go back like you want – if you'll buy me going to agricultural college later.'

'Hey, let's take this one step at a time,' Andrew interrupted, alarmed. 'I'll barter A-levels at your current prison for college here; I'll even buy a gap year in Timbuktu if that's what you really want, but I should hate to think you might decide to be a son of the soil on the strength of a few hours' work flogging Christmas trees, before you've at least tried university.'

Toby's mouth took on a stubborn line. 'Oh, get real, dad; I'll never make it to uni; this is the first thing I ever enjoyed doing.'

Andrew was cynical, 'The wages you'd earn as a gardener wouldn't exactly let you lead the life to which you have become all too well accustomed.'

'I'm not going to be a flaming gardener,' Toby exploded, 'I want to go on a proper college course, learn all about plants an' trees an' stuff; get into garden design like Sam.' He held his breath. *If he laughs at me, if he even bloody grins, I'll never tell him anything ever again...*

Andrew knew stubborn when he met it. *Bloody marvellous...* he closed his eyes briefly. *He's going to be a fully-fledged, diploma-gaining Capability Brown. Now how does an idle little tyke like him think he'll manage that?*

Opening his eyes he met his son's tense and challenging stare. 'One of your better ideas,' he said, and hoped the effort not to scream didn't show.

Toby's smile came slowly; came from within, lighting first his eyes then curving his mouth into a brilliant grin of pure delight. 'Great,' he said, 'so can I do it?'

'I should think it possible, if you buckle down and get some good grades in your exams: you certainly won't get into any decent college without them. Is there anything else you want to surprise me with before we show ourselves at the dining table?'

'Yeah,' Toby looked him straight in the eyes. 'Sorry I made it crappy for Kate and you, pissing off like that.'

'Keep going,' said Andrew dryly, 'and you might just get a motorbike for your next birthday. At least that would mean the weekly allowance I'm about to make you won't all go in payment for George's and my services as taxi drivers.'

*   *   *

Andrew waited until Toby had sloped off to find Gus and Heck before he returned to the study, frowning when he saw the only occupant of the room was Fliss who was stretched full length on the couch, an open book in her hand. He asked 'Where is she?' His sister lowered her book and raised a delicately arched eyebrow.

'She left ten minutes ago; said she needed some simmering down time.'

Andrew dropped into a chair by the fire. 'Sometimes I could cheerfully wring that woman's neck. She is the most irritating, bloody-minded female I've ever come across. We need to *talk*…clear the air, stop faffing around.'

Fliss gave an audible sigh. 'She seems a pretty level-headed woman to me, and if simmering down is what she needs, my suggestion is you give her time to do it.'

'I don't have time to arse around and I'm too old to play games… each time I think I'm getting somewhere she backs off. For Christ's sake, she's still talking about returning to London; I'm not in the market for being stop-gap until she can get back home again to the love of her life.'

'What makes men so bloody dumb?' Exasperated, Fliss cast aside her book and sat up. 'Any woman with half an eye can see she's a damned sight more than interested, but at the moment you're both going nowhere. She doesn't know you any more than you know her, because neither of you give out with what you're really thinking and feeling. Considering you've been working side by side for the past few weeks and already made it to bed together, you still seem to know bugger-all about each other.'

He took up a poker and stirred the logs, sending a shower of sparks up the chimney. 'When you get to my age, you've learned not to show every bloody thing you feel.'

'When you get to your age, Andy, you should be past being uptight about letting the woman you love know everything there is to know about you. You start the ball rolling and she'll follow.'

'That some kind of Celtic wisdom you've picked up from north of the border?'

'No, just logic – you know, that stuff you men don't think we have.'

'First my son surprises me; now my kid sister...and another thing,' he stirred the logs again, 'George tells me he found young Hector hiding in the boot room in tears this afternoon because his dad wasn't going to be here for Christmas. You'd better not be mucking those kids' lives up for nothing.'

Fliss scowled. 'Don't blame me, blame Duncan, he started this... you don't know the half of it.'

'No. I bloody don't,' he was suddenly furious. 'You just swan in here, giving the minimum of explanations and expect everyone to be on your side. It's high time you came clean about what happened to make you decide to put the length of the country between you and Duncan.'

Her lower lip began to push out and for a moment he thought she was going into a sulk, then she suddenly gathered herself together and gave him a long, haughty look. 'OK, you work it out for yourself, smartarse...for the past four or five weeks he's taken to sneaking off at all kinds of odd times. Last week I followed him and he ended up at old Rothsay's stud the other side of the glen – and guess what? – that tart Jeannie Dalgliesh bounces up to the car and greets him like they were bosom buddies. Two seconds later they disappear into the stables, both of them laughing like drains.' She banged her fist on the table. 'They were in there together for *half an hour* and the bastard came out grinning all over his face. I took off before he saw me, but I let him have it right between the eyes soon as he stepped back through our doorway.'

Andrew raised an eyebrow. 'So?'

'So he went all mulish and said it was just business and what was I doing spying on him anyway? After that we just slugged it out for a couple of hours until I told him he was a lying, conniving sod, and to piss off out of my life. He called me a brainless ungrateful cow and wouldn't stay now if I went down on my knees and begged. Then he slammed out of the house.' Tears began to course down her face and she fumbled for her handkerchief. 'When he didn't come back and I found he was staying with the Camerons, I couldn't face Christmas alone with the boys; they would have been so bewildered. I thought coming here would make it easier for them...just like a big adventure.'

'Okay, Okay.' With a sigh Andrew gave in; he moved to put an arm about her shoulders. 'Let's just let it ride for a day or two...give yourself a breathing space and we'll all make sure Gus and Heck have a decent Christmas.'

Tomorrow, he thought, he would ring his brother-in-law. One way or another, even if just for the sake of those two little boys, something had to be salvaged from all this mess.

But as it turned out, Duncan beat him to it.

15

The phone was ringing as Kate arrived in the kitchen with her arms full of logs; impeded as she was by the logs and Heathcliffe circling her legs she only just made it before the ringing stopped. Snatching up the handset she announced breathlessly, 'Hello, Kate here.'

'Well I didn't expect the Archbishop of Canterbury!' Megan chuckled. 'I thought it time to check you hadn't been bored to death yet.'

'No chance of that. I'm kept too busy.' Kate sat down reaching for an apple from the dish on the kitchen table. 'How about you: still tottering around and trying to keep old Frank on the straight and narrow?'

'I couldn't even begin to do that. No, mostly I'm sitting around and drinking unsuitable amounts of gin.'

'That should do your liver a power of no-good.'

Megan laughed. 'At my age I don't think I'm going to start worrying about my liver.'

Kate grinned at Heathcliffe, who was trying to infiltrate his head between her arm and the telephone. 'Okay. You haven't rung to discuss Frank, how much booze you're putting away *or* the state of your liver. What do you really want to know?' she asked and heard Megan's familiar huff of laughter.

'How you are getting on with Andrew Parradine for a start.'

Kate said smoothly, 'As employer and employee we get along just fine.'

'And the house?'

'That's getting along just fine too.'

Megan said bluntly, 'You know James is selling as soon as it's finished?'

'I know that's what he plans.' Kate was non-committal.

'I thought you should know he might come over sometime to check on progress.'

Shit, thought Kate, Now what's he going to think about Andrew's plans for Rosscannan's future – and from a purely personal point of view, how mad might he be to find *she* was ready to aid and abet those plans? She took a bite of her apple, chewed thoughtfully, swallowed then said, 'Why tell me? It's none of my business and if he does come I'll most likely be up in London – I have to go back sometime and sort out my things. I'm sure Andrew would have Heathcliffe for a while.'

'We-ell, that brings me to another thing...'

Kate closed her eyes. 'Go on,' she said ominously, 'give with the bad news.'

'Frank is going home the end of January but I'm not ready to face winter in Cornwall that soon. If you can hold the fort at Pendragon I'd like to stay on here until the spring. James has suggested I move into the villa, and as it's big enough for us to share without getting under each other's feet, I'd like to accept his offer.'

With a sinking feeling in the pit of her stomach and the total conviction that Fate was shoving her relentlessly back into the inexplicably seductive warmth of Rosscannan and Andrew's equally seductive arms, Kate gave in. Though not without a passing thought towards such well-worn clichés as the reckless burning of boats, tears before bedtime, etc, she said bravely, 'That shouldn't be a problem. Stay as long as you like. God knows there's nothing much to draw me back to London permanently.'

There was a moment's silence before Megan answered gently, 'I should hate to feel you were lonely and I know things must be tight financially. I can't magic up any company for you but you must at least let me provide for housekeeping expenses...'

'I have company when I want it and I'm earning enough for the groceries,' Kate's independent spirit rebelled, but she kept her voice light, 'I don't need to take from you. Just promise you won't leave me anything really crap in your Will – like your car or the contents of your freezer, and I'll stay on as long as you like.'

'What happened to the big-city girl?'

Kate's mouth crooked in a grin. 'She's living in shirts, jeans and old sweaters and wondering what she'll do with that wardrobe full of *haute couture* she left behind!'

*   *   *

'How is she doing?' asked James as Megan put the phone down.

'Better than I expected after such a short time. Although she's not giving anything away, reading between the lines I'd say your son may have something to do with the resurgence of her fighting spirit.'

'Perhaps,' James pursed his lips. 'Fighting spirit apart she sounds as cool and independent as he is, although he can spark all right if someone rubs him up the wrong way.'

'Oh, Kate will do that, never fear!' Megan chuckled. 'That

depression she was heading for after the break-up with Paul seems to be fading rapidly. I guarantee there'll be enough fireworks along the way to keep the adrenalin flowing – and the lack of a sex life when you are nowhere near old enough to do without it can be a powerful incentive to find a mate.'

He gave a wry smile. 'From what I remember, courtship is a very tiring business for very little reward.'

'James, you sweet old-fashioned thing,' she gave an uninhibited hoot of laughter. 'Courtship is out; these days its orgasms that count!'

*   *   *

Kate set a match to the paper and kindling in the drawing room grate, then sat cross-legged before the hearth, her back against the fireside chair, and fed logs onto the growing flames. Beside her, Heathcliffe rested his great head on her shoulder, whining and snuffling her hair.

"Isn't it rich; are we a pair; you with your feet on the ground, me in mid-air..."' she sang softly, letting a small sliver of melancholy shiver through her. What was she going to do, she mused, then corrected herself swiftly, what *could* she do but let go and drift with the tide? It would be a first, she thought, and although just drifting was a new concept and slightly scary, it was not an entirely unpleasant one.

She wondered what was happening back at Rosscannan: if Andrew was doing one of his silent fumes because she had slipped away before he had a chance to take charge again; if Sam was back home yet in his cheerless little cottage; if Andrew had handled the situation with his son badly or well, and if Toby was crushed in defeat or elated with victory. Fliss and George, she thought, would each be watching from the sidelines and putting their own ten cents worth in at what they deemed to be the right moments. She threw another log on the fire and watched the sparks fly up the wide chimney. 'Four of them *and* Rosscannan,' she said aloud, 'and only one of me; it hardly seems fair. But what's fair about anything in this ruddy life?'

When memories and longing, the need to feel loved, and just plain unvarnished sex got all tangled up together anything might happen. *We all have our "something nasty in the woodshed"* she communed silently and gazed broodingly into the fire. *I have to stop thinking about what might have been and start concentrating on what I have, or Christmas, and possibly the rest of my life, could be a disaster.*

But still the old ache started up around her heart. What would she have bought and wrapped, decorated with ribbons and bows and put

157

under the tree for him/her this Christmas and other Christmases to come? A train set or a doll's house – perhaps a macho black, or Barbie-pink, bicycle? Tears gathered behind her eyes and she laid her head back against the arm of the plush covered Victorian chair, aching with the knowledge that not all the counselling in the world could ever erase that particular agonising memory.

No, life wasn't fair. It wasn't fair at all.

*   *   *

Kate wasn't the only one taking time out. When his young cousins were at last in bed and dinner over, Toby left his father and aunt playing backgammon with the vicious rivalry known only to siblings and padded along to his own room, where for a long time he perched on the cushioned window seat, staring out across the moonlit grounds.

His day, entered into so light-heartedly, had been a revelation. The work had been hard and menial but unbelievably satisfying; even flogging Christmas trees had been more or less a pleasure. But it was the glasshouses filled with plants, shrubs and trees from humble winter pansies to tropical palms, that had lighted some hidden spark, ambition bursting on him like a tidal wave. He blushed now to remember his confident declaration of his innermost thoughts. Hell, but the old man must have had a job keeping his face straight. What a wanker, blurting it out like that...and how the hell would he ever achieve high enough passes to get into a decent college when he'd spent most of his schooldays doing the minimum amount of work to scrape by in the classroom while creating general havoc outside of it?

Dimly he perceived that the reputation of a Bolshie sod he had so carefully fostered would make it very hard, if not impossible, to convince anyone he was now in deadly earnest about getting down to work; he was finding it difficult enough to convince himself. But he did mean it and somehow he would do it, whatever it cost.

*   *

When Kate returned from her run the next morning, she found Andrew seated on a rock beside the steps up to Pendragon. He rose to his feet as she came along the beach towards him with Heathcliffe at her heels, and stood waiting, hands in the pockets of his Barbour, his head tilted back, his gaze fixed on her face.

A shaft of mixed pleasure and pain shot through her and for a moment she lost step; love, she thought dizzily, did that to you. She flashed him a guarded smile and asked, 'Hello, did you come to join my morning run?'

'The spirit may be willing, but...' he shrugged and stooped to pat a fawning Heathcliffe who was greeting him with moans of delight and slobbering all over his boots.

She stopped a little distance from him. 'I do know about your problem. Remember, I've seen the scars.' She began to climb the steps and he followed. 'Going to bed with a man, a girl notices little things like bullet wounds, but as you never volunteered any information, this girl didn't like to mention it. My parents,' she said feelingly, 'taught me to mind my manners and not ask questions; on the other hand Megan taught me the exact opposite.' She looked at him over one shoulder. 'I had a very confused childhood.'

'Yeah, it shows!' He followed her as she began to climb the steps.

'We can talk about it, or not,' she volunteered. 'I don't mind; it's up to you.'

'It's quite OK; not much to say, really. I got shot, I lived. Some do, some don't; all part of the job.' He shrugged. 'I didn't want to talk about it at the time – or afterwards – counselling isn't my style, but I don't mind telling you anything you want to know. George tells me I still yell a bit in the night from time to time, so be warned.' He fell silent for a minute then asked quietly, 'How about your bullet holes? Were *they* all part of the job?'

She shrugged. 'In a way.'

'Tell me, Kate, please. I want to know what it is you can't or won't, talk about. I'm damn' sure there is more than just a love affair that went wrong. Come on, you can tell me,' he coaxed.

'Not sure I can...' She shivered suddenly, 'and not here or we could both end up with pneumonia. Come on, I'll race you to the house.' She began to run up the steps, Andrew following with less agility, Heathcliffe bumping at his heels.

Swearing beneath his breath and with chest heaving, he reached the kitchen well behind her. 'Coffee,' he gasped. Sinking down onto a chair he rested his head on his arms. Kate switched on the kettle and reached for the jar of instant coffee.

'That'll teach you!' she said and grinned, hoping, but not really expecting, that the challenging run and a little light badinage to follow might put him off his disturbing line of questioning.

He waited until he had taken his first sip of the reviving coffee and, as she had dreaded but expected, returned to the attack. 'Please: begin at the beginning if you like, or tell it backwards if you prefer, but for God's sake get whatever it is off your chest,' he implored.

'Finding what makes you tick is on a par with getting information from an Afghan War Lord – and,' he added, 'don't think I haven't tried that in my time!'

'I can believe it.' She gave a crooked smile, 'but if I let you into my world, you have to let me into yours – first.'

'OK – but there isn't a lot in mine – no skeletons, I'm afraid.'

She said lightly, 'Stop beating about the bush, and just dish the dirt.'

'We-el' he wrinkled his brow, 'I went into the Army straight after University…not entirely sure why; probably to get away from home. My mother died when I was not much older than Toby and pa wasn't all that easy to get along with…although at least he was always *there*, but very wrapped up in his vineyard and pretty pissed off I wasn't willing to stick around and learn the business. I had my baptism of fire in the Falklands, met Vanessa on one long leave – a case of instant lust on both sides, but the marriage never really worked. I was posted all over the place and she wouldn't live with me in married quarters in any part of the globe.' He sighed and rubbed his chin.

'Poor old Toby got the worst of it – shuffled off to prep-school at eight; having to put up with a succession of his mother's boy friends …' he shrugged. 'No wonder he's a mess. Van had never really wanted a child and I was hardly ever home to pull my weight. She and I finally parted company four years back, Toby spent his vacations with her, when she was around, and with school friends when she wasn't; I saw him occasionally during the holiday periods. The final break this year and the divorce cut me up badly at first; I was bloody angry and blamed it all on her, which was unfair…' he shrugged again. 'We did have some good times at first, but they just didn't last. She was lonely and needed a man – quite a lot of them as it turned out, and I suppose in the end I just didn't care. Selfish pair of buggers, weren't we?'

'Perhaps, but she knew you were a career soldier when you married. Why didn't she want to travel the world with you?'

He made a wry face. 'The term "peace time soldier" has a pretty ironic ring now; believe me, there are not many safe cushy postings these days where wives would wish to come along.'

She said shrewdly, 'Particularly if the man in question wouldn't take a safe cushy one if offered?'

'Possibly,' he grinned suddenly. 'Very boring sitting behind a desk…anyway, that's about it: you know how it ended. I thought I had a couple more years to go, but I'm not complaining; there have been compensations.' There was a silence. Andrew broke it. 'Your turn,' he said.

Kate stared down into her cup. *You don't have to tell it all,* said an insidious inner voice. *Oh, yes I do* her conscience answered.

She took a deep breath. 'Remember, you started this.'

16

She told him, sitting at the table, sipping her coffee; admitting for the first time, in all its shameful, hideous detail, the real truth about the end of her relationship with Paul. For all these weeks she had kept up the pretence that their parting had been amicable and without grief – now, as she related honestly the bare facts of their life together and its explosive end, she could see from the expression in Andrew's eyes that he was both angry and baffled that she had spent eight long years in such a volatile and exhausting relationship.

'You see,' she endeavoured to explain, 'I was ripe to really fall for someone; ready to find some kind of stability in my life. When I left Art School I knew I wasn't likely to make a living as an artist; I just didn't have the spark, so I drifted into the theatrical world *via* the London Fringe Theatres. In those early days I wasn't exactly Little Miss Confidence, so working backstage, out of the limelight, I was reasonably settled and happy.'

She took another, pensive draught of her coffee. 'It was lousy pay of course, but I was quite successful at set design and in a few years had worked my way up as assistant to a guy who created sets for the larger provincial theatres; it was at one of those that I met Maestro Verdassey...and you don't have to pretend you know who he is.'

Andrew said loftily. 'But I do know. Saw him conduct at the Festival Hall when I was on leave from the Gulf...a Mahler evening: Symphonies 4 and 5. Took a tottie I'd met at a mess 'do' the previous night and she slept all the way through.'

'Good job she wasn't in the front row; if Paul had spotted her snoozing he'd probably have thrown his baton.'

'No sidelining,' he said, 'and no more digressing; get on with your life story.'

Kate finished her coffee and sat, holding the cup between her hands, rubbing her chin against the fading warmth. 'It was all very Some Enchanted Evening: eyes meeting across a crowded room, or rather, a theatre foyer, and I fell like the proverbial ton of bricks.' She sighed. 'I should have been immune by then; I was thirty-five, I'd had my share of unsuccessful relationships, when I'd thought I was in love then found I wasn't. In retrospect, I'm not sure Paul fell quite as hard as me, but it was the beginning of a very happy, stimulating, and for me, educational relationship. I discovered I had a talent for PR and progressed rapidly from live-in lover to the organizer of his life, both professional and private. In return, he taught me how to dress, how to talk – when we met I was still an Essex girl with vowels to die for – but above all else he gave me confidence and the certainty that I could cope with any person, any situation and achieve anything I wanted to.' She gave a throaty, reminiscent chuckle that stirred a sudden unreasonable jealous rage in her listener. 'And he taught me to enjoy the high life. God, but he was quite something, on *and* off the rostrum; his sheer *joie de vivre* more than made up for his temper tantrums, his intolerance, his massive ego, his total inability to see any point of view but his own...oh,' she threw up her hands, 'I could go on forever...and you know, it's only in these past few weeks that I've realized how incredibly hard I worked: entertaining, dealing with the media, holding him back from insulting people who mattered, seeing he was charming towards the people who could be influential in his career, smoothing his path, keeping him on the pedestal on which his fame had placed him... you name it, I did it.'

'Why?' Andrew spread his hands in angry disbelief, 'Why slave like that for a man, however talented, who was such an arrogant, selfish egomaniac?'

'The heart,' she said simply, 'and sex' she added honestly, 'the two went together...at least, they did until a couple of years ago...'

Her face was suddenly devoid of all animation; in her eyes Andrew saw clearly a depth of sadness he had only glimpsed before. Rage welled until it was an actual pain around his heart. *I really do love her,* he marvelled at the realisation, *but all I want to do right now is yell at her for being such a bloody fool and wasting her life on that heap of shit...* With a supreme effort he controlled his rage. Not trusting himself to speak he took her hand in both of his, holding it in a tight, almost crushing grip.

There was a long silence before she spoke again. 'A little over two years ago, I discovered I was pregnant. Up until then I hadn't thought I wanted children, and I certainly didn't want marriage, I'd seen too much of my parents' own stultifying version of wedded bliss to want that. For heaven's sake, I'd just hit forty, and to be honest, children weren't on my agenda, ever; not until I sat in the bathroom one morning and watched that little blue line appear on the do-it-yourself kit from the corner pharmacy. Then it was like a dam bursting. Before I really knew what I was actually celebrating, I did the most utterly crazy dance all around the house. I couldn't wait for Paul to get back from rehearsals and tell him the news.'

She paused for even longer before giving a bleak, dismissive shrug. 'You know those cartoons where someone explodes with rage and a great big "POW!" lights up over their head in a burst of jagged light? – *Yeah,* mused Andrew, *that's what I feel like doing right now* – Well, that was Paul: "Houston, we've had a problem" was very small beer compared with the drama that ensued – the tantrums and the sulks lasted for days – weeks, but eventually he won...' She forced a bleak smile. 'At that time I still loved him; couldn't even begin to imagine life without him – and of course he was right. In my heart I knew the impossibility of having another baby when the one I already had, even given he was forty-five and well out of nappies, took all of my time and energy to care for and cosset. So, eventually and before it was too late, I did what he wanted, demanded: I had an abortion. Since when there hasn't been a day when I have not had regrets...and it was all for nothing; I could never forgive him, nor lose the guilt over what I'd done, and from that time we began to drift apart; I'm surprised it took him so long to find someone else.' She looked down at the hand still clasping hers. 'I don't think I have ever felt so utterly powerless and alone as I did after he'd gone; I spent the next couple of weeks alternately bawling my eyes out and cursing him to hell and back, until salvation came with the offer to look after Megan's house and dog whilst she was in Italy.'

'Je-sus...' Andrew let out a long breath. 'But...the baby...you must have told your parents – surely they could have helped – and what about your friends?'

She said simply. 'I didn't tell anyone, least of all my parents, that I was pregnant, let alone that I'd had an abortion. Paul wouldn't talk about it; refused even to acknowledge it had happened – it was over, ergo: forget it. Later, when it came to the break-up, I played that down too; told my parents and the rest of my family, that we parted by mutual consent. Face-saving, you see.' She withdrew her hand from his and smoothed her hair, the façade of control back in place. She said, 'Actually, I didn't tell my girl friends either...you are the first to hear it. Isn't that odd?'

'Odd? It isn't odd; it's bloody tragic.' He put both his hands in his hair, ruffling it distractedly. 'I just don't understand...Christ, I may not be that close to my father, but I could always rely on him to lend an ear if I was in trouble.'

She said quietly, 'I think some people shouldn't have children; I'm sure if they thought a lot harder about it first, a good many wouldn't; my ma and pa for a start. I suspect when they embarked on parenthood, which they only did when they were both nearing forty and pretty set in their ways, it was so as to have at least one child to carry on their genes. When I finally arrived I don't think they knew quite what to do with me.' She shrugged again. 'My mother was, and still is, the epitome of a professional housewife and committee woman. She belongs to a half dozen local societies and has friends round to the house every Thursday to play Whist. She even has afternoon tea on Sundays. Since I hit eighteen she's nagged me, in a nice, sweetly soulful way, to "Find a good man and settle down."'

'What about your father? What does he do?'

She gave her little, twisted smile. 'My father is a retired assistant bank manager. He plays bowls and enjoys river fishing and visiting museums. He has a particular liking for the Natural History Museum and used to take me there when I was a child, when what I really wanted was to go to the V&A where I could gaze at all the beautiful costumes and furniture.'

She was suddenly pensive, looking down at her hands again, her eyes narrowed. 'I do love them, you know, in my own way, and in their way they love me. We can enjoy each other's company in short bursts, but we simply never jelled as a family and the love has only ever worked at a distance; I guess I'm closest to my father, but think I disappointed him, well, both of them probably, by being: a) a girl, and b) "Arty". I'm sure they would have been proud and happy if I'd been a boy, passed all the right exams and worked in my father's bank.'

She looked up again and now there was a hint of sly amusement in her voice. 'What you might call a dysfunctional family – perhaps it sounds a little familiar to you – with a slight role and gender reversal?'

For a moment he was uncomprehending – then her meaning hit home. He covered his face with his hands then drew them slowly downward before looking up at her with a rueful smile. He said, 'Dysfunctional doesn't even begin to cover Toby, Van & me, does it?' Absently he smoothed his rumpled hair. 'However you look at it, once the initial attraction and lust had run its course, neither she nor I ever understood, or even tried very hard to understand each other, let alone Toby. We just led our separate lives and made damn all effort to be a family for our son. If I'm honest, the Army was probably my perfect excuse to be an absent husband. As for Van...' he shrugged. 'Sufficient to say, she was never lonely.'

Kate was already regretting opening up old wounds for this basically kind and caring man. What right had she to prod and push at the flaws in others? And would telling all really relieve her own nagging sense of guilt and help her regain a long lost peace of mind? Right now, all she knew for certain was that the top layer of sophistication a once-shy and unsure Kate Shaw had acquired over the past eight years seemed to be slipping away, leaving her almost as vulnerable and exposed as she had been as a child.

She said quietly. 'When I was a child, and through all my growing-up years, I lived for the holidays; for Cornwall and Megan, the one person I wanted to see and be with. She was my rock; she had time to talk and listen, really *listen,* to me.' Suddenly she was desperately, achingly tired. She said wearily, 'With a bit of luck there may be a Megan for Toby. It may be you, or George – or more likely Sam – it doesn't really matter that much, so long as it's someone who'll care enough to try and understand what makes him tick, and listen to what he's really trying to say.'

For a long moment there was silence. Andrew was still, watching Kate as she sat with her fingers clasped loosely together on the table top. She looked exhausted and as though she were about to relinquish life itself. After a while he stood and putting an arm about her shoulders led her, as she had led him that first evening, up the stairs to her room. Once there he took off her running shoes, helped her out of her jog pants and sweatshirt then eased her onto the bed, tucking the duvet about her as gently as a nanny with a tired child.

'Sleep', he said, 'and then we shall have breakfast.' He raised an eyebrow. 'No Ena today, I hope?'

Kate gave a pale grin. 'No Ena – and I'm not tired, you know; not really.'

'Your brain is,' he answered, 'so give it a rest.'

She murmured, 'If there's one thing I can't stand, it's a bossy man.'

'Tough,' he said and pulled the curtains closed. 'You have an hour to switch off before I put the eggs in the pan,' he added and left the room.

Kate lay still, listening to the sound of the waves on the shore and the sudden bursts of rising wind against the windows. Stormy weather ahead, she thought, so what was new…she smiled again and closing her eyes did her best to give her brain a rest, which wasn't easy because despite all the trauma and exhaustion of the past few hours one thought was running like a startled hare through her mind…

'I love Andrew Parradine,' she said aloud into the darkened room, 'and I think he loves me.' She paused then added, 'and that's quite enough to be going on with for now.'

*   *   *

166

She dozed, but didn't sleep and after some forty minutes, slipped out of bed to head for the shower. Downstairs, Andrew heard the gurgle of water in the pipes and took a pan from the shelf. Poached eggs, a couple of slices of buttered toast each and a pot of strong coffee would just about set them both up for the day. When she appeared in the doorway he slid two perfectly poached eggs over the waiting slices of toast on each plate.

'How about that for timing?' he reached for the coffee pot. 'Black or white?' he asked.

'Black, I think. Nothing quite like strong coffee to kick-start the day,' seating herself she began tucking into the eggs. 'Lovely...you have hidden talents.'

'Oh, yeah, Jamie Oliver, that's me.' He cast a quick glance at her face and saw she looked calm but still heavy-eyed. 'Think you'd better take some time off.' He smiled, 'On full pay, of course.'

'I'd rather work.'

'Well at least rest this morning; then come over to lunch if you feel up to it.'

She looked as though she would refuse, but to his relief nodded her agreement. 'All right, I'm too whacked to argue.'

'Kate.' He put down his knife and fork and leaned his arms on the table. He said quietly. 'I'm sorry if I pushed you – I thought it was just your love life that went wrong and that it would clear the air between us to talk about it; I had no idea you were hiding something so tragic and personal. Now I feel a total heel.'

'Don't...' she shook her head. 'You were right; it needed to be said. One can't continue to live in the past, wishing things had been different,' she took his hand. 'You know, I don't think I want to go on fighting to keep an independence I never really had, or refuse to let myself love for fear I might get hurt again. Because at the end of the day, no one is ever totally independent, and if one gets hurt...' she lifted her shoulders, 'well, I guess that's just too bad. Life still goes on regardless, doesn't it?'

He nodded gravely. 'Only poets die of unrequited love.'

For a few charged moments they looked deep into each other's eyes. Then Kate smiled. 'Do you want to go to bed?'

He returned the smile. 'I thought you'd never ask,' he said.

*   *   *

Much later he asked. 'Would you like to hear how my idiot sister and her equally daft husband almost made it to the divorce court?

167

'We talked, I know the bare bones, but fill me in. Does it have a happy ending?'

'I hope so; I'm doing my best.'

'I'm all for happy endings.'

He grinned and nuzzled her neck. 'Glad to know that; I'll keep it in mind.'

'Stick to the story.'

'OK, but I'll still keep it in mind...' he settled his arm more comfortably about her shoulders. 'It seems old Duncan kept taking off at odd times and behaving like a man with a secret, so eventually the next time he whizzed off on his tod, Fliss followed him and discovered him disappearing into the stables at the local equestrian stud with the very dishy female owner. When they reappeared half an hour later laughing their heads off and looking very satisfied with themselves, she thought the worst. Being Fliss, she jumped on him the second he walked back through the door. They had a blazing row; she told him to piss off; he accused her of not trusting him and being a suspicious bitch and roared off to stay with friends; the next day she high-tailed it down here.' He shook his head. 'Stark, raving, mad, the pair of them.'

'So where's the happy ending?'

'I'm coming to that...Duncan phoned me yesterday in one hell of a state: seems he'd been secretly negotiating with the dishy stable boss for a horse to replace Fliss's old mare she'd had to put out to grass. Poor chap was trying to keep it under wraps until Christmas when my daft sister jumped the gun, and as I said, all hell let loose.' Kate started to laugh and he joined in. 'Quite a tangled web, you might say,' he chuckled. 'Anyway, I suggested he came down tomorrow and they all stay for Christmas; he jumped at the idea. I think he feels it might take the heat off the reconciliation if they meet on neutral ground.'

'He'd better be right about that,' she said, 'or Christmas could just be cancelled this year!'

17

Glass in hand, James stared out across the valley and the straight lines of his vines. He said, 'I think I'll take a trip over to the UK in the New Year. Care to come with me?'

Megan shook her head. 'Cornwall in winter has quite definitely lost whatever charm it once had for me.'

He said moodily. 'It doesn't hold much charm for me either; in fact, I wouldn't bother going if I didn't feel something was a little off with Andrew. He's being damned evasive about the whole business of Rosscannan.'

'In what way is he evasive?' Megan had her own private thoughts about Andrew and Rosscannan, but knew when to keep her own counsel.

James frowned. 'Too much talk about how wonderful it is to bring the place to life again, and not enough about when he expects it to be ready to put on the market.'

Megan, an expert at reading between the lines and suspecting a hidden agenda in her niece's increasingly up-beat descriptions of her employer and his dedication in bringing Rosscannan to life again, guessed Kate might also have something to do with Andrew's evasion. 'Perhaps you should give him a little more time before you descend on his neck,' she said.

'The sooner I go over and light a fire under him, the sooner it will be finished and off my hands.'

Megan thought about Andrew's photograph on James' desk, and doubted if anyone, even his determined father, would have any great success in lighting a fire under that particular gimlet-eyed and author-itative figure. She gave a little tucked in smile. She was sure that if it came to a showdown and a locking of horns, the old stag would, sooner or later, give way to the younger.

Interesting, she thought; it might almost be worth going along, just to stand on the sidelines and watch. But that wouldn't be very charitable of her. She said prudently, 'If you take my advice you'll let sleeping dogs lie. It sounds as though he's doing a competent job – give him the chance to finish it without hassling him.'

'You could be right...' he gave a sudden grin. 'Mind you, I'd quite like to have a look at his woman and see if he might be getting it right this time.'

*   *   *

Andrew stood at his study window, casting a weather eye at the lowering clouds and what looked suspiciously like a breeze-blown drift of fine snow. The house itself really was coming together now. Although the installation of the new radiators, at present stored in the barn, would have to wait until the New Year, the replacement for the old boiler had arrived on Monday and been fitted, so now the house was warm throughout. The interior had needed far less work than at first expected, and once Christmas was over, the expert plasterer recommended by the National Trust would arrive with his scaffolding to replace the odd missing or damaged parts in cornices and ceilings. Given a spell of reasonable weather, the exterior painting shouldn't take more than two to three weeks; that done, all the other work on the house itself should be finished well before the end of January: by which time, he thought gloomily, the old man would most likely be on his neck to get the place on the market…

His mind shied away from the problem of how much the present market price would turn out to be once house and grounds were in first class order. Even with his share from the sale of the London house, plus the generous sum James had promised for his input towards the restoration of Rosscannan, he would still need to raise a pretty hefty mortgage.

His reverie was interrupted by the sight of a dark blue Volvo SUV pulling up before the house. Almost before the wheels had stopped, a tall, red-haired man stepped out; there was a combined shriek of 'DADDY!' and two little boys raced down the steps to leap into their father's arms.

This, decided Andrew, was one reunion he would allow to run its course before *he* turned out to greet his brother-in-law, particularly through the could-be-explosive first meeting between Duncan and Felicity.

He gave it ten minutes then walked cautiously out into the hall. Gus and Heck were crouched, squabbling *sotto voce* over a garishly coloured giant floor jigsaw-puzzle of dinosaurs, the wrapping paper of which was strewn around the hallway. George, he noted, was nowhere in sight. Both boys looked up as Andrew approached. Gus jerked a thumb toward the ceiling. 'They're up there,' he said in a resigned tone.

'Snogging,' supplied Heck.

'How d'you know that?' asked Andrew.

170

Hector looked at him scornfully. 'Cause it's all gone quiet.'

With great care Gus placed a piece of dinosaur claw in the right spot. 'And when they go quiet up there; that's when they snog,' he said.

Andrew sighed and returned to his study. *Out of the mouths of babes and sucklings...* – how the hell did kids get so flaming knowing so early these days?

*   *   *

Kate awoke to leaden skies and a slight flurry of snow in the air. She swung her legs out of bed and stretched luxuriously. After Andrew had driven her back from Rosscannan the previous evening, she had gone early to bed and slept the deepest sleep she could remember having since childhood.

'Only four days to Christmas,' she informed Heathcliffe as he returned from a hasty visit to the garden. 'Wouldn't it be great to have snow on Christmas morning?'

He peered intently from beneath shaggy brows, his look telling her plainly to stop yattering and get some breakfast in his dish. Kate sighed. 'No great conversationalist in the mornings, are you, I suppose I'd better –'

She broke off as the telephone rang and snatched the handset up quickly, expecting to hear Andrew's warm tones. Instead a deep, resonate voice demanded: 'Katarina, why you haf left London – and changed your mobile number? I haf one 'ell of a job to find you; your mama would not tell me where you were, and your friends, they say they do not know...but I think they are telling the porkies.'

'Paul!' Kate's knees buckled and she sat down abruptly. Her first instinct was to slam the handset down, but long experience told her it would be pointless; that if she did, the phone would just keep ringing all day – and night – until she did answer. She said faintly, 'How did you know I would be here?'

'If you are not in London, and not with your parents, where else would you go to 'ide away but that so ugly 'ouse of your charming cousin?'

Kate struggled for composure; the shock of hearing his voice was arousing a tumult of emotions she'd thought securely dead and buried. *I can't, I can't let him do this to me...* She took three deep steadying breaths so that when she spoke again her voice was clear, with only the slightest catch. 'What is it you want, Paul?'

'I want *you* Katarina: now, at once...tell Megan goodbye and take a plane tonight.'

'I will not. Megan is in Italy and I'm house-sitting Heathcliffe – and I have a new job.'

'But Katarina, I need you...all is...how you say it: all cockeled up.'

Kate asked coldly. 'What is all cocked up? Dopey Opie made a balls-up, has she? '

'What are these balls? Bertie ...poof...she make my schedule all cockeled. You must come...in two days I am flying to Vermont with Panos Papadopulos – 'e has a private plane – you remember. We skied with 'eem last year? Meet me there. We will ski and dance and make love and be 'appy again.' His voice dropped, became warm, seductive. 'Come, my lovely Katarina...we were happy, yes? Forget what 'appen – it was nothing: we were hafing the bad patch, you and I: you spend much time with your friends; you go away to those so tiresome lectures, and I think you stop being my 'eart, my soul...'

'Stop!' Kate wanted to crash down the phone; cover her ears to shut out the sound of his voice, but hadn't the willpower to do either. 'Paul, have you forgotten what happened: how we fought – really fought and hurt each other?'

'But Katarina, ve alvays fight...'

'Not like *that* we didn't – but then I'd never before caught you shagging that half-wit harpist.'

'But I tell you – that Alberta: it was nothing. She is not you. It is you I need.'

Suddenly Kate found her voice. 'Well you can't have me,' this time she made to slam the handset down then snatched it up again at the last second to yell, 'and in case you hadn't noticed, I smashed every last one of your bloody porcelain figurines!'

Very carefully she placed the handset beside the phone and topped the whole with a large cushion. 'Damn your hide, Paul; ring again all you like...I won't be able to hear you,' she said, and a moment later felt the first scalding tear begin to trickle down her cheek. Furious she jumped to her feet. 'Come on Heathcliffe, breakfast can wait. What I need is a damned good run along the shore before the day's work begins.'

*   *   *

'Is everything all right?' asked Andrew.

She answered breezily. 'Absolutely fine; why?' She stripped off her duffel and, easing off her Hunters, carried them and the coat through to the boot room.

Andrew followed her and as she turned back peered searchingly at her face. He said bluntly, 'You've been crying.'

'Who wouldn't in this cold? My eyes have been leaking like taps all the way here...it's warmer out than inside Megan's car.' Kate's tone was brittle and defensive.

He shrugged. 'OK; whatever you say. Come on into the drawing room and meet Duncan; George has just brought up a vast jug of coffee and Fliss has put so much wood on the fire you'd think she was building a funeral pyre. After coffee I thought we could go out to take a look at the stables...see if between us we can come up with any new ideas for making money without spending a fortune. Duncan's volunteered to help George and Toby finish off any odd jobs, sort the beds and bedrooms out properly and haul down some more furniture for the long gallery...' he grinned. 'So you and I can take it easy.'

She cocked a satirical eyebrow. 'Since when did I ever do that in this house?' she asked, but followed him into the drawing room where the newly-arrived Duncan and his wife were snuggled together on one of the sofas. Across the room George presided over a laden tray, with Gus, Heck and Toby on the window seat behind him making inroads on a plate of cakes. Andrew introduced the newcomer and the long, rangy Duncan stood, clasping Kate's hand warmly.

'Good to meet you, Kate – hey, hear a lot of this is up to you...' he swept an expansive hand around the room, 'care to come up to the Highlands and try your hand at re-vamping our place?'

She managed a smile. 'Not at this time of year,' she said.

George passed her a coffee. 'You be careful what you says, Miss, or you could find yerself spending the summer there up to yer neck in paint and the guv'nor wouldn't like that now, would he?' and he gave a leery wink.

'Neither would I, George,' she returned. 'Neither would I!'

She settled into a chair with Andrew perched on the arm beside her; the warmth of his arm against her shoulder was comforting and she thought she might just manage the next few hours without falling apart in front of all these people. Covertly she studied Duncan and could hardly repress a smile; he was fair and sandy haired with a rugged, lived-in sort of face, and gave the impression of solidity, as though he could stand any buffeting that life might throw at him. Kate judged him the perfect foil to the mercurial Felicity; she must have really gone over the top, she mused, to have roused this man into the kind of blazing row that had sent them both roaring in different directions from the marital home, and in the teeth of a snowstorm...Kate

173

shied away from the thought: it was too close to her own confrontation with Paul, and she didn't want to think of Paul at this particular moment. Time enough for that when she was alone again.

Andrew was saying: 'Kate and I are going to leave you shortly – we want to take a look at the stables and barn – see if we can find a way to make money out of them.'

'Don't see what you need to beat your brains out over,' Fliss yawned. 'Why don't you tart them up a bit and set up a Pony Trekking Centre.'

For perhaps half a minute there was a dead silence, then Kate said cautiously, 'Well, to do that I imagine one would need to know all about horses.'

Felicity opened her eyes wide. 'Well Andy does know all about them; he was riding almost before he could walk. We both were; in fact we've ridden all our lives. He even played polo at one time.'

Kate turned to Andrew. 'You really know enough about those big hairy things that bite at one end and kick at the other, to entice ignorant oiks like me and their pony-mad kids to hire your nags and go trekking over them thar hills?'

'Well, I wouldn't put it quite that way, but I do know which end bites and which end kicks and I could probably run an outfit like that with my eyes shut – if I had a first class business brain to keep it all together – a what-d'you-call-it – a PA.' Andrew grinned and winked at Kate. 'Brilliant idea, Fliss…I'd never have thought of that in a million years.'

She sniffed, 'That's the trouble with the Army; you get tunnel vision. You can't see beyond blasting the other bloke before he blasts you.'

Andrew rubbed his chin. 'Trekking…we could do that by the day – no need to provide accommodation…' Kate could almost see the cogs start whirring in his brain as he began to pace back and forth across the room. 'We're in a good spot here with Penzance and plenty of local Inns & B&Bs nearby. If we started in a modest way, say with a half dozen good mounts, it wouldn't cost all that much to set up – the main outlay would be on horses and tack; there are always plenty of pony-mad teenagers around to hire for stable work. Getting the stables up to scratch I could manage with a bit of outside help…' he turned to Kate. 'What d'you think?'

'Well, I could probably get into the Guinness Book of Records as the person who knows least about horses, but fill me in on the details and if you like I'll draw up a business plan and see what it all looks like on paper.'

Andrew stood, pulling her to her feet. 'OK, pardner – let's go take a mosey around the old corral,' he said.

'I'm coming,' said Fliss.

'Count me in,' said Toby.

Duncan uncoiled his long legs again and stood up. 'Me too,' he said.

'Me too,' said Gus & Heck in unison.

'Oh, my Gawd,' George said.

Andrew led the way, almost towing Kate along by the hand; a warm surge of excitement stirring his blood. God bless Fliss…he had been groping in the dark, trying to find what he might do once work on Rosscannan was finished; dreading a return to the awful state of boredom and depression that had begun to settle on him when fate forced his retirement before time, The necessity to make any plans for the future hadn't even begun to occupy his thoughts before that because his chosen profession had always carried a second agenda: that there was little point in beating his brains about retirement and what to do with it when there was a more than a 50/50 chance that a sniper's bullet, or a stray mine, would mean his old age was something that might never happen.

*　　*　　*

It had been a long day and Kate was exhausted, but at least all the talking and planning, helped along by far too many cups of whisky-laced coffee, had kept her from thinking too deeply about her present dilemma re Paul, although she hadn't been completely successful in hiding her feelings. She knew Andrew hadn't been entirely fooled; he would soon start asking questions, and she would soon have to tell him of her ex-lover's sudden re-appearance; albeit if only on the telephone.

She fell asleep, feeling guilty at her spiteful parting shot to Paul and spent a restless night filled with spasmodic dreams and images of him, waking well before daybreak to lie staring into the darkness, battling with the undoubted fact that the sound of his voice and his plea that he needed her was playing hell with her peace of mind; giving lie to her belief that she had been successful in cutting him out of her life…

One could not just walk away from eight years of living and loving without having some part of those years survive, she thought mournfully. 'If only,' she said aloud; 'if only you had been able to accept our child.'

175

But Paul never would have, never *could* have shared her with another being, even his own flesh and blood; so what was the use of going over old ground? Surely she had done enough of that to Andrew to last a lifetime.

Andrew... Kate gave an involuntary smile; now if she stood face to face and told him she was expecting his child, what would *he* do? She gave a sudden snort of laughter. Probably say if it was a boy she could send it back, then kiss her breathless...she shook her head. Was she really that sure of him? She'd thought she was over Paul and found she wasn't entirely; was she really in love with Andrew...had it all happened too soon?

'No!' she sat up and snapped on the bedside lamp. 'It happened just right.'

She drew her knees up to her chin and sat with her arms wrapped around them, watching the first light of a new day steal through the un-curtained window. She had loved Paul, and he in his way had loved, may still love, her. He would always be a part of her as she would be of him, but truthfully, they had never been destined to go on into a peaceful old age. Somehow she doubted that she and Andrew were likely to do that either...she was confident that they would go on together, but it could be a bumpy road they'd travel from time to time...

*   *   *

Toby and Sam were seated side by side on a pile of filled compost sacks, each with a mug of coffee in one hand, a slice of George's fruit cake in the other. The Christmas rush was over and all but a few late shoppers wandered the garden centre; another hour and the gates would close. It was the last working day before the holiday and Toby just had to ask the question that had been hovering in his mind for several days; any minute now dad or George would arrive to take him home and the opportunity would be lost...

'Sam,' he cleared his throat, 'I've been wondering...what's your scene over the Christmas ... I mean, are you spending it with your girl?'

Sam grinned at him over the rim of his mug. 'Too right, I am. Things are getting serious: I've been invited to her parents' place over in Roseland for the holiday.'

'Wow. Cool.' Toby tried not to show he'd been about to ask dad if Sam could spend the time at Rosscannan. He felt a bit jealous and disappointed and left out but couldn't blame Sam: he'd once seen him out with his girl in Penzance – she was pretty alright, and clever too, Sam said.

'You're all fixed up, of course?' Sam asked.

'Sure – my Aunt and Uncle and the kids are staying...and Kate, I guess.'

'I'll have to start looking for some extra work in January...the boss'll keep me on, but only part-time and until some other bad boy comes along.' Sam took a thoughtful bite of his cake. 'Dosh will be a bit tight. I start college in September; before then I'll need to have done a bit more hands-on gardening than I get just working at The Friary. Thought I might put an ad in the local paper soon as Christmas is over; see what turns up.'

'Yeah.' An idea began to wriggle its way into Toby's mind. He gave Sam a thoughtful sideways look. 'I'll ask around for you too,' he said.

18

Christmas day at Rosscannan, complete with tinsel-laden tree, an enormous amount of food, and over-excited children, was the sort of Christmas Kate had never had, and she savoured every minute; thrusting to the back of her mind all the possible complications the return of a determinedly amorous Paul might bring, she just concentrated on the pleasures of the present and let the future go hang.

Toby had appeared after breakfast lugging his and George's combined gift to Andrew of a large, sleek black cat, wearing a red tinsel bow about its neck and a malevolent expression, whom Andrew immediately christened Darcy. The newcomer's arrival had sent Heathcliffe first into a state of shock, followed by deep suspicion of the interloper, but after a few cautious sniffs and growls from him and a couple of determined swipes across his large intrusive nose from Darcy, a kind of armistice had been declared between cat and dog, with the feline commandeering an armchair and the hound setting up his own territory on the hearthrug. Although both Andrew, who was clearly besotted with his gift, and Kate, who was slightly less so and entirely on Heathcliffe's side, doubted a close friendship between the pair would ever be what one might term close.

That night, for the first time, she slept at Rosscannan, warm and secure in Andrew's arms while they made long luxurious love in his own reclaimed bed; afterwards lying entwined and drowsily content, Kate snuggled closer and Andrew whispered, 'Loved my tapestry: clever girl.'

'Loved my set of workman's overalls, complete with silver Celtic lapel brooch!' she returned, and he chuckled.

'Duncan reckoned you'll look dead sexy in them,' he said.

'Well, we'll see about that when I've tackled the stables and they're less than Persil white.' She gave a prodigious yawn. 'Now, not only my brain, but all of me is tired. 'Night, Andrew.'

'Goodnight, my love.'

Long after she slept, Andrew lay awake, watching the moon make a pathway across the polished boards. It had been a perfect day, he thought, and he would be completely and utterly content if he could just figure the reason for that almost haunted expression that from time to time he had caught lurking in Kate's eyes. After she had opened her heart that morning at Pendragon, confided so much more to him than she had to anyone else, he had thought she could have no more secrets tucked away, but still there was something…

He traced a finger over her sleeping face. When had he ever felt this tender, this protective, this *loving*? He wanted to keep her safe; here, at Rosscannan; to banish forever the uncertainty beneath the outward show of composure and control…he loved her, dammit…loved her…his mind groped for a phrase: *"…by sun and candle light"* – no, too hackneyed, too sugary. He tried again… Ah, Yeats, of course: who else.

"…But one man loved the pilgrim soul in you,
And loved the sorrows of your changing face…"

Yes! That was it… *the sorrows of your changing face…*.

He smiled and closed his eyes. If over the past weeks he had learned any one thing about the woman who now slept in his arms, the woman he loved, it was that, whatever troubled her, she would tell him about it in her own good time.

*   *   *

The day before the old year ended, Fliss, Duncan and the little boys returned to their own home, Duncan stating firmly that his family's Hogmanay had to be spent in Scotland.

Holding Darcy in his arms Andrew watched their departure with mixed feelings of relief and regret. It had been great having his family around him for the festivities, but he was ready to get back to the real world of work; most of all, he wanted to have Kate to himself again.

Fliss had been an enormous, enthusiastic help, relating the ups and down of her own considerable trekking experiences gained in the saddle during her years in the Highlands; putting in ideas – some of those a touch wild – warning of possible pitfalls and, most importantly, leaving the addresses of a half dozen useful contacts across the country: in fact, she had left his head fairly buzzing with plans and possibilities. He was confident that with a half dozen horses to start with, he could manage the day-to-day work of giving lessons, leading rides and cleaning tack. Hopefully there would always be plenty of help on offer from those pony-mad teenagers willing to groom and muck in – and out – for a reasonable wage packet. Now all he needed was Kate's return from her visit to check on Pendragon when she would draw up a battle plan and help him make a start on getting the stables, office and barns up to scratch; that done, the hunt for suitable mounts could begin.

As the VW and Range Rover disappeared from sight, his reverie was interrupted by Toby's 'Hi, dad – got a minute?' An innocent enough query but one which had him immediately on the alert; experience telling him that that particular note in his son's voice usually presaged some unlikely, possibly unwanted, information or request.

'Ye-es...' he answered cautiously.

'You know how Aunt Fliss said the grounds looked awful and you'd have to do something about them – well, I've had an idea.'

Andrew's tone increased in caution. 'Whatever it is, let's get inside before you unburden yourself or we'll both freeze to death.'

Behind them George cackled, said something about 'Big Jessies,' and disappeared towards the kitchen.

Toby followed his father into the drawing room. For a moment he struggled with the attempt to find the right words; the process of communicating with the old man was getting easier but could still hold some pitfalls...he took a deep breath. 'Sam says he'll need more practical experience before he goes to college than just working at the centre. So I was thinking; I mean, like, he could work here and earn some dosh...I could help in the vacs and all that...' he stopped suddenly, went bright red and muttered, 'well, just an idea I had.'

Andrew sat down, Darcy settling on his lap. *Better get this right, or in no time at all we'll be back to the grunts and "yeah – whatevers"...* He gestured to the chair opposite. 'Park it,' he said, 'and we'll talk this through.'

Toby sat forward on the edge of his chair. 'Really, dad, he's good; he knows a lot about trees and plants and all that...and he works really hard.'

'I'm sure he does, and if he took on this place single-handed he'd need to!'

'I could help – I said I would – I've got another two weeks before I go back to school and then there'll be the vacs. You wouldn't have to pay me!' he added hopefully,

Andrew looked into his son's pleading eyes, thought of Kate and her wry comments about dysfunctional families and how perhaps Sam might be a Megan for Toby. He might have his suspicions about the enigmatic Sam's past, but if there was a chance to add a little more cement to this burgeoning father/son relationship, he must accept Toby's new hero as he was, warts and all.

'OK,' he said, 'Let the poor guy enjoy his Christmas break, then he can come up and we'll sort something out...that's if he *wants* to work for an ex-murderer of freedom fighters like me.' He watched Toby's rising colour and knew that, even on their admittedly brief acquaintance, he'd read Mr Sam Trevene's politics pretty well. 'Don't worry,' he said dryly, 'my past, like your friend Sam's, is now well and truly behind me.'

Relief surged through Toby like a flood. He grinned. 'Wick-ed!' he said.

Andrew, who had neither the time nor inclination to pursue gardening in any shape or form, could see there would be more than enough work to fill Sam Trevene's time between now and his planned departure to college in September. The walled kitchen garden was a disaster; the woodland a wilderness of fallen branches and overgrown saplings; the small lake overtaken by rushes and weed…as for the rose garden and the straggling ornamental borders around the house…

'It needs one hell of a lot of work,' he said.

Toby shrugged. 'We can do it.'

Andrew stopped and looked at him. 'Well, as your grandfather was always so fond of telling us: anyone can do anything if he tries hard enough, so you probably can,' he said, and added silently, *let's hope he's still of the same opinion when he discovers I plan to keep hold of this place, although God only knows where the money to do that is coming from!*

19

JANUARY

After the full house over Christmas, New Year's Eve at Rosscannan was relatively peaceful; although the three adults might have awoken the next morning with varying degrees of hangover and a desire to lie peacefully in bed for as long as possible, Toby, in a burst of un-teenage-like energy was up before breakfast and out into the grounds with Heathcliffe, to greet the respectable two or three inches or so of snow that had finally fallen overnight after several half-hearted attempts over the past week.

Roused by whoops of delight from Toby and Heathcliffe's yowls of pleasure and excitement, Kate, wrapped in Andrew's towelling robe, looked down from the bedroom window at the spectacle of dog and boy rolling together on the soft white carpet below. Turning her head, she smiled back at Andrew where he lay propped up against the pillows. 'It might not last long but they are certainly making the most of it. Feel up to a snowball fight?' she asked.

He said lazily, 'I feel up to something but I don't think a snowball fight is it.'

'Ain't that just like a man,' Kate returned to sit on the edge of the bed. She took his hand, her smile fading. 'Darling, we have to talk; or rather I do,' she said.

'At last!' he said

'Smart arse, aren't you?' She gave a little grimace.

'So tell me what has been buzzing around your brain these past few days,' he said.

'I have to return to London very soon – don't panic; just for a visit.' She kept her gaze steady on his face. 'Paul phoned me just before Christmas – wanted me to fly out immediately and spend the Festive Season making love on the ski slopes of Vermont, before returning to my former post as lover and PA … Alberta Opie,' she added dryly, 'has, as he put it, "cockled up" his itinerary.'

'And of course you turned him down?'

'Of course I did, but…I know Paul; he doesn't take "no" for an answer and if I don't go to *him*, then he'll be down here like a shot.' She squeezed his hand. 'I don't want him here in Cornwall – either at

182

Pendragon or, God forbid, Rosscannan, so I'm going to suggest we meet at the Ealing house.'

His reply was swift. 'I'll come with you.'

'No. I have to clear this up myself – sort it once and for all.' She leaned to kiss his troubled mouth. 'Don't worry…I'm a big girl now; I can manage, although I had a nasty couple of hours after he'd called me out of the blue like that. Eight years is a long time you know, and some of those years were very, very good. I loved him once and I think in his way he loved me, but,' she gave a defeated little shrug, 'he is a genius, and geniuses are hard to live with. I think it's difficult for anyone with that amount of talent and drive for perfection to live in any world but his own…all that focus, all that energy, all that dedication channelled into one thing: it doesn't leave much space or time for other people, other lives.'

They were silent for a few moments, each wrapped in his own thoughts. Eventually Andrew said, 'I don't like to think of you going back alone: let me at least come with you until he shows up, then I can make myself scarce, if that's what you want. That way, when it's all over, I'll be around to help you pack and do what you have to do. I'm a practical sort of guy, you know.'

Kate's first impulse was to refuse: but this was a seminal moment in their relationship. She could say no, and go it alone, or she could step out onto a new road of mutual dependence and trust…*Decision time*, she thought, then smiled and lifting his hand, turned it and kissed the palm. 'Thank you,' she said, 'you're my sort of guy, so please come.'

'When?'

Paul's next engagement is in Atlanta on the tenth – he flew to Vermont in the private plane of one of his millionaire pals, and he's returning the same way, probably sometime today. He'll need a couple of days to finalise the arrangements for his last concert in the US. I'll call him back later this morning and see if he can make it over here sometime next week, before the concert, if that's OK with you.'

'On one condition,' he said.

She raised an eyebrow, 'Which is?'

'You get that robe off and back into bed again.'

'God,' she said, 'but you drive a hard bargain.'

*　　　*　　　*

Later that morning she returned with Heathcliffe to Pendragon. Feeling a deep reluctance to have Paul any part of her life with Andrew, albeit if only by telephone, she had refused his suggestion to make her call from Rosscannan, and he had understood; only said, 'Call me if it gets hairy and I'll be there.'

Now she sat at Megan's desk, staring at the 'Message Received', light as it repeatedly blinked its red malevolent eye. Of course, it could be Megan, or her parents, but then getting no answer here they would have called her mobile; only Paul didn't have her new number

Heathcliffe, catching her anxiety, sat close and thrust his head onto her lap. 'Oh, *God*, Heathcliffe!' she pushed the hair from his eyes and peered into their liquid depths. 'Why the blue-blazing hell did that idiot have to drop his bloody great bomb just when my life and love was as near perfect as any woman could want?'

Heathcliffe blinked at the sudden excess of light. 'Sorry,' she dropped his fringe, returning him back to the comfortably blinkered world behind the shaggy outcrop of hair. Reluctantly she pressed the 'Play' button on the answer phone.

'Katarina,' this time the voice was softer, seductively playful, *'that vas naughty of you to be so unkind; to destroy hall my figurines...but no matter; you and I, ve can purchase more together. Call me and ve vill make the new arrangements, yes?'*

'No,' Kate mouthed silently as the bleep heralded another message, the machine whirred and Paul's voice sounded again; this time gently chiding and faintly amused.

'Still you are not there; vere are you, my darling – and vy not with your Paul 'ere in this beautiful plice of sun and snow? Now I must return to Atlanta with Panos – not to vorry though, soon back in England I shall be and all vill be vell...I am asked vill I conduct five concerts in Russia in May...should ve go, or do you think they might still vant to send me to Siberia?

Do widzenia, until ve meet in London. Call me soon my lovely Katarina...

There was a click as the machine switched off. Kate breathed, 'Oh, God...' then bracing her shoulders lifted the handset and keyed in the well-remembered number. There was a long pause, then it rang twice and went straight to voice-mail and she almost wept with relief.

'Paul,' she gripped the receiver tightly, willing herself to be calm; not to let her voice shake. 'I know you, when you return from Vermont you will need a day or two to prepare for the last concert. I aim to be at the Ealing house for a few days from next week and will meet you there. Let me know when you plan to arrive. We have a lot to discuss....' She hesitated. 'Paul, I'm truly sorry about your porcelain and for being such a cow – and I wish we hadn't fought like that. Give Panos my regards and enjoy your flight back to Atlanta.'

She replaced the handset, switched the answer phone back on, and letting out a great breath of relief, sat back in the chair and began to swing it gently from side to side. There, it was done. No going back now.

After a few minutes she left the house to walk out onto the headland, Heathcliffe padding alongside. A great swelling sea was running ahead of a bank of dirty grey/brown cloud that presaged more snow. She thought of all the Christmases she and Paul had spent together: of the white ski slopes of Vermont; of Panos's lodge where last year they had stayed over Christmas: of the long, exhilarating races down the mountain, the blue shadows of approaching evening as they returned to blazing fires, fine wine and a perfectly cooked supper... She pulled her coat more closely around her and lifted her face to the rising wind. Yes, it had been good – very good; in retrospect, there was little she now regretted of their life together, although the loss of the child would always haunt her: that, and the devastatingly sudden and violent end to their relationship.

But she wouldn't look back, only forward to her future with Andrew and Toby, and George at Rosscannan; perhaps, she thought with a grin, in time she might even try riding one of those large pungently-smelling beasts that would soon invade their world.

'I have so much,' she said aloud, 'I can at least make this meeting with Paul as painless as possible for him. When he comes I'll offer an olive branch: find him a new, good, reliable PA, preferably male, so that there will be no more mixing business with pleasure.' She gave a little chuckle. 'Then my replacement will be able to have a life of his own – and Paul will be free to find his pleasures of the flesh elsewhere. One never knows, with a good PA to run his professional life, perhaps he and Dopie Opie will give it another shot.'

On a sudden impulse she decided that, before her return to Rosscannan, she would drive into Penzance. There was a small antique shop tucked away in one of the old streets that often had a few pieces of good porcelain on display. The prices were usually ruinously expensive but perhaps she would buy a piece as a further gesture of goodwill and thanks for the good times...heaven knows, she thought, the meeting would be difficult enough; even a small piece of good porcelain might help soften the blow she was about to give that supremely confident and self-assured man.

*   *   *

185

The Hornet had been air-born only a few minutes when Paul Verdassey switched on his mobile and checked for messages: smiling, he listened to Kate's voice.

'Ah, my little Katarina…' he snapped the mobile shut and tapped his companion on the shoulder. 'I knew it: she will be waiting for me – cannot you make this plane go a little faster, Panos?'

They were almost the last words he spoke.

20

In the antique shop the old man lovingly wrapped swathes of tissue paper around the four-inch high figurine of a shepherd boy holding a lamb under each arm. 'I think someone is going to be very lucky,' he said, as he fitted it into a stout cardboard box. 'It is for some special person?'

'Quite special, in his way,' she said.

'Then I wish him joy of it; and you too, madam.'

She thanked him and left the shop, wondering just how joyful Paul would be when she had finally managed to convince him their life together really was over. It would be good if they could remain friends, but even in her most optimistic moments she knew that was unlikely. Paul only ever had time for matters of the moment: for his work, and the immediacy of those presently around him.

She drove back through falling snow, musing on the vagaries of the British climate of late: a very wet summer, a dry warm autumn that had begun with record temperatures, only to change rapidly to rain and icy, near gale-force winds. Now snow in the West Country for the New Year…and cold with it! She would be glad when she was off these treacherously slippery roads and safely back at Rosscannan, where her presence at the house over Christmas had passed so easily and without dissent from anyone: Toby, their guests, and even George accepting the fact that she was sharing their lives – and Andrew's bed – without comment or any sign of either surprise or disapproval. She thought of Fliss's confident avowal that Andrew was the marrying kind and wondered if marriage might be on the cards at some time in the future…*And how would you fancy that?* she asked herself but didn't wait for an answer: things were very satisfactory as they were, so: *che sera, sera* and all that jazz.

*   *   *

Andrew perched on the desk in the study turning over an old copy of *Horse and Hound* while Kate sat at his computer juggling figures on a spreadsheet beating a business plan for the Trekking Centre into shape. Completely absorbed in her task she worked in silence, only occasionally throwing a terse question over her shoulder at him; once, giving a small cry of pain when he admitted the probable initial cost of the horses and ponies required, and the going price for a bale of hay.

They were four days into the New Year and Andrew was already restless and becoming increasingly impatient. Tomorrow the plasterers would arrive to deal with the small amount of detailed repairs to cornices and ceiling mouldings; his own part in the restoration of Rosscannan was over and now only the present icy conditions outside stood between him and a serious assault on the stables. Even if the weather improved dramatically, he thought gloomily, there was the London trip to be got through: a couple more days and they would leave this warm and peaceful place for what could only be at best a pretty traumatic few days. He didn't know how *he* was going to handle it, let alone Kate...and it was almost more than he could bear to think of leaving her, as she wished, to face her ex-lover alone in the house where they had lived together ...

This last unwelcome train of thought was interrupted by the sudden jarring jazz tones of Kate's mobile which lay on the desk beside him. Without looking up from her task, she said, 'Get that will you, Andrew' and he grabbed at it, welcoming the distraction.

'Hello, Parradine speaking...who? Yes, she is here. One moment...' he covered the mouthpiece with his hand. 'It's for you, Kate...your father.'

'*What?*'

He waggled the mobile and repeated, 'It's your father.'

She leaped from her chair. 'Oh, God – I only spoke to them a couple of days ago...something's happened to mother...or Megan.' She snatched the instrument from his hand. 'Dad, what is it? Why are you calling?'

'Steady Kate...' David Shaw's voice was carefully calm and measured – *like he'd have been when telling someone they couldn't have a bank loan*, Kate thought with a kind of frantic, terrified hilarity – 'first, take a deep breath, sit down, and ask that chap who answered to fix you a drink.'

'Oh, my *God,*' Kate sank into a chair and raised disbelieving eyes to Andrew, 'he wants you to fix me a *drink!*'

'Whisky or brandy?'

Andrew's tone was as calm as her father's and Kate made a huge effort to match it.

'Whisky,' she hissed. 'All right, dad. I'm sitting down and a drink is on the way. Now give with the bad news. It has to be bad if you're calling me so soon.'

'Kate, did you know Paul was flying back to Atlanta with that

Greek chap?'

'Yes,' she took the drink Andrew handed her; holding it so tightly her fingers were white around the glass, 'he said he'd be travelling back with Panos in his private plane.'

'Look: There isn't any way to do this gently,' for a moment her father's voice faltered. 'The aircraft crashed soon after take-off…they think it was bird-strike.' In the silent room Andrew could hear every word spoken. 'Kate, a rescue team was on the spot within an hour, but there were no survivors. I'm so sorry … Paul's solicitor tried to call you at the Ealing house and on your mobile yesterday; when he still couldn't get an answer this morning he contacted us.'

Kate said dully, 'Oh, poor Mr Hankin…he must have been in a state. It was my old mobile number… I never thought to tell him before I left Ealing – and I wouldn't give Paul my new one…'

She gulped at the whisky, her teeth chattering against the glass. Andrew took the mobile from her cold hand and said quietly, 'Mr Shaw, this is Andrew Parradine again. Kate is staying here at Ross-cannan for a few days and we will look after her…I'm sure she'll need to travel home as soon as possible and she won't be alone; I'll go with her whenever she's ready to leave.'

'Thank you.' Now David Shaw voice sounded sad and shaken. 'This is a bad business. I don't suppose any of us will sleep much tonight…'

*   *   *

Too numb and shocked even to find release in tears, Kate forced herself to concentrate on the immediate future: on all the practical things, like packing suitcases, calling her parents again and making an appointment to see Mr Hankin, who had been Paul's solicitor for the ten years since he had had moved from New York to London.

'What made him leave America?' asked Toby as they sat over a delayed lunch. He was fascinated by what he'd been hearing about Maestro Verdassey over the past few hours, and clearly unable to grasp why anyone in their right mind would forsake the Big Apple for grimy old London.

'He was smuggled out with his parents to the States from behind the Iron Curtain when he was about fifteen,' Kate explained patiently. 'The family settled in Newark but Paul was never really at ease in America; I think it had unhappy connotations for him: both his parents were dead before he was twenty. They'd been imprisoned during one of the many Soviet purges of Polish intellectuals and apparently died as a result of their ill-treatment.'

Toby gave a low whistle. 'Awesome! Were they in one of those Gulag places – did they get tortured?'

'Toby!' Andrew frowned at this demonstration of the heartlessness of youth, but Kate shook her head at him. 'No, it's all right, Andrew; in a way it helps to talk about him…keeps me from feeling so guilty. I don't know,' she answered Toby's question, 'he didn't talk much about his past. He came to the UK to do a series of concerts with the LSO when he was in his late thirties and fell in love with London…' she smiled for the first time since her father's telephone call that morning, 'he was a pretty impetuous guy.'

*   *   *

But the following afternoon when, accompanied by Andrew, she met with Mr Hankin in the offices of Hankin, Barlow and Hankin, Solicitors, of St Giles Square, Bloomsbury, she discovered Paul Verdassey had not been quite as impetuous as she imagined. Had in fact, thought very much ahead and left a very comprehensive and detailed will.

'It was imperative that you came to us as soon as possible.' Mr Hankin looked over his half-moon spectacles, a benign expression in his eyes. 'As you know, Miss Shaw, we have acted for Mr Verdassey since he came to this country, and you and I,' here his expression became even more benign, 'have met often over the past eight years have we not, to sort out one tangle or another for the Maestro?'

Kate smiled. 'Yes, we have…and you can still call me Kate, as you have for most of those years!'

Mr Hankin's eyes positively twinkled at Andrew. 'Kate is a very clever business woman, Mr Parradine, and an expert in public relations.'

'So I've discovered,' replied Andrew dryly.

'Now,' the old man opened a folder lying on his desk. 'In his will Mr Verdassey left very clear instructions to be carried out in the event of his demise. First, that he should be buried alongside his parents in the Cemetery of the Church of Saint Sebastian in Newark, for which a plot has been reserved. It is to be a private ceremony attended only by yourself, Kate, and a few designated friends. Secondly, any Memorial Service is to be arranged here in London at a later date by two close friends: a Mr Peter Livesy, at present domiciled in New York, and Sir Alan Haversham of St James Square, London.' He looked up over his glasses again. 'Both of whom I believe you know well, Kate.'

'Yes. I imagine Peter is already dealing with everything

immediate that needs to be done in the States.' Kate gripped her hands together. She really didn't want to sit here listening to dear old Hankin reciting the contents of Paul's will; she wanted all talk to be over and done with...and if there were any mention of Albertie Opie she thought she might possibly scream... Doing her best to distance herself from hearing more than the gentle rise and fall of the solicitor's voice, she missed the larger part of his recital, only coming fully to her senses again when she realised the solicitor had stopped speaking and was now looking at her expectantly. Only vaguely aware that beside her Andrew appeared to have gone rigid as a steel pole, she gave a guilty start.

'I'm sorry...it's been a long day,' she made a feeble attempt at a grin. 'Did I miss something important?'

Andrew breathed: 'Oh, *Jesus!*' The solicitor coughed, his face changing rapidly from expectation to disbelief.

'My dear Kate,' he reproved, 'you really should pay more attention...apart from several bequests to personal friends of some small items ...' *Please,* she begged silently, once again feeling hysteria begin to bubble perilously near the surface, *not any of his porcelain collection...* 'and the monies to found a music bursary to the Royal Academy of Music in London and another in New York, the whole of his estate, which includes the house and contents of 15 Kynaston Place, Ealing, goes to you.' As she continued to stare at him in shocked disbelief, he added gently, 'Paul had no family living that he knew of and he has named you as his sole beneficiary. After all expenses and bequests pertaining to his estate are met, the remainder will come to around three million pounds.'

'Did you have to faint quite so dramatically?' Andrew closed her nerveless fingers around the glass of water Mr Hankin had provided. 'I only just managed to catch you.'

'But I can't – I just can't...' she felt she was fighting her way through an impenetrable fog. She took a huge gulp of the water. 'Mr Hankin, you don't understand...' her voice rose in panic. 'Paul and I parted back in September last year...he was with someone else. Don't you see: he just hadn't got around to changing his will?'

'Oh, I know all about the trouble between you – well, perhaps not all,' he looked faintly embarrassed. 'Paul came to see me a few days before he left for America; he mentioned there had been some trouble and you would – ahem – not be accompanying him on this particular tour, but he wanted to make sure the *status quo* with regard to your position was maintained until he returned. I can assure you that he had no intention of altering his will. I gathered from what he told me that he was feeling a little guilty, but...' he spread his hands, 'I don't have to tell *you* that is something he couldn't actually admit.'

'No,' Kate said slowly, 'he would never do that.' She fell silent then, conscious that the two men were watching her closely, shook her head vehemently. 'I still don't feel everything should come to me – is there any way I might contest it?'

'Certainly not,' Mr Hankin was clearly scandalised at the mere idea; he lifted an admonitory finger as she again opened her mouth to protest. 'Kate, listen to me: Paul was well aware how much of the smooth running of his professional life was due to you. When I first knew him he was not making a good impression over here: he was not then very well known in the UK and was a difficult man to deal with. *You* enabled him to maintain a good standing in this country, both in his professional life and in society in general; you were always loyal; always there to smooth his path. He knew and thought of little beyond his music, and it was only through you that he was able to live at reasonable peace in a world he didn't really understand. So let's have no more guilty feelings about the recent past.' He smiled, his voice softening. 'Now I think Mr Parradine should take you away somewhere to have a rest and follow that with a good dinner. Do nothing until tomorrow, when you will have had time to think more clearly.'

But Kate was already thinking, clearly – and furiously. Of course it would be wonderful to be able to face the future now without worrying about how to pay the bills, but she'd always earned her wages by sheer hard work: the mind-numbing amount Mr Hanson had dangled before her eyes was positively obscene –she didn't *need* that much money...

Or did she?

Suddenly it was as though someone had switched on a very bright light, right in the middle of her muddled brain. Firmly she gathered together her whirling thoughts; she must have time, a lot of it, to think this through. What she needed was a battle plan; time to load her weaponry, and then find the right moment to open fire...

*   *   *

'You know,' she said later that evening as they sat over their 'good dinner', 'it's comforting to know Paul didn't feel too badly about me after all. I'm glad I left that message to say I was sorry, and that I'd meet him at the house, and I'm glad I bought the shepherd boy as a peace offering. He'll never know about that of course, but I will.' She put her hand over Andrew's. 'Come with me to Newark; I don't think I could bear it without you.'

'Just try to stop me.' He smiled. 'Want to go and see your pal Sir Alan Havisham first thing tomorrow?'

'Yes, then down to my parents, I think. They never liked or approved of Paul, but still, they are kind-hearted and will be upset on my behalf – or will at least make a good show of being so.' She made a wry face. '*Then* I suppose we should come back here. Everything in the Ealing house will have to be placed into store at least for a few weeks...there won't be time to sort things out before we have to fly to Newark – and I must call Megan, although I guess my parents have already done that. Oh...' she gave an impatient huff. 'I just want all this tangle of feelings and people and doing what must be done to be over so we can get back to Rosscannan and start making plans.'

Andrew said, 'What plans?'

'Oh, you know,' she was suddenly vague, 'taking Toby back to school; tarting up the stables; getting the outside painted; making sure Sam wants to work for a mass murderer and persuading George he needs more help in the house, which he does...shall I go on?'

'No, please don't.' Andrew held up a hand 'You're giving me indigestion,' he said.

*   *   *

Megan was sympathetic, practical and supportive when Kate phoned her before they made the journey to Essex. 'If you want to be free of Pendragon, just say the word and I'll return; if you need somewhere to come and lick your wounds, come to Italy and I'll be right here to provide it...'

'I'm OK, Megan, really I am, and I need to be busy, not sit around feeling sorry for myself.'

'Hmm. Well, I have some news to give you, but as it seems you have enough on your plate already, perhaps it should wait until you are back from the funeral.'

'Don't be coy, it doesn't suit you.' Talking with Megan, Kate felt herself getting back into her stride. 'So come on: what's your news – no, don't tell me – you're going to marry Andrew's father.'

Megan chuckled. 'Not in a million years – why risk spoiling a beautiful friendship? The matter is that I have decided to sell Pendragon. It's much too large for me now and I haven't been coping well with winter in England for the past year or two. I've found a pleasant little villa on the outskirts of Florence and plan to buy it and live in Italy more or less permanently. I'll probably come back to Cornwall for a few weeks each summer and either rent somewhere small or make do with a hotel.' She hesitated for a moment. 'I have only one problem... I don't think Heathcliffe would cope with this climate – and I couldn't in any case keep dragging him to and fro each summer.'

'So, would I like to adopt a big, hairy, smelly, lazy hound who farts for England and eats enough for a half dozen normal canines, is that it?' Kate gave a derisive snort, followed almost immediately by a peal of laughter that made Andrew look up with a smile from where he was seated at his PC, hunting for tack on eBay. 'Well, I know one young man who will be delighted to have Heathcliffe around permanently...of course I'll keep him,' she laughed again. 'I've actually got fond of the great ox. You go ahead and buy your villa, Megan.'

'And you? Where will you and Heathcliffe live when both Pendragon and your temporary dwelling place of Rosscannan are sold?' asked her cousin shrewdly.

'Ah,' she answered cagily, '*that* is what one might call in the Lap of the Gods.'

'Well the Gods had better watch out, because James is getting very impatient about progress on the home front and wants to be shot of the house, once and for all. You might warn your chum Andrew to start talking to Estate Agents PDQ, before he gets papa on his back in person. '

Conscious that Andrew was half-listening to this conversation, Kate took a deep breath and grabbed at the opportunity she had been waiting for. 'Just tell Andrew's daddy not to grind his teeth too loudly,' she said calmly, 'because he already has a buyer for Rosscannan.'

'Really?' said Megan.

'Yes, really,' said Kate and killed the call.

Andrew said, 'You don't know how good it felt to hear you really laugh again –' he raised one sceptical eyebrow, 'but you won't buy me much time with that whopping great fib.'

Kate said with dignity. 'I never lie.'

'Oh no...so who's the supposed buyer for this pile?'

'I am,' she said.

She gazed at his stunned expression with interest. 'You've gone quite pale,' she said.

'I'm not surprised,' he recovered himself quickly. 'Don't be ridiculous, Kate. This place would probably fetch a cool million and a half –I can certainly twist pa's arm for the share he promised me for getting the house put to rights, and raise a fair bit towards the rest...but you've contributed one hell of a lot already to this place in sheer hard graft, I won't have you chucking your money at it as well. When and where in hell did you get such an idea?' he finished explosively.

'About two minutes after Mr Hankin told me I was a rich bitch.' She fixed him with a determined eye. 'Are you going to give me grief about this?'

'You bet your sweet life I am – of all the bloody harebrained, un-thought-through ideas...' he flung both arms wide as her jaw set in what was becoming a familiar stubborn line. 'Oh, for God's sake, don't go all mulish on me, woman...if you start sinking great chunks of your inheritance into Rosscannan now, everyone will think I'm marrying you for your money!'

'Whereas before if *I'd* suggested it, they'd have thought I was after yours...Oh,' she stopped, her eyes widening with shock, 'did you just mention *marriage*?'

'Yeah,' he was belligerent, 'you got something to argue about with that idea?'

For a long moment she looked at him in silence; he glared back and saw something like a shaft of gleeful malice suddenly light her eyes.

'You know, I'm not surprised somebody shot at you,' she said.

Andrew clenched and unclenched his hands and took a menacing step forward. 'Just repeat that, will you?'

She said dutifully, 'I'm not surprised that –'

Snaking out a hand he grasped her wrist and pulling her to him wrapped his arms around her. The following prolonged bout of intense and masterful kissing effectively rendered Kate incapable of saying anything very much for a full two minutes. When she did finally surface and regain the power of speech, it was only to gasp, 'Was that a proposal?'

'You bet.' He stood her back and taking both her hands in his own asked solemnly, 'Kate Shaw, will you marry me?'

'I believe I will,' she said.

'Well that's a relief,' he said. 'So now that's settled we'll discuss the little matter of you, me and Rosscannan...and don't think I'm giving in without a fight.'

*   *   *

Megan's phone call, and the subsequent bout of lust on Andrew's part, had proved something of a catalyst in helping to clear some of the turmoil of guilt and sadness from Kate's mind; effectively returning her to her customary determined, persuasive self, so that by the time they arrived at the Ealing house, Andrew found he had agreed that a fifty-fifty partnership in property, as well as in life, might be a very sensible, nay desirable, goal for which to aim, and that what people might think had never been a good enough reason for not doing pretty well anything one wanted to do.

Afterwards, he wasn't at all clear how he had come to such a momentous conclusion, but had a lurking suspicion that his own clear, logical, military brain was no match for his Kate's equally clear, logical, but infinitely more devious one; honed to perfection as it had been by years of dealing with the temperamental and totally illogical, Maestro Paul Verdassey.

*   *   *

On Andrew's insistence they stopped en route for Colchester to visit Bond Street for the purchase of a ring, Andrew declaring firmly that he wasn't going to turn up at her parents' house without having first staked his claim.

As their taxi drew up before the trimmed laurel hedge of number sixteen Acacia Grove, Kate examined the diamond and sapphire band now gracing the third finger of her left hand. 'My mother,' she said, 'will probably swoon with joy at the sight of this. She's entitled, I suppose; God knows she's waited long enough for someone to make an honest woman of me!'

*   *   *

A week later as the Boeing touched down at Heathrow, Kate felt an overwhelming sense of relief; the eight days since they'd left Rosscannan had been too frantic, too full of the myriad tasks to be done before the flight to Newark and Paul's funeral, that there had been little time to relax, to properly take in the unexpected shift, not only in her fortunes, but in her personal life as well.

She sighed, stretched and took Andrew's hand in her own. He turned his head towards her. 'Glad to be back?' he asked.

'I shall only feel we're really back when we walk through the door of Rosscannan tomorrow.'

'On Monday morning I shall have to leave you to take Toby back to school…unless *you'd* rather go and smooth things over with his headmaster?'

'What – and cause that poor child even more embarrassment!'

He laughed. 'Well, perhaps not.'

Kate looked sideways at his profile and felt her heart shift a little. How would she have managed this past week without him? Always a comforting presence, even when he was on the far side of a room: knowing intuitively when she needed him by her side but never crowding her. Even now, as the plane taxied along the runway and they began the mundane tasks of unfastening seat belts and checking hand luggage and pushing magazines into bags, she felt his strength surrounding her like the comfort-blanket she would snuggle into as a small child.

She loved him, more than she had ever loved anyone in her life before, although she was still not quite used to all the baggage that came with such a love…the total rapport, the sharing, the tenderness, the wonderful new togetherness, the desire to make love at every opportunity…not, she thought with an inward smile, that such feelings and desires were likely to preclude the odd falling out, but if Andrew loved her as much as she did him, and she was pretty sure that he did, then together they could ride out any old storm…

She said suddenly. 'Let's not stay over tonight: let's go straight home.'

He grinned. 'OK, but we won't make it back before midnight. We'll be bushed.'

'I don't care. I just want to be back at Rosscannan with you and Toby and, God help me because I never thought I'd say this, George as well!'

'You're on!' He seized her arm as the plane stopped, 'If we hit the ground running when the taxi reaches Paddington we might just make the last train.'

They made it, with rather more time to spare than Andrew had at their first meeting, and at mid-week, on a late train, they at least had a choice of seats. Settled side by side, holding hands, they smiled at each other as lovers all down the ages had done.

'We're going home,' she said.

He raised her hand to his lips. 'But *this* time we're doing it together,' he said.

By the same author

A Year Out of Time

A Year Out of Time is the story of one twelve year old girl from a "nice" middle-class background and a "nice" private school (where her mother hoped she might learn to be a lady) who, in the Autumn of 1940, finds herself pitched into the totally foreign environment of a small Worcestershire hamlet.

For the space of one year her life revolves around the village school and its manic headmaster; the friends she makes, notably Georgie Little the "bad influence"; the twee but useful fellow evacuees, Mavis and Mickey Harper, whose possession of an old pigsty proves the springboard to some surprising and sometimes hilarious happenings; and Mrs 'Arris, the vast and formidable landlady of The Green Dragon Inn.

In the company of Georgie Little she awakens to the joys of a new and exhilarating world: a secret world which excludes most adults and frequently verges on the lawless.

The year comes to an explosive end and she returns unwillingly to her former life – but the joyous, anarchic influence of the Forest and Georgie remains, and sixty years on is remembered with gratitude and love.

ISBN 978-0-9555778-0-2

Available from Sagittarius Publications
62 Jacklyns Lane, Alresford, Hampshire SO24 9LH

By the same author

And All Shall Be Well

And All Shall Be Well begins Francis Lindsey's journey through childhood to middle age; from a suddenly orphaned ten year old to a carefree adolescent; through the harsh expectations of becoming a man in a world caught in war.

Set mainly against the dramatic background of the Cornish Coast, it is a story about friendships and relationships, courage and weakness, guilt and reparation. — *The first book in a Cornish trilogy.*

ISBN 978-0-9555778-1-9

**Chosen as the runner-up
to the Society of Authors 2003 Sagittarius Prize**

"The author has succeeded to an extraordinary degree in bringing Francis to full masculine life. The storyline is always interesting and keeps the reader turning the pages. All in all it is a good novel that can be warmly recommended to anyone who enjoys a good read."
– Michael Legat

"Seldom do I get a book that simply cannot be put down. The settings and characters are so believable, the shy falling in love for the first time and the passion of forbidden liaisons written with feeling. Many of the sequences left me with a smile on my face, others to wipe a tear from my eye." – Jenny Davidson, The Society of Women Writers and Journalists Book Review

"A beautifully written novel. Eve Phillips' writing is a pure joy to read and her wonderfully graphic descriptions of the Penzance area of the Cornish Coast made me yearn to be there."
– Erica James, Author

Available from Sagittarius Publications
62 Jacklyns Lane, Alresford, Hampshire SO24 9LH

By the same author

Matthew's Daughter

Matthew's Daughter is the second book in a Cornish Trilogy and follows Caroline Penrose, as she returns from her wartime service in the WAAF to her father's flower farm in Cornwall. But once home she finds a number of obstacles and family conspiracies impeding her path to peace…

ISBN 978-0-9555778-2-6

The Changing Day

The Changing Day the final book in a Cornish Trilogy, begins in 1940, when a meeting between WREN Joanna Dunne and Navy Lieutenant Mark Eden is the start of a love affair that at first seems unlikely to stand the test of time. She is 22, single and an Oxford graduate; he is 36, married and in civilian life a country vet. She is attracted but not looking for romance, he is attracted but not looking for commitment and, as Joanna soon discovers, he is the black sheep of his family and has a very murky past.

ISBN 978-0-9555778-3-3

Available from Sagittarius Publications
62 Jacklyns Lane, Alresford, Hampshire SO24 9LH

A Very Private Arrangement

When in the spring of 1934, fourteen year old orphan Anna Farrell is transported from a life of drab, penny-pinching, genteel poverty with her cousin Ruth, to the elegant, affluent Bloomsbury household of distant cousin Patrick Farrell, and his manservant, Charlie Caulter, she is at first blissfully unaware of the well hidden secret kept by the two men, until a meeting with the quasi-charming Madame Gallimard and her sons becomes the catalyst that threatens to tear her world apart.

Against the backcloth of WW2 and a diversity of places and people, with her beloved Patrick and Charlie to smooth her path through the inevitable pitfalls of first, second and last love, Anna matures from naïve young girl to confident young woman, well able to cope with the men in her life – and some of the women in theirs.

ISBN 978-0-9555778-4-0

Return to Falcon Field

Ryan Petersen, a professor of European Literature at a New England University, accepts a year's exchange lectureship in London. But in coming to England the cynical, detached Ryan has a hidden agenda: to find the woman with whom he had a passionate wartime love affair over twenty years before.

He returns to the now derelict airbase of Falcon Field and the nearby Hampshire village of Hawksley, to begin a journey into the past; one that proves both painful and inspiring as he re-discovers the man he once was, and perhaps could be again.

ISBN 978-0-9555778-5-7

Available from Sagittarius Publications
62 Jacklyns Lane, Alresford, Hampshire SO24 9LH

By the same author

A Very Artistic Affair

The year is nineteen sixty-five. After twenty years of marriage Olivia, a forty-five year old wife and mother, discovers that her husband, Giles, has fallen in love with a young actress half his age.

Already feeling the first stirrings of discontent as the conventional and dutiful wife of her far from faithful husband, and conscious that the Swinging Sixties is rapidly passing her by, a humiliated and angry Olivia leaves the family home, moves from Hampshire to Devonshire, discards her twin-set and pearls image, resumes her earlier career as an artist, acquires her own occasional lover and copes successfully with her teenage son's burgeoning affair with a sculptor's daughter.

But as the months pass neither Olivia nor Giles find the separate paths they have chosen free from difficulty. There is confrontation, conflict and pain as events take many unexpected, sometimes tragic, and sometimes farcical twists and turns, before either can leave the past behind them and move forward into a new, and hopefully more peaceful, future.

ISBN 978-0-9555778-6-4

Available from Sagittarius Publications
62 Jacklyns Lane, Alresford, Hampshire SO24 9LH

By the same author

The Turning Point

Growing up is hard to do. Even at twenty two...

Landscape photographer Cassandra Chisholm is permanently hard up. She has an absent father in Paris and a not very satisfactory lover in Cornwall. When she agrees to take publicity photos for middle-aged author Michael Niven, the process of growing up begins to accelerate at an alarming rate.

Unrequited love; unwanted revelations about her past, and the frightening prospect of leaving her Cornish home, has Cassie arriving at her own personal Turning Point. Aided by her thespian friend Jono, she begins work at a London Arts Centre, until a series of romantic misunderstandings and family disruptions send her bolting around the Home Counties pursued by an irate Michael and her bewildered father. Ultimately it is left to Michael's own irascible octogenarian father Archie, whose many eccentricities include taking his pet ferret into battle on D Day and keeping a herd of politically incorrectly named pigs, to finally run Cassie to earth and restore peace and harmony between the warring parties.

More or less

ISBN 978-0-9555778-7-1

Available from Sagittarius Publications
62 Jacklyns Lane, Alresford, Hampshire SO24 9LH

www.ingramcontent.com/pod-product-compliance
Lightning Source LLC
Chambersburg PA
CBHW072103170626
46813CB00004B/1447